THE PORTRAIT

Nada's portrait hung in Sir Philip's bedroom.
Looking at it, Gwendolyn was overcome by a
strange feeling. She could not take her eyes
off the hauntingly beautiful face or the
compelling eyes of that girl, who had died so
tragically for love . . .

"We'd better go," said Elizabeth. "We mustn't
be caught here."

"But that's her. Nada. The woman he will love
until he dies," said Gwendolyn.

Gwendolyn felt sorry for Elizabeth. She had spent
the best years of her life pining over Sir Philip.

Would Gwendolyn make the same mistake?
Would she give her heart to this man who could
never return her love?

LOST
LOVE

(original title: THE BLACK PANTHER)

Barbara Cartland

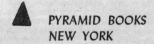

PYRAMID BOOKS
NEW YORK

To
MISS EDITH E. GREAVES

Matron for twenty-seven years of the
City of London Maternity Hospital,
in deep admiration of her unfailing
sympathy, efficiency, and understanding.

LOST LOVE
(original title: THE BLACK PANTHER)

A PYRAMID BOOK

Pyramid edition published July, 1970
 Seventh printing, February 1975

ISBN 0-515-02621-2

Printed in the United States of America

Pyramid Books are published by Pyramid Communications, Inc.
Its trademarks, consisting of the word "Pyramid" and the
portrayal of a pyramid, are registered in the
United States Patent Office.

PYRAMID COMMUNICATIONS, INC.,
919 Third Avenue, New York, N.Y. 10022

And after death, through the long To Be
    (Which, I think, must surely keep love's laws),
I, should you chance to have need of me,
    Am ever and always, only yours.

INDIAN LOVE LYRICS

I

It is difficult to know where to start this story. Birth is the obvious beginning of anyone's history, just as death must be the end. And how can I tell the story of these last dramatic months without including the years of development, the slow awakening to realisation, which preceded them?

They were dull years, yet now they seem to me to have had a purpose, to fit neatly into the pattern of things, so that in their greyness I can perceive an occasional golden thread, a note of colour which synchronises with the whole. I can never escape from them, they are with me, just as my body is with me, altering, developing, ageing, but indissolubly part of me and of my life. And so they must be included here if I am to give a coherent as well as truthful account of myself.

All my life I have tried to escape from a consciousness of myself; perhaps I was instinctively afraid of learning too much, or it may have been a deliberate attempt to avoid emotion.

In adolescence most human beings shrink from the natural emotions—they sense their strength and try vainly to stem the rising flood. Most schoolboys have no use for girls and little girls go through a phase of hating boys.

I hated myself. I remember the moment when I first saw my face clearly. I can't recall the room, the occasion, or the actual mirror into which I looked but I can still see my reflection staring back at me. The plump pink and white cheeks, the pale corn-coloured hair, the half angry, half startled expression in my blue eyes.

I loathed what I saw. I must have been very young;

7

there was a blue satin bow at the side of my head and a frilled collar of white muslin round my neck.

Another moment in my childhood is even more vivid. There was a garden party or a fête in the grounds of our home, I forget which. I cannot remember the setting; I only recall the band playing on the lawn. The music thrilled me—certain music has always conjured up strange feelings in me—I started to dance. For the first time in my life, I was aware of other people. I wanted them to applaud me. I believed that I could float gracefully over the grass before them. I thought of myself as a swallow in flight, I had a definite idea of what I could do, of how I would appear. Suddenly—I can experience it again now—I saw my knee. It was fat and naked, rising awkwardly from among the frills of my starched frock. I stopped dancing and ran away. I ran and ran, where to, or for how long, I do not know, but the misery of my flight remains.

Yet I have always admired my mother whom I resemble, and I think at sixty she is still one of the loveliest women I have ever seen. She is taller than I am and has more dignity than I shall ever have. Perhaps her loveliness lies in her serenity. Nothing seems to trouble her. She goes through life like a ship in full sail, taking everything as it comes. I have never heard her complain; and as long as I can remember she has never expressed any desires or wants beyond those of daily necessities.

As a child, I realised that my nature should in all justice have been like hers, but I have never had anything in common with her, unless it be the large bones, characteristic of her family, the classical features, and her golden hair which earned her the description as a girl, of the 'English rose'.

It was popular, in the Edwardian days, when the Jersey Lily was claiming the King's attention, for beauties to be described as flowers. It was obvious, I suppose, that Mother should have been written up in the press and talked of as a 'rose'. Yet I remember how nauseated I used to feel years later to hear people speak of me as a 'rosebud'. I longed to look like Angela. It was inevitable that I should passionately admire my only sister; she was so much older than I—nearly eleven years—and David was only three years her junior.

I was an afterthought. Father has often referred to me

as that, and on more than one occasion Mother has told me how much she disliked having to start a nursery all over again, just when she thought she had dispensed for ever with nurses and all the difficulties that they entailed in a household.

When parents are old they are supposed to spoil their children. At the same time I think they find it very difficult to enter into their children's thoughts and feelings, to have much sympathy with the years of youth, which are so far behind them.

Certainly as a child I felt terribly alone; Angela was in the schoolroom with a very superior governess who didn't get on with my nanny; David I very seldom saw, he went to his preparatory school soon after I was born and by the time I was old enough to be aware of him in the holidays, he had reached the stage when he had no use for girls.

Angela was dark with thin, pointed features and a slim, almost willowy figure which was characteristic of my father's family. I used to long to be like her; when I was about eight, I was severely punished for blackening my hair with coal dust to see what the effect would be. Angela went to school when she was sixteen and after that time I saw very little of her. When she came out mother and father gave her a short season in London. I was still a little girl, but old enough for lessons, and Nanny used to teach me reading and writing every morning while she washed and ironed my dresses.

It is funny how as a child one never realises what money means or its importance. Each year as I grew older, more rooms were shut up in my home, fewer servants were employed and the times when mother or I had new clothes, became increasingly less frequent. I used to hear father talking, planning economies on the estate, saying at meal times that it was impossible for him to fulfil all the demands that were being made on him. It made no impression on me because my idea of poverty was the children I would see playing outside the cottages in the village, or at harvest time working with their parents in the fields. Now I understand how really difficult those years were; David was at an expensive public school, Angela was anxious to have a good time like other girls of her age.

It was funny that I was not happier, for after all, the usual child's dream of bliss is a huge garden in the country, a pony to ride and very little supervision. I remember sitting, staring out of the window in my nursery, feeling a kind of misery, which now I can best describe as homesickness—I know no other feeling which approaches that I experienced so often as a child. I was subject to nightmares, too, and fits of crying which bewildered my mother, for they were quite out of keeping with the placid, contented, temperament she expected from a child who looked the spit of herself.

Later I had a governess; she was shared with two children in the neighbourhood, and Nanny stayed on to look after me and my clothes.

I was backward for my age and I hated learning. I found all that they wanted to teach me, dull and uninteresting. I daresay I was badly taught. Our governess was a harassed genteel little woman, who found three girls of different ages far more than she could cope with, and she made little attempt in the hours we spent with her to do more than recite a wearisome repetition of dates and facts.

Yet strangely enough it was through her that one tremendous interest came into my life.

We had a gramophone at home—an old, rather creaky affair, which had been given to David when he first went to school. The records were old too; they were mostly of the comic variety, songs or jazz pieces, which made the maximum amount of noise. For my birthday in the summer Miss Jenkins bought me two records. I was disappointed at the present, thanked her politely, and forgot all about them for nearly a fortnight. Then one Saturday when it was raining, I played them. The moment the first one started a new world was opened to me: a world of sound. I had never expected anything like it; I had never experienced before such feelings that rushed over me as I listened. I played those records again and again until they were almost worn out—I have them still.

When I was sixteen there was talk of sending me to school, but it came to nothing for father decided he could not afford it. Actually, I believe my parents, thinking that I was pretty and likely to be a great deal prettier by the time I had grown up, concluded that an extensive education would not be necessary. After all, they argued, Angela had married exceedingly well in her first season. She had met Henry Watson, only son and heir to one of the richest brewers in the country. Of course, it was not an ideal match—the Watsons were not the family that my father would have chosen for one of his children to marry into—but he was delighted at the prospect of Angela being rich, rich and free from all the problems which had beset her family ever since she was born.

Henry Watson was nearly thirty-seven when he married her. He was stockily built, slightly pompous, but pleasant. He was Member of Parliament for a north country seat and very anxious to have a wife to entertain for him, in his constituency and in London. I have no doubt that Angela filled the bill admirably; when I grew to know my brother-in-law better, I was soon aware that he enjoyed both Angela's title and the status that his marriage gave him in society.

We were all brought up to realise that in his own way, which we shouldn't underestimate, father was important. After all, the earldom dates back to the seventeenth century and Maysfield had been in the family for nearly a century before then. When he was a tiny boy, David had drummed into him that the most important fact in his life was that he would inherit both Maysfield and father's name.

The worst father could ever say to us when we had been naughty was 'I don't expect one of my family to behave like that'. He said it with a kind of sternness which was far worse than if he had been angry. It made us feel completely unworthy of being his children.

I was only eight when Angela got married, so except for the excitement of being a bridesmaid and walking behind her up the aisle, I remember very little of the ceremony or of Henry Watson and his relations. Five years later when mother and father went up to London to stay with them for Ascot, I remember hearing on their return, father make a somewhat disparaging remark about Henry's father, and mother saying: 'One can't expect everything, Arthur, after all, Angela has a lovely home.' I thought about that and wondered why mother had not said a nice husband, or nice children, because Angela had two by then. But she hadn't, and when I tried to ask her about Angela and Henry, she was non-committal and insisted on telling me about Ascot instead.

I saw my sister two or three times in the passing years,

11

but not more. She and Henry would come down for the week-end, or sometimes stop for luncheon or tea, on their way to stay with other people in the neighbourhood. When I was sixteen she greeted me with 'Darling, how terribly fat you've got', and I almost disliked her at that moment. She was looking so lovely herself. Beautiful clothes and good jewels are shown at their best on Angela; and she had the right figure for the modern square-shouldered fashions. She was bright and gay, too, but with an almost feverish manner as though she were frightened of missing something, and had to go on ceaselessly, striving towards some goal which she could never reach.

Henry used to watch her when she was talking. Once I saw an expression on his face which made me shudder. I got the idea that he was like some circus proprietor watching an animal he was very proud of, at its tricks. I didn't like Henry, he used to patronise me in the wrong sort of way. I know now that it was just that he was naturally awkward with children, but somehow the ten shillings that he used to give me when he went away, never meant as much as the half-a-crown, or even the hand shake, from some of our other guests.

So I grew up at Maysfield. There was never a lack of things to do, but I did them almost automatically, just as one can eat a meal and not taste it. I was not living, I was dreaming. Perhaps it was just a usual stage in adolescence.

I had one friend, the Vicar. He was an old man, well over sixty, but he had an understanding and a sympathy which drew to him people of all ages and made him their confidant. His daughter, who did lessons with me, was a weak, rather whiny child for whom he had endless patience and affection which, I believe was based more on duty than on spontaneity.

He was always nice to me. He was a great admirer of Father's, but I think also he was more than a little relieved to find that the expense of his daughter's education would be shared by myself and another neighbour's child. He lived a frugal life at the Vicarage and he must have been lonely, for his wife had been dead for some years. The governess who taught us, who also took charge of his household, was a distant relative of his.

We had lessons in the Vicarage and as soon as they were over in the big cold schoolroom which was originally intended for the dining-room of the house, we used to rush into the garden, the two other girls to whisper secrets and eat sweets, I to find my host. I would generally find him gardening; he loved his garden, it was his only passion in life. It was he who made me understand flowers, how one could group colours so as to make a pattern of beauty when the time for blossoming came, and how a small delicate plant in a rockery could be made to glow like a jewel.

But we did not always discuss flowers; he talked to me of people, of events, of history, geography and literature. Every word he said remained in my mind, while my lessons were forgotten as soon as they were finished. At last he introduced me to his library. He had a miscellaneous collection of books, mostly tattered and dirty, for he bought them second hand in the Charing Cross Road, or picked them up at sales where they had been too dilapidated for other collectors. There were whole shelves of biographies and of memoirs. They appealed to him most, the stories of people who had led full lives; they thrilled him who lived, perhaps, the quietest, most humdrum existence it was possible to imagine.

At first it was more to please him than to please myself that I borrowed a volume. I suppose it was inevitable that after that the desire to read more should possess me. I couldn't put a book down once I had started it; if I had to go to bed, I used to creep on to the landing outside my bedroom and sit reading by the light of the chandelier in the hall. I didn't dare switch on my own light—the old motor which snorted and chunked through the day making the light for the house, was woefully inadequate. The light grew dimmer and dimmer every Sunday evening, when the gardener who attended to it was off duty. On ordinary weekdays in the summer it would just last out, but in the winter we often had to grope our way to bed. When I was too sleepy to read more I used to go back to bed—often shivering with cold. I used to crawl under the bedclothes to try and get warm again. I would often wake at five or six in the morning, driven by an urge to continue reading where I had left off.

Perhaps that was when I was conscious of being really happy: when I was lost to the world I knew, following some explorer across the Sahara, indulging in the intrigue at the

13

Court of Louis XIV, or weeping at the death of Mary Queen of Scots. I seemed to be able to live the lives of these people with them. I concentrated on a book so fiercely that if anyone spoke to me I did not hear them. Often I would be roused by someone who I had no idea was in the room with me.

My parents mildly teased me about it. 'I must say I never expected to have a child who was a bookworm,' father would say. Having spent most of his life out of doors, he had little use for books and *The Times* was about all he could manage in the evening before his eyes drooped and he dozed in his chair by the fire.

I seldom saw my mother read. She would sew and knit innumerable garments for the Personal Service League. When she wasn't doing that she would be writing letters. Mother belongs to the old school who keep up a frequent, and I imagine, animated correspondence with all their relatives; even friends whom she has not seen for years, she will regularly write to, although what she has to tell them in her closely written sheets of notepaper, I cannot begin to imagine. She writes to David, who went out to India with his regiment when I was eighteen, once a week. I watch her cover page after page, while I who write irregularly, wonder what on earth to say that would be of the slightest interest to him.

When I was eighteen, father's brother died and we went into mourning for six months, so that it was quite impossible for me to 'come out' while we were all wearing black and unable to accept any invitations. As my birthday is in June, it meant a whole year wasted, and although I didn't expect a season in London as Angela had had, I hoped that mother would arrange for me to stay with various people who would make some effort to do their best for me. It was disappointing, because I had looked forward for some time to getting away from home. I had visited relations once or twice in the past years, but it seemed ridiculous to think that I had never been abroad, that I had never stayed in London for more than one night, and I knew practically nothing of the world, or even of the country in which I lived, beyond thirty miles of my home.

Father and mother were not the sort of people to whom one could ever complain, or even try to put into words thoughts of that sort; I had hoped that my coming out would mean a change—if only for a short while.

14

When they told me that Uncle Granville was dead, I sat down and cried. I think father was rather pleased at my grief—Uncle Granville had always been his favourite brother and he had spent a lot of time at Maysfield. He was a High Court Judge; personally I found him a dull, pompous old man, entirely self-centered as old bachelors are apt to be. I couldn't explain that I was mourning, not for him, but for my own hopes, and my tears remain a tribute to his memory.

2

My whole life changed on that May morning when mother called 'Gwendolyn!' as I was doing the flowers in the housekeeper's room.

Mother is the only person who calls me by the name I received at my baptism; it was her mother's name and she has, naturally, an affection for it. Everyone else has always said how awful it sounds, and since I was a baby, has called me 'Lyn'. Mother, however, is never swayed by other people's opinions.

'Gwendolyn,' she called, 'come here.'

I put down the flowers with a sigh. It is impossible to get a job done at home before one is called to do something else. There is so much to do in the morning; the dogs to be brushed and combed; the flowers to be rearranged; the china dusted in the drawing-room, innumerable messages to be carried backwards and forwards between the kitchen and the morning-room, as well as the food to be ordered from the village. There was only myself to do it all, for mother had suffered from arthritis all the winter and had been told to keep her leg up as much as possible. Once she got down to the sofa in the morning-room she seldom moved from it, except for meals, until it was time to go to bed.

'Coming!' I shouted and I ran across the hall and up the short flight of steps which led to the morning-room.

Mother was in her usual place in the big bow window. The sun was shining on her hair, which even now retains much of its goldiness, she looked at me with such a radiant smile that I said to myself—'How pretty she is!'

'I have got news for you, Gwendolyn,' she said.

'News for me?' I questioned.

She held up a letter and I saw it was in Angela's writing.

'Angela wants you to stay with her in London,' she said. 'Would you like to go?'

I felt my heart leap with excitement.

'When?' I asked.

'As soon as we can spare you,' mother replied. 'She says that she had meant to ask you last year, only, of course, Uncle Granville's death made it impossible. But she feels now that we are out of mourning that you must have some kind of coming-out. She has written and asked if she might present you and has received her command for the third Court.'

'Oh mother!' I said.

Mother put on her spectacles. She always has to wear them to read.

'She adds that you needn't worry about clothes. *"Henry has been very nice about it,"* she writes, *"and when I explained that things were a little difficult for you now, he said he would stand Lyn a trousseau, so that's that!"* '

'When can I go, when?' I asked.

Mother took off her spectacles again and looked at me.

'I shall miss you,' she said gently.

'But, mother, I must go, I must.'

'Of course, my dear,' she answered. 'I want you to go and I want you to have a good time. I often feel very guilty that we didn't send you to school. Angela enjoyed her year at Mademoiselle Jacques', but you do understand, that income tax is so much worse now than it was then. We can't afford to do anything nowadays.' She gave a sigh.

'I'm not complaining, mother, but I would like to go to London.'

She looked at me with a smile.

'I hope you won't be disappointed,' she said. 'I remember hating my first season.'

'But you had a wild success,' I said.

'Afterwards, not the year I came out. But then, girls are so different now. I was shy, desperately shy and I knew so few people.'

'Well, I shan't know anybody,' I said, 'except Angela and, of course, Henry, but in a way that makes it all the more interesting. It will be like going off on a voyage of exploration. Can't you see me, mother, a traveller in a strange land?'

'Oh Gwendolyn, your imagination!' mother laughed. 'I am afraid that one day it will get you into trouble.'

17

'My imagination?' I questioned. 'You make it sound like a deformity.'

Mother looked up at me with a quizzical expression in her eyes.

'Ever since you were tiny,' she confessed, 'I have wondered how much you have realised of what is going on around you and how much you have lived in a world of your own.'

I laughed, almost in a shamefaced way. It is always disconcerting to find that other people have noticed things about one, when one has hardly been aware of them oneself.

'I will keep my imagination severely in check,' I promised. 'How long will Angela keep me?'

'She doesn't say,' mother replied. 'But I suppose that the third Court is hardly likely to be held before the middle of July.'

'Over two months!' I cried. 'Oh, how exciting! Can I go at once—tomorrow?'

'There's the Sale of Work on Saturday,' mother said. 'You must be here for that, you promised the Vicar.'

'Sunday, then?' I asked.

'Angela is certain to go away for the week-end. You had better go on Monday and arrive about teatime.'

'I can catch the 2.45,' I said, remembering the many times I had driven our guests down to catch the London train and watched it steam out of the station, waving them good-bye as they journeyed away into the unknown world outside. 'What shall I wear to go to London? What can I wear?'

'What have you got?' mother asked.

I knew that she could not remember—mother never was interested in clothes, either for herself or for us. I can hear Nanny now in my childhood saying, 'But, mi'lady, the child hasn't got a rag to her back and her shoes are right through at the toes.' Mother would stand and listen, a vague look of anxiety on her face. 'How distressing, Nanny,' she would answer. 'Well, I am afraid you will have to write to London for some patterns.' When the patterns came, Nanny would take them triumphantly in to my mother, only to be met with surprise. 'Clothes! Surely Gwendolyn doesn't need anything more? I thought it was only a month or so ago that she had something new.'

'It will have to be the blue serge,' I said. 'It is frightfully shabby, but I am thinner, aren't I, mother, and it might be possible to get into something of Angela's until we have time to shop.'

I walked across the room and looked at myself in the long Queen Anne mirror, dark with age, which hung between the two big bookcases. I was a little thinner, but my figure seemed to me voluptuous. Looking at it I thought of Nanny saying: 'She is beautifully covered, mi'lady, and firm as anything, it is muscle, not fat!'

I was still beautifully covered—there was no getting away from it. There was no pretence of my having the slender hipless and chestless outline which was fashionable and which Angela had managed to attain and keep ever since she was seventeen.

I was so big; my feet were well shaped, but I took sixes. My neck was white and firm but almost—well Junoesque! I hated myself and I turned away from the glass.

'I hope Henry is prepared to spend a good deal of money on me,' I said sharply. 'He will need to if I am to be anything like fashionable enough for a London Season.'

'Supposing I'm a failure?' I thought. 'Supposing I disgrace them?' I felt almost terror at the idea. Supposing after a few weeks they suggested that I should come home, that I needn't wait for the third Court? Wouldn't it be better not to go, not to risk humiliation?

I tried to shake myself free of my fears, but I knew they would pursue and terrify me, circling around me like ghouls and giving me no peace, I should lie sleeplessly tossing hour after hour at night, or wake before day to find the question still irritating, still unanswered.

'You are quite certain that Angela wants me?' I asked mother desperately.

She looked startled at the tone of my voice.

'But of course she does,' she said, 'why, she says in her letter . . .' she picked up her glasses again and turned over the pages . . . 'yes, here it is, *"You know how much I would like to have Lyn, Mother dear, and how carefully I would look after her. I promise you that she shall have a lovely time, so don't have a moment's anxiety about how she will be getting on".'*

'She really is an angel, isn't she?' I cried in a tone of relief.

'I will write and accept,' mother said, 'the 2.45 on Monday! You are sure it is running?'

'Quite certain,' I answered, 'but I shall call in at the station this afternoon to make sure.'

I went towards the door. When my hand was on its handle, mother said:

'I will lend you my small row of pearls, Gwendolyn, while you are away, but you will be careful of them, won't you dear?'

'Oh Mother, how sweet of you!'

Her small row of pearls that she wore more often than the heavy family jewels, was a particular treasure. I knew that it had been given to her by her father when she came of age. The pearls were well matched, slightly pink with a diamond clasp. Angela had borrowed them for her coming-out dance; now I was to be allowed to wear them.

I love jewels, I always have. When I was a small child I used to creep into mother's room when she had gone down to dinner and look into the jewel box that was left out on her dressing-table. I would try on the heavy diamond rings and clasp her bracelets round my wrists. Once I was caught, for father came back to the room for something which mother had forgotten. I was too terrified to move and only stood staring at him with frightened eyes, the diamonds glittering on my arms and round my neck. But he laughed, said I was a little peacock, and picking me up in his arms, carried me downstairs to show me to mother. She too had laughed at the time—there were people there—but next morning she had told me that I must be very careful, that all the jewels had been in the family for a great many years and they were a trust which each generation handed on to the next. One day David's wife would have them all.

It seems ridiculous to think of Maysfield with its family treasures, pictures and tapestries, which are mostly National Treasures, and mother's jewellery, all worth hundreds and thousands of pounds, and nothing cashable. When I think of the local girls we have to train as housemaids, rough handed, willing enough, but far too few to begin to keep that vast place clean; when I think of the food, thin, meagre little cutlets for dinner, coming up in the heavy crested silver dishes which were kept polished by old Grayson, who has been with father for over fifty years, I want to laugh and to cry. There are empty stables and the gardens going to rack and ruin for want of money, with only one gardener and the fruit garden let out to a local man who sells back to us at cost price our own vegetables and potatoes. And what is so terrible is that its only hope of survival lies in David's marrying money.

Of course we never mention the fact, that would be a vulgarity of which father and mother are quite incapable, but we all know it in our innermost hearts, and I suppose David does too. When father dies and the heavy death duties have to come from the estate, it will be quite impossible to keep even two housemaids and old Grayson, unless more money is found from somewhere. Perhaps David will find an heiress in India, perhaps he will be lucky like Angela. If he doesn't, that is the end of Maysfield. I suppose it will be sold as a school and David will try to cram the pictures, the tapestries, and the silver, which are entailed on to his son, into a small villa at Aldershot, or into a low-ceilinged modern flat in London.

It was only when I came to leave Maysfield that I found how much it meant to me.

All through the preceding days I had been buoyed up with excitement; I had been unable to concentrate on anything: I had forgotten duties which had become so much part of my routine that ordinarily I could have done them in my sleep.

The Sale of Work in the village hall, which the Vicar had held to wipe off the debt on the church, was its usual social success and financial disappointment. We cleared only fifteen pounds where we had hoped for at least thirty, but everyone in the neighbourhood had come in during the afternoon to gossip and enjoy a cup of tea. I found myself for once the scene of attraction.

'I hear you are going to London,' everyone said to me the moment we shook hands. Needless to say the news had spread all over the county by that time. And more than one neighbour added, 'We shall miss you, Lyn, the Court won't seem itself without you.'

I felt flattered. I had grown so used to taking a very second place to father and mother that it was surprising to find that I was noticed at all, or that people minded whether I was there or not.

Then came the one good-bye I minded saying—to the Vicar. I went down after tea on Sunday for a last farewell. We had had people at the house who had motored over unexpectedly to see mother, so I was late in getting away and only arrived when the church bell had begun to peal for evensong.

21

I did not go to the front door. I walked straight into the garden where I knew I should find the Vicar walking up and down on the lawn, thinking out his sermon.

'I have come to say good-bye,' I said.

He held out his hands and took both of mine in his.

'Lyn, my dear,' he said, 'I hope you find great happiness and that you come back to us safely.'

'You say that as though I was going on a long voyage,' I said. 'That's how I feel myself. It is all very strange and almost frightening.'

'Of course it is,' he said gently. 'You have lived such a very quiet life here, but I don't think you need be frightened. It is extraordinary how easily we all get used to wider horizons.'

'I've wanted to go away so much,' I said, 'but now I am afraid—perhaps really I'm only frightened something will stop me.'

'I will come to the station and wave good-bye to you tomorrow,' he said, 'to make quite certain that you go.'

'Will you?' I asked. 'I would love you to. I shall feel rather lonely otherwise, because Mother, of course, can't come to see me off and father has a Hunt meeting at two o'clock.'

'I promise you I will be there. Bless you my child.'

The bell had begun to toll the five minutes to half-past. Picking up his books he walked through the little door in the wall which led from the Vicarage garden into the churchyard. With a final wave of his hand, he disappeared.

When he had gone I sat down on the wooden seat and looked at the garden around me. How dear it all was, the rockery which I remembered being started nearly ten years ago; the stump of a tree which had fallen down in a summer thunderstorm and which was now a mass of Paul Scarlet; the sunken lily pond, which had taken nearly six months to make and which had threatened to be a failure because the water wouldn't run away—it was all so familiar, but for the first time I seemed to see it clearly as a part of myself.

It was there, where the lupins were just breaking into blossom, that I had heard the story of the taking of Quebec. The Vicar made Woolfe with his irritabilty, his frenzy, his impatience and his genius, seem a living person, as when we were nailing up the honeysuckle on the summerhouse, he had made me feel the same about Clive of India. We had sat together for the first time in that sum-merhouse to read Browning, and here on the seat where I was now sitting, I had begun Childe Harolde and read it right through in the afternoon, while the Vicar mowed the grass, backwards and forwards, backwards and forwards, in front of me. Yes, the mellow red brick walls enclosed not only the garden, but also my education.

After a long while I got up and walked slowly into the house and into the library. I looked along the untidy shelves. The books were badly kept, for the one daily maid at the Vicarage had little time for dusting.

I wanted something to take to London, something I thought that I could read if I wanted to escape, as I might, from gaiety and excitement. I opened one or two of the books. Which should it be? I knew most of them so well. They were my friends, the real friends which I was leaving behind me.

I heard the front door slam, a voice speaking in the hall. I had no desire to see anyone else, not even the girl with whom I had shared my lessons for so many years. I picked up the book that was nearest to me, walked quietly through the french-window which led in the garden and crept away as I had arrived.

3

Angela's house was quite overwhelming. I had expected
something very luxurious and grand, but it exceeded anything I could possibly have imagined. Henry had apparently employed all the most expensive decorators in
London and they had really let themselves go. There were
tapestries; period furniture; pictures of everyone's
ancestors except Henry's; statues done by the latest and
most sensational sculptors; chandeliers glittering and shining and filled with real candles which were changed every
day. It was not surprising that I felt over-awed and tongue-
tied when I arrived.

Luckily there weren't many people to meet. Angela was
lying on the sofa looking, as usual, exactly like a picture of
Vogue. Henry was standing in front of the fireplace
which—being the summer—was massed with all sorts of
expensive flowers, and Henry's mother, Mrs. Ernest Watson, was sitting in an armchair looking far too young, I
thought on my first glance, to be his mother.

This first impression, I soon found, was only an illusion.
Mrs. Watson was about the most synthetic woman of her
age it was possible to meet. She had a good figure, but that
was the only thing about her that was her own. Her hair,
her teeth and her complexion were all bought, and although she looked a passable forty in electric light, at any
other time of the day she quickly disillusioned one.

I kissed Angela and shook hands with Henry before
Mrs. Watson exclaimed:

'Gracious, Angela, I had no idea that your younger
sister was going to turn out a beauty! She certainly won't
be on your hands for long this Season.'

Her remarks somehow broke the rather awkward moment of my arrival.

'Wait until I have finished with her!' Angela said looking

at me affectionately and slipping her arm through mine. 'I have made appointments with hairdressers and dressmakers and goodness knows what else. Tomorrow morning we are going to have a lovely time. Henry will faint when he gets the bill, but otherwise everyone will be pleased.'

'Thank you,' I said shyly to Henry, trying to smile gratefully at him.

He patted my shoulder awkwardly, just as he did when I was a child.

'That's all right,' he said. 'In for a penny, in for a pound. You deserve a good time and it is nice for Angela to have someone to take about with her—getting a bit too keen on running around on her own.'

There seemed to be a double entendre in his words, for Angela gave an uneasy laugh.

'You flatter me,' she said. 'Come Lyn, I want to show you your bedroom.'

She led me out of the room and we walked across the landing to the lift. As she shut the door and pressed the button, she said:

'I am sorry, Lyn, but Henry's like that.'

'Like what?' I asked.

'Oh don't you realise,' she said irritably, 'he can't help labouring the point when he pays for anything, but unless one coaxes money out of him one doesn't get any.'

The lift stopped before I could think of any reply, and we got out at the third floor. I followed Angela down the passage wondering what I ought to say, wondering also whether she was happy as father and mother had always believed.

She led me into a large room with two big windows overlooking the Square. There was a bathroom leading out of it and twin beds covered in quilted pink satin.

'Darling, it is heavenly!' I said. 'But surely this is your best spare room—won't you want it for somebody else?'

'There are two other rooms,' Angela said. 'As it is we have Henry's mother here incessantly—I am getting sick of it, I can tell you.'

She walked to the looking-glass and patted her hair.

'How do you think I am looking?' she asked.

'Lovely,' I answered. 'I have never seen you look better, really I haven't.'

'You really think so?' Angela questioned anxiously as though she valued my opinion.

25

'Of course I do,' I said. 'You are doing your hair a new way, aren't you?'

She nodded.

'You don't think it makes me look a little older?' she asked.

I laughed.

'You talk as though you were a hundred,' I said. 'After all, you were only twenty-nine last birthday.'

'Don't,' Angela said. 'It sounds awful—I never tell anyone my age, it is such a mistake, for even if you are honest they always put you on five years.'

'I shouldn't have thought you wanted to look as young as all that,' I said without thinking. 'After all, Henry must be forty-five, or is it forty-six?'

'Oh Henry!' Angela said with a shrug of her shoulders and turned away from the glass. 'The maid will unpack for you, and tomorrow we will have to get you something to wear. We'll burn that terrible coat and skirt. Where did you get it?'

'I've had it three years,' I answered.

'It looks like it,' Angela said. 'I am sure Mother chose it for you—it is just the type she made me have when I was eighteen.'

'I think she did,' I answered.

'Darling Mother,' Angela said, 'she has got absolutely no taste.'

I felt almost shocked. I was so unused to hearing mother and father criticised. While I suppose I knew that mother was a bad dresser, who never worried about her own clothes or mine, I had never dared to put the criticism into words, even to myself.

Angela was scrutinising me.

'You know, Lyn,' she said, 'Margaret's right, you are going to be a beauty.'

'Margaret?' I asked.

'Henry's mother,' she explained. 'You don't suppose we are allowed to call her anything so ageing as "mother", do you? Christian names, dear, every time. She likes to think she is still thirty-five. She's got the most terrible gigolo whom she insists on taking out every evening to dance. He's a wretched little boy of about twenty-five who, I am sure, loathes the sight of her.'

Quite suddenly I sat down on the bed and started to laugh.

26

'What are you laughing at?' Angela asked suspiciously.

'I was laughing at how far I had to come from Maysfield,' I answered. 'Can you imagine mother's face if you talked like that. I don't suppose she has ever heard of a gigolo.'

'You will hear of them here, all right,' Angela answered. 'And a good many other things too. I've thought sometimes that I am wrong to bring you up to London, Lyn. One is much happier, really, at home, knowing nothing, meeting nobody, not getting mixed up in all the intrigues and difficulties of this social hell.'

'What's the matter Angela?' I said. 'Aren't you happy?'

'Happy?' she echoed. 'Is there such a thing? Well, perhaps there is, but not for me at any rate.'

'But darling . . .' I began.

'No Lyn,' Angela said turning away. 'You will see, hear, and understand quite enough if you stay here a month or so and if you take my advice, you will just be discretion itself and not take sides.'

'But I don't understand.'

'It isn't important, anyway,' Angela said wearily. 'Take off that awful hat, and come downstairs and have a cocktail. There are some men coming in later, friends of Henry's from the House of Commons. We will try you out on them before we put on the finishing touches.'

I looked down at my coat and skirt and home made blouse.

'I can't come to a party like this,' I said.

'Well, I can't lend you anything,' Angela replied. 'You really ought to bant, Lyn. You must be at least thirty-eight inches round the hips—and I'm just thirty.'

'Well I will stay up here,' I said, 'and wait until tomorrow when I have some decent clothes.'

'No,' she said. 'We'll find you something. Come down to my room and have a look.'

I don't think I ever hated my appearance so much as when I stood in front of Angela's long fitted mirrors in my old faded camiknickers and found that dress after dress wouldn't go over my shoulders, let alone my hips.

'It is hopeless,' I said eventually.

So I put on my own clothes again and because she insisted, went downstairs to the drawing-room, feeling hot, ruffled and exceedingly irritable.

Actually the cocktail party went off far better than I had

expected. The men were either contemporaries of Henry's who wanted to talk politics and who were, therefore, not interested in women, pretty or otherwise, or Angela's intimates who being full of the latest gossip about people of whom I had never heard, ignored me. Mrs. Watson's boy friend duly arrived and I must say he seemed to me far better than Angela had led me to expect. He was a thin, rather intelligent looking young man, with a high forehead and a nervous habit of flicking his fingers together whenever he was not talking. He was quite pleasant to me and I was just beginning to enjoy our conversation together, when I saw Mrs. Watson glowering at me, and realised that I was being tactless.

I moved away from him across the room to where Henry was standing. Jovially my brother-in-law put his arm round my waist and said to the man standing next to him:

'What do you think of my little sister-in-law? She only arrived this evening from the wilds of the country—she is going to stay with us for the Season.'

'I hope you enjoy yourself,' Henry's friend said.

'I mean to,' I answered.

My words were trivial, but at that moment they meant something to me, and they were almost in the nature of a vow. Already I saw difficulties ahead, but I meant to circumvent them. I had come to London for a good time and I had every intention of having it. My visit to Angela wasn't going to be anything like I had anticipated—I saw that. But I could at least make the best of everything that presented itself. I had always thought of Angela as ideally happy with her husband, getting everything she wanted from a man who adored her. Already I had learnt that was not a true picture and I was almost afraid of what else I might discover.

Yet, I told myself fiercely, it should not affect me. I had my own life to lead! I was going to meet people; I was going to see places and things which in the past had been only names to me. I had so much to do and such a short time to do it in, and I vowed that come what may I would live fully every moment of my new life.

I woke in the morning with the same determination. Everything came flooding back to me after the first sensation of wonderment as I opened my eyes. Where was I—I wondered? Then I remembered. I got up and drew back the curtains. It was only eight o'clock but I was used to getting up early, although Angela had told me that I mustn't think of being called until half-past nine.

Outside in the Square gardens a few wood pigeons were cooing, and they reminded me of home, but they did not make me feel homesick. I felt on tiptoe for the adventure that was before me.

Last night we had dined quietly in the house, then we had gone to a cinema. There were just six of us: Mrs. Watson and her young man whose name was Peter Browning; Henry; Angela, and a man who arrived for dinner, and who, from the way that she introduced him, I sensed instantly was of importance. His name was Captain Douglas Ormonde. He was tall and fair, goodlooking in a somewhat conventional 'Brigade of Guards' manner. The moment he arrived Angela was a different person. Gone was her air of weariness, of restlessness, of irritability. She literally sparkled; her eyes were shining; amusing witticisms came quickly to her lips, one after the other. It was so obvious that she was delighted with Douglas Ormonde's presence that more than once I glanced nervously at Henry, wondering what he thought about it. This, of course, was the explanation of Angela's unhappiness; the reason why she wished to be young and beautiful; the reason why she was finding her present married life difficult.

It would not have taken a very imaginative person or a very sensitive person to understand that here, just in front of me, was what is known as the eternal triangle; Henry, old for his young wife but rich, Angela infatuated with a man of her own age and someone who, I gathered from the conversation, was not well off.

Henry, I thought too, was at his very worst; he seemed to enjoy embarrassing his guest on the question of money. During dinner he said to Captain Ormonde:

'Aren't you playing polo this summer—I thought your regiment was so keen?'

'I am afraid I can't afford to,' Douglas Ormonde answered with a laugh. 'It is an expensive pastime, you know, Watson.'

Henry raised his eyebrows.

'Surely you could economise in other ways,' he suggested. 'Not so many night clubs, for instance. Women never were a cheap luxury, as I have found—haven't I, Angela?'

29

'It depends very much on the woman,' Angela said shortly.

'But of course!' Henry answered good-humouredly. 'For instance, if they have money of their own, it makes things so much easier.'

There was an uncomfortable pause which Mrs. Watson broke in giving one of her shrill laughs and saying:

'All women should have money of their own. I am not a feminist on most things, but I certainly believe in that—don't you, Lyn?'

'I have never thought about it,' I answered, rather shy at being brought into the conversation. 'But I would certainly like to have some of my own.'

Henry laughed.

'You will have to marry a rich husband my dear, and get him to settle a good allowance on you.'

'Just like your sister has done!' Angela said in a bitter voice.

'Well, well, and why not?' Henry questioned. 'I hope Lyn finds both a rich and charming husband.'

'So do I,' Angela said. 'But I assure her that the two don't often go together.'

Henry was hurt. I could see it in his face, though he laughed in a hearty sort of manner and Mrs. Watson changed the conversation by asking what cinema we were going to.

At once the conversation became general again, everyone suggesting some preference of their own. They argued for so long that it seemed likely we should miss half the programme, whichever was decided on, until finally, Henry made up his mind for us and we drove off in the Rolls Royce to the Empire.

4

Why do clothes mean so much to women? They do, however much we may try to deny it, however much we may laugh at our yearnings to be fashionable. Every woman loves clothes and there are few more enjoyable sensations than being really well dressed, and knowing that one is being admired.

Angela took me first of all to shops where I could buy some clothes ready-made, then to the more expensive and exclusive dressmakers, who promised to copy models as quickly as they could, so that by the end of the week I had a wardrobe full of dresses, as well as drawers packed with new chiffon and silk underclothes, and a shelf full of shoes which made my feet look half their usual size.

I enjoyed choosing the clothes; but wearing them was bliss, so when I came to dinner wearing a picture frock of white chiffon and found Henry alone drinking a glass of sherry in the drawing-room, I tried to thank him and ended by kissing him affectionately on the cheek. He was surprised and, I think a little touched.

'You aren't to thank me, Lyn,' he said. 'I like to give them to you and, damn it, it is a long time since anyone's been enthusiastic about anything I have given them.'

I felt a sudden pity for him which I quickly tried to quench, because whatever Angela might say about being impartial, my loyalty must lie with my sister. All the same it was difficult not to see a little of Henry's point of view. He was, it was true, being awfully difficult about Angela's friendship with Captain Ormonde, but I couldn't help feeling that any man might have behaved in the same way except, of course, father, or anyone just like that, who would simply have turned Douglas Ormonde out of the house and said no more about it. Henry was, I think, too frightened of Angela to do that, so he merely nagged at her, getting in nasty, spiteful remarks when he could, and being at times so rude to Douglas that we all felt embarrassed. Angela was quite capable of holding her own, but I despised Douglas Ormonde both for putting up so meekly with Henry's sarcasm and for relying on Angela to defend him.

Mrs. Watson did not make things any better. After a week in the house I came to the conclusion that she did not really like Angela. She used to come into the drawing-room before dinner when Angela wasn't down, she was generally late, and say:

'Now, how many are we going to be tonight? Let me see if I can guess—six, and the sixth guest's name begins with a "D". Aren't I a clever little woman?' Or else she would say, 'Angela will be late, Henry dear! I shouldn't wait for her, she has only just come in. She has had a lovely afternoon—a run in the country!'

'Oh, has she been to the country?' Henry would ask, perhaps quite innocently.

'Oh, didn't you know?' his mother would say. 'Dear dear, how tactless of me, perhaps I oughtn't to have mentioned it.'

I thought that she was a cat, only she was such a silly woman that one couldn't really be angry with her for long about anything. The more I saw of her and of Peter Browning, the more I realised the only way to grow old was to be like mother—not to run away, to let age come upon one slowly and graciously. There was something pathetic and at the same time horrible in this striving after youth, in this groping after love, when one was twenty-five years too old for it.

Sometimes I would come upon Mrs. Watson unexpectedly, when she was alone, relaxing in a chair, and I would see that without her party expression she was just a tired old woman, fighting a losing battle without even commendable courage.

Every night we did something and every evening we either went to cocktail parties or people came to us for drinks. At luncheon time Angela took me round to all sorts of her friends and made a real effort, I think, to see that I met the people who would be useful to me, who would invite me to the balls they were going to give, or who had daughters and sons of the right age. It was awfully sweet of her and I really appreciated it because I realised that she was making a sacrifice in giving up some of the time she might have been with Douglas.

Often before luncheon was hardly finished, she would get to her feet and say:

'Don't hurry, Lyn, you have got a fitting at half-past three, but nothing else this afternoon. I have an appointment I must keep, so everyone will have to excuse me.'

She would rush away to snatch an hour or so with Douglas, knowing that Henry would be safely at the House of Commons, or playing golf outside London.

I think that Henry genuinely began to like me after the first Saturday I spent in his house, when I suggested going round the golf links with him. I had come down to breakfast because although I had been to a dance the night before, I still found it difficult to sleep late in the morning, and I have always hated breakfast in bed. I was just pouring myself a second cup of coffee when Henry came into the dining-room.

'Good morning, Lyn,' he said. 'You look blooming—aren't you tired?'

'Not a bit!' I answered. 'Did we wake you up last night?'

Angela, Douglas and I had gone to a ball. There had been a three line whip at the House and Henry had been unable to come with us.

'I got in at one o'clock,' he said, 'but I suppose you were long after that, although I didn't hear you.'

'It was after three,' I confessed. 'It was a lovely party. I did enjoy myself.'

The butler came into the room while we were still talking.

'Sir Henry Gratton has telephoned, sir, to say he is very sorry he is unable to play with you today, as her ladyship is not at all well.'

'Damn!' Henry said. 'That ruins my day, and I haven't had a round this week.'

'Can't you get someone else?' I suggested.

'At the eleventh hour?' he asked. 'Not a chance. These near London courses are always the same—people make up their games before they arrive and there's never a chance of picking anyone up in the club house.'

I hesitated; then I suggested:

'If it will make you feel less lonely, I will come and walk round with you. I can't play; I've never learnt, so do say frankly if you would rather I didn't come.'

33

'Will you really come?' he asked in surprise. 'That's jolly nice of you, Lyn. I would love it; and I'll give you a lesson. What do you say?'

'You will be sorry if you do!' I answered. 'I couldn't be worse at games. I have never had a chance of learning any, except tennis with the Vicar's daughter.'

Henry laughed.

'That's a change,' he said, 'from the modern young women who can beat us wretched men at everything, and don't forget to let us know it. Get your thick shoes on; I am looking forward to this, Lyn,' he added almost boyishly.

I left a note for Angela because she wasn't called, but I knew she hadn't arranged anything special for me. In fact, the night before I heard Douglas say to her "Can't you lunch tomorrow and come down to Ranelagh?" and she had answered, "I will try, but don't count on it". With me out of the way and Henry safely employed until teatime, she could do what he wanted. I left the note with her maid and hurried off with Henry.

I had expected him—I don't know why—to drive himself; it seemed too luxurious to sit at the back of the Rolls in golfing clothes, being driven by a uniformed chauffeur, but Henry lit a cigar and bent forward to shut up the glass window between ourselves and the chauffeur.

'Now we can talk,' he said comfortably. 'Tell me all your secrets, Lyn.'

'I haven't got any,' I answered.

'Haven't fallen in love yet?' he asked.

I shook my head.

'I have met so many young men in the last week that I don't think I should recognise one from the other again.'

'Well, there's plenty of time,' he said.

'I don't want to get married unless I am quite certain it is the right person,' I said, then felt a fool for having made such a trite, conventional remark.

Henry however did not laugh at me.

'You are quite right, Lyn,' he said slowly. 'Don't be in a hurry.'

'You know, Henry,' I went on, 'I don't think I really want to live this sort of life for ever.'

He took the cigar out of his mouth and turned and looked at me in surprise.

34

'I thought all women wanted a social roundabout,' he said.

I shook my head.

'It is lovely for a short time,' I answered. 'Don't think that I am not enjoying myself because I am. I wouldn't miss a moment of it for the world, but do you think it makes for real happiness? Look at father and mother, for instance, they never got away from Maysfield, they never seem to do anything but just the usual humdrum routine, day after day, yet they are terribly happy together.'

'I have often thought that I would like a home in the country,' Henry said. 'When my father died, I wanted to keep on his estate, but Angela didn't like it—said it was too far from London and the house was gloomy.'

'Angela loves London,' I remarked quickly.

'You are right, Lyn,' Henry said violently. 'It is a damned rotten life—one oughtn't to live in it all the time, wearing out one's health going to parties, drinking too many cocktails and sitting up late, night after night. I shall buy a house in the country and we will go there. The children will like it in the holidays.'

I was frightened at the storm I had unwittingly produced, wondering what Angela would say if Henry really made up his mind to do that which she would dislike.

'You might find the country awfully dull,' I suggested. 'After all, you are a busy person yourself, aren't you, Henry?'

'I used to be,' he answered. 'You know, Lyn, I made a terrible mistake when I gave up working in the business. I had the chance of going on as a working director, or sitting back as my father had done in his old age, just drawing the profits and taking no active part. I liked the work in a way—it was a family business—and it gave me an interest. Now I have only got the constituency, too safe to be interesting, and a lot of time to mooch about at Angela's parties, thinking how much I dislike them and her friends.'

It was really very difficult to know what to say to this sort of confidence. I felt that Henry had no one to whom he could talk, and I sensed that he was dying to unburden himself to me, to tell me how worried he was about his life with Angela. Once again I remembered Angela's words about being impartial. At the same time I longed to help them both.

35

I decided that Henry was a nice person at heart, although I could quite understand how he annoyed Angela. But after all, he was her husband, she had married him, and even though I liked Douglas Ormonde, I felt in many ways he would be a poor exchange for Henry. He was good-looking, but he had very little character. Henry had a rough but definite personality and it was obviously lack of occupation that had made him moody and disgruntled. He came from a class which had always worked. His energy unemployed was turning sour within him, making him unhappy over things which, had he been busy, he might have passed by with a laugh.

'Isn't there anything you could do?' I suggested. 'Not in your old business, but something new? Couldn't you take up some new invention, start a new factory, run it yourself? You would enjoy it, you know, Henry.'

He took my suggestion seriously.

'That is certainly an idea,' he answered. 'You think I am capable of running a business? Thank you for the compliment, Lyn. But after all, the only one I ever tackled was going along very well before I put my hand to the wheel and it has managed very well without me, since I retired. Suppose I failed?'

'I don't believe you are as modest as that,' I said. 'So I shan't bother to answer that question.'

'You've got sense,' Henry said. 'I will tell you the truth, you may like to know it. When you first arrived the other day, I thought "here's a jolly pretty girl, but I will bet my bottom dollar that she hasn't got a brain in her head—brains don't go with those sort of looks". I have known women who looked like you, Lyn—pink and white blondes—and they have always been half-wits. Well, my dear, I take off my hat to you, you have got both brains and beauty and that's saying a good deal.'

I blushed, I really couldn't help it because I was frightfully pleased. I had never thought of myself as having any brains and I have certainly never thought much of my looks, but it was very nice to be appreciated.

'Thank you, Henry,' I said. 'If you are so nice to me I shall have a swelled head as well.'

'I'm not worrying about that,' he answered. 'If people have enough brains, they are seldom conceited. They have self-confidence, but that's a different thing. We get all our values mixed up these days. That is the trouble with your sex, Lyn, they've got all the wrong values. They're so proud of the limbs that God gave them, that they never have any time to consider what they might acquire for themselves, unless, of course, it is money.'

'Don't,' I said quickly without thinking.

'Don't what?' he questioned.

'Always be nasty about women and money,' I said bravely. I wasn't quite certain how he would take my remark, but he accepted it gravely and didn't answer for a moment.

'Am I?' he asked at length.

'You are rather,' I answered, feeling rather frightened now at what I had said. 'It makes people uncomfortable, you know, at least it does me. I think money's a lovely thing to have, if you have it and it is a bore not to have any, but if you keep talking about it, you make it far more important than it really is. I can't explain—I am saying this awfully badly, Henry, so don't be annoyed with me—but you know, if you labour a point of view too often, it becomes rather nasty, almost vulgar.'

I stopped then, horrified that I had said too much; in fact when Henry said: 'Well, I must say, you have got a nerve!' I wasn't surprised. I quaked inwardly, thinking that I had been crazy to be so frank.

'I am sorry . . .' I started to say, but he stopped me.

'No, no, don't apologise,' he said. 'That's honest and if we are going to be friends, you and I, Lyn, let's have honesty between us. Are we going to be friends?'

'Yes, let's,' I answered. 'And you mustn't mind if I say awful things like that to you, it is my country upbringing which hasn't got a very sophisticated polish yet.'

'Thank God for that,' Henry said gravely and he held out his hand. 'Friends, Lyn?'

'Friends,' I answered and put my hand into his.

5

I had been staying with Angela nearly three weeks before I
said to Henry, somewhat shyly because I didn't want to
bother him:

'Can I come down to the House of Commons, one day
when you are not too busy to show me round? I would like
to see the Mother of Parliaments.'

Henry looked pleased.

'Of course,' he said. 'I would have suggested it myself
before, only I didn't think it would amuse you. Angela always calls it a deadly hole and whenever she has to have a
meal there, says the food is uneatable.'

'Well, I would like to sample it just once,' I said
laughing. 'If you are not busy.'

'There's an interesting debate tomorrow,' Henry said, 'on
unemployment. I think I shall be able to get you a couple
of tickets. Can you persuade Angela to come?'

'I'm sure I can,' I answered.

'Don't be disappointed if you find it dull,' Henry said. 'It
is very seldom anything sensational happens in the House.'

'I won't be disappointed,' I promised. 'And I certainly
won't be bored. I have wanted to see the House for years.'

When Angela came in—she had been out with Douglas
Ormonde as usual—I told her what we had planned.

'Do say "yes" Angela,' I pleaded. 'I want to go so much.'

'All right,' she said not very enthusiastically. 'I have got
nothing very important to do tomorrow, nothing that can't
be cancelled, at any rate. But you don't mean to say that
Henry has persuaded you to lunch there?'

'We have got a new kitchen committee,' Henry said.
'The food is better and I will order you all your favourite
dishes beforehand.'

'Don't bother,' Angela said. 'If I don't eat anything, all
the better—I am slimming.'

'Angela!' I cried. 'How ridiculous you are! You are only
38

saying that to shame me. I know I ought to diet, but the food here is so delicious, I just can't refuse a single course.'

Angela looked at me critically.

'I honestly think you are fatter than when you arrived,' she said.

I gave a cry of despair.

'Don't tease the child,' Henry commanded. 'She looks very nice as she is and I will promise her plenty of strawberries and cream on the Terrace to put on another ounce or two.'

'And I shan't be able to say "no",' I said in mock despair.

I looked forward to going to the House of Commons and I realised, as I was dressing the next morning, that it would be the first bit of sight-seeing that I had bothered to do since I had come to London. I remembered, somewhat guiltily, that before I had left home I had talked to the Vicar of seeing the Tower of London; going to the various museums; looking at the pictures in the National Gallery, and that I had promised to write him a full description of the new sculpture rooms at the Tate. 'There doesn't seem to be time for anything,' I told myself, but in excuse, I realised it would be rather difficult to go off all on my own, and there was certainly no one to go with me.

I was finding too that not getting to bed until the early hours of the morning was making me late in getting up. When I wanted breakfast in bed I had only to leave a note outside my door and on one or two occasions I had said I would ring when I awoke, and found myself sleeping until it was nearly lunch time.

'I am deteriorating,' I told myself solemnly.

I knew I looked smart by the time I was ready to leave home. I had asked Angela what I should wear and she had said:

'Oh, nothing showy, the members are all like a lot of schoolboys—they don't want their belongings to be conspicuous. When I go to the House with Henry, I always feel I might be going to Parents' Day at the boys' school.'

I put on, therefore, a neat but very attractive little dress of pale blue crêpe de chine, with a white collar and cuffs which matched a white straw hat trimmed with blue ribbons. It was no use my trying to look sophisticated like Angela, who came down in exquisitely cut black crêpe de chine, with a huge bunch of parma violets pinned on her

39

shoulder. So I had to be pretty-pretty, and while I rebelled over some of the things Angela wanted to choose for me, I knew that she was right, and that it was no use for me, with my fat fairness to try and look chic.

I had learnt a lot about dressing since I came to London. The first thing that Angela had taught me was how to make my face up. I didn't need to use very much, but I must say, lipstick and eyeblack made a difference and while I would have given anything personally to have changed my appearance, it was gratifying to know that I was a success at dances and seldom had a dance free after I had been in the ballroom a few minutes.

We drove down to the House in the Rolls and as Angela had kept us all waiting, we had no time to see anything before luncheon, but went straight into the dining-room. Henry had done as he had promised and ordered the meal beforehand and I must say, everything seemed delicious, although Angela grumbled and tried to pretend that she could not eat anything. As soon as we were settled, I looked round the room and Henry pointed out one or two celebrities.

'There's Maxton, over there,' he said, 'with two friends.'

I looked where he directed and was excited to find that the leader of the I.L.P. looked exactly like his caricatures.

'It isn't often we see him in the dining-room,' Henry remarked.

He also pointed out Sir Patrick Hannon, who looked to me like a jovial John Bull; but Henry said he had never heard that John Bull had a strong Irish brogue on him. There was Megan Lloyd George and tiny, red-haired Ellen Wilkinson, but what excited me more than anything, was to see Winston Churchill coming through the Lobby afterwards. I had heard stories about him ever since I was a child and I only wished that Henry had known him well enough to introduce me, because I would have liked to have had the opportunity of speaking to one of my heroes. I admired him so much, perhaps because I had read some of his books, but perhaps too, because he had always seemed to be against the conventional order of things.

Father's politics had always been of the good die-hard solid kind; every change to him brought us near the time of revolution. I had learnt too much from books and far too much from the Vicar, to believe as Father would have

40

liked us to believe, that what was good for him, must be good enough for us and for our children after us.

'You had better see the Speaker's procession,' Henry said. 'Then I will put you in the Ladies' Gallery.'

He took us into the Inner Lobby where everyone was gathered, waiting for the Speaker to arrive. When he came there was an impressive hush, only broken by a girl who was standing next to me, saying, in a broad cockney accent: 'My, but mustn't 'e be 'ot in that wig!' She was quickly hushed into silence, but it made me want to laugh and spoilt what I am sure should have been a memorable moment.

Then Henry took us up to the Ladies' Gallery and we managed to get two seats in the front row. I stared down into the Chamber below. I was disappointed because I could not see the Speaker, being directly above him, but Henry pointed out one or two members of the Government on the front bench, and then hurried away to get to his own place.

The questions were amusing and members kept popping up and down, while others came in and out the whole time, some of them just looking round as if for a friend before they went away again. Then the debate opened and several old gentlemen spoke, one after another, most of them in such droning voices that I could hardly hear what they were saying. I must confess I didn't much want to. A speech from one of the Labour members was full of vitality, so I listened to that and felt inclined to clap at the end. Then, from directly behind the Government Bench, a man rose to speak. I don't know why, but the moment he got to his feet I felt my attention riveted upon him.

He was tall, very dark, and thin, so that I could see the square cut lines of his cheekbones from where I was sitting. He spoke in a low clear voice and I could hear every word. I can't remember anything of what he said—it is odd, because not for a moment did my attention waver, but there was something in his voice, something in the way he spoke, which stirred me. I sat staring at him. He must have spoken for nearly half an hour and when he sat down I felt myself relax as though I had been taut and strained during the whole time that he had been talking. He received quite a lot of hear-hears. I turned to Angela.

'Who is it?' I asked.

'Sir Philip Chadleigh,' she replied. 'He's good, isn't he?'

I didn't answer her. The name seemed to strike some chord in my memory. Where had I heard that name. Why did I know it—Philip Chadleigh? I must have read about him, I thought to myself.

Someone else had risen on the opposite side of the House. They made a reference to Sir Philip's speech which was obviously incorrect; he rose to his feet, corrected the speaker, then sat down again. There was something in the way he moved, a quick, almost feline grace, that once again seemed to hold some connection for me with the past. What was it, I asked myself, but I could find no answer; I could only sit looking at him, staring down at his dark head, finely cut nose and broad shoulders.

How long I sat there just looking at Sir Philip I have no idea, but I was startled to feel Henry's hand touch my shoulder.

'Come on,' he whispered.

I got to my feet and found to my surprise that Angela had already left me and was disappearing through the door.

As we got outside Henry spoke.

'It's a quarter past four. I thought, perhaps, you would like some tea.'

'A quarter past four!' I said in surprise. 'Have we been there an hour and a half?'

'I am very glad it has passed so quickly,' Henry said with a smile. 'Most people say "I thought you were never coming".'

I felt dazed as we went down in the lift; as we stepped out into the passage, who should come walking alone straight from the Chamber, but Sir Philip Chadleigh himself.

Henry spoke to him.

'Very good, Chadleigh,' he said. 'It was a fine effort.'

'Thank you,' Sir Philip replied.

'You know my wife?' Henry went on. 'And my sister-in-law—Lady Gwendolyn Sherbrooke.'

Sir Philip shook hands with Angela, then turned to me. I put my hand into his and felt in some extraordinary way as though something momentous was taking place. I felt breathless and at the same time bewildered, as though my brain was asking me why, how and what all this meant.

'I thought your speech was marvellous,' Angela said gushingly.

'Thank you,' he said. 'We don't often have the pleasure of seeing you here, Lady Angela.'

She laughed.

'I confess that it is not usually my idea of spending a happy afternoon,' she answered. 'But I had to come today, because this is my sister's first visit. She has never been to the House before.'

'I am very glad I had the honour of speaking on such an auspicious occasion,' Sir Philip said mock seriously. 'You must tell me,' he added to me, 'what you thought of my speech. Be honest.'

Without formulating the words, without thinking, I spoke.

'I thought you looked like a black panther.'

As soon as my lips opened I knew that I was about to say something awful, but I could not prevent myself. As though in a dream I heard myself utter the words. I saw Sir Phillip stiffen, then a strange, almost frightening look came into his eyes. There was a second of utter silence.

'Lyn!' Angela said in astonishment and I knew without looking at him that Henry was furious.

'Why do you say that?' Sir Philip asked sharply, and there was a fierce note in his voice.

I felt the tension break and a humiliating blush came flooding into my cheeks.

'I don't know,' I stammered.

Without a word Sir Philip turned and walked away down the passage.

'Lyn!' Angela said again, but she was interrupted by Henry.

'Really, Lyn,' he said angrily. 'There's surely no need to be rude to Sir Philip.'

'I didn't mean to be rude,' I said miserably.

'Well, you couldn't have gone a better way about it,' Henry said. 'Don't you realise that he is a very important person and you shouldn't talk to anyone like that.'

'Really, Henry!' Angela said in a drawling voice. 'I don't see there's anything to make so much fuss about.'

I knew that she was taking up the cudgels on my behalf simply to be disagreeable to Henry, although I felt that she too thought I had behaved in an extraordinary manner.

'Well, it was a jolly queer thing to say, anyway,' Henry said.

'Now I come to think about it,' Angela answered slowly, 'that is exactly what he does look like.'

'There was no need to be rude,' Henry said solemnly sticking to his guns.

'And there was no need for him to go off without saying good-bye,' Angela retorted.

We had walked along the passage by this time and were going down the stairs which lead to the Terrace.

'I am sorry,' I said meekly. There seemed to be nothing else I could say. I was so surprised at myself; the words seemed to have jumped from my lips.

Somewhat gloomily we found a table on the Terrace and sat down. Henry ordered tea and strawberries and cream.

'You might have asked someone to have tea with us,' Angela said, breaking an awkward silence.

'I couldn't think of anyone you would like,' Henry replied. 'You always abuse all my friends.'

'I must admit I prefer the absence of most of them to their company,' Angela said. 'I can't think why it is, Henry, that you have a penchant for all the biggest bores in Europe.'

'Just as well I didn't ask anyone to tea then,' Henry said. 'If that is what you feel about them.'

'Surely there must be some amusing Members of Parliament?' Angela asked. 'Now, who is that young man over there, for instance—the smart, clean-looking one?'

'No idea,' Henry replied. 'He's a visitor, not a Member.'

'I was afraid so,' Angela said with a sigh.

'May I have some more tea?' I asked.

She poured me out another cup. Just as I was taking it from her, a voice beside me made me start so much that I nearly dropped it.

'Can I come and join you?'

We all three looked up to see Sir Philip.

'But of course!' Angela answered. 'Henry, ask for another cup, will you?'

'I am sorry I had to rush off like that,' he said easily. 'I had a man waiting for me. Well, he's disposed of and I feel I need some pleasant relaxation.'

Angela was all smiles and Henry's anger vanished like a summer thunderstorm. Only I sat silent, hardly daring to look at Sir Philip, but concentrating on my strawberries

44

and cream. Angela started to engage him in animated conversation about various people whom they both knew. But after a moment he said:

'And is your sister enjoying the Season?'

He looked at me.

'We are doing our best to entertain her,' Angela said. 'I feel like a dowager with a debutante daughter, for I sit on the dais night after night, don't I, Lyn?'

'I am having a lovely time,' I answered.

I looked up as I spoke; I saw something in his eyes which made me catch my breath, just as I had that first moment of introduction. What was it about this man, I asked myself? Why did his name and his looks seem to haunt me? Where could I have heard about him before?

'Do you like music?' he asked me.

'Yes,' I answered, feeling my monosyllable was stupid, yet being incapable of making any answer save the bare truth.

'Then you must all come to the concert I am giving on Tuesday,' he said, turning to Angela. 'It is at Chadleigh House, I needn't add that it is in aid of charity—everything is, these days. But perhaps you would dine with me first?'

'We would love it,' Angela said. 'How sweet of you to ask us.'

'That's splendid,' Sir Philip answered. 'I will tell my secretary to send you the tickets and I shall expect you all to dinner at eight-thirty.'

'It is very kind of you, Chadleigh,' Henry said. 'Although, I am afraid, concerts aren't much in my line.'

'You will enjoy this one,' Sir Philip said. 'We have Dezzia coming over from Paris specially for it, and two or three of the stars from Covent Garden.'

'It is simply years since I have been to Chadleigh House,' Angela said. 'Have you still got that wonderful ballroom decorated with murals?'

'The ballroom's still there,' Sir Philip answered, 'but the murals aren't. They faded terribly. The Frenchman who did them used some sort of pigment which couldn't stand the damp. However, it has been redone by an Austrian, and I think you will find them equally lovely, if not more so. I personally am delighted with his work. Have you seen the murals in Peterborough House?' he added speaking directly to me.

I shook my head.

'I don't think I have ever seen any,' I answered, 'not modern ones, at any rate.'

'Lyn has lived in the country all her life,' Angela explained. 'It seems incredible these days, but my parents are terribly old-fashioned and this is the first time Lyn has ever been to London.'

'It doesn't sound very modern!' Sir Philip said with a smile.

'I am a real country cousin,' I answered, losing a little of my embarrassment and shyness.

'May I say you don't look it?' he said.

'I think you are entitled to make a few personal remarks,' I replied, trying to speak lightly, but in spite of myself feeling the blood rising again to my face.

'One day,' he said, 'I am going to ask you why you made that particular remark to me.' He spoke very seriously, in a low voice as though he were speaking to me alone. He looked at his watch. 'I am sorry, but I must go. Good-bye, Lady Angela.'

'Good-bye,' Angela answered. 'We shall look forward to Tuesday.'

'So shall I', he replied and it seemed to me that he glanced in my direction as he spoke.

6

'Really, Henry!' Angela said when he had gone. 'After making such a fuss, abusing poor Lyn, the man wasn't annoyed at all. You seem to go out of your way to find fault, but that's nothing new.'

'That isn't fair, Angela,' I said, feeling I must defend Henry. 'It was unpardonable of me to say what I did, but I have got no explanation about it at all. I just can't explain why I said it.'

'Anyway, it has got us an invitation for Tuesday night,' Angela said gaily. 'I have always wanted to dine at Chadleigh House and so has Henry—only he has never managed to squeeze an invitation for himself before.'

'Chadleigh has always been very pleasant to me,' Henry answered.

'By which you mean he's said "good morning" and "good evening",' Angela said tartly. 'Don't pretend you have been on intimate terms with him, Henry, because you haven't. What is more, you know you are snobby enough to be delighted to be asked to one of his parties.'

'Is he very important?' I asked.

'Frightfully,' Angela answered. 'Ask Henry to tell you about him. He will enjoy it.'

I looked up at Henry who cleared his throat rather pompously, before he said:

'Of course Chadleigh's important. His father was a fine Prime Minister, although he held the post for a very short time owing to ill health. When he retired he was offered an earldom, but said "I have served His Majesty to the best of my ability, and I would like to leave the same opportunity to my son". So they gave him the Garter and his son inherited only the baronetcy, which has been in the family for hundreds of years.'

'Go on,' Angela said sarcastically. 'I am enjoying this.

Henry talks exactly like a mixture of Debrett and a snob's memoirs.'

'Oh please go on, Henry,' I said, for I was genuinely interested.

'Well, there's always been a Chadleigh at Court, just as there has always been a Chadleigh in the House of Commons. This one went to the War and did extraordinarily well. When he came back he stood for the family seat and, of course, romped in. Then after he had been in the House a couple of years, there was some scandal, I can't remember what it was all about now, but anyway, he gave up his constituency and went abroad for some years. Then he came back and took up his old life again, reopened Chadleigh House and Longmoor Park, their place in the country. Royalty stay there, just as royalty attend most of the parties he gives in London.

'It is difficult to explain why Philip Chadleigh is politically important—socially, of course, it is obvious. He has got one of the most respected names in England and a huge fortune. But he does count for something in the Party. He has held various government posts at different times and I was very surprised that after the last election he didn't take office. There is, however, a strong rumour that they are keeping him for something else—the Ambassadorship in Washington, perhaps, or the Viceroy of India, I shouldn't be surprised at either. Philip Chadleigh's a dark horse.'

'Or rather a dark panther,' Angela said with a scream of laughter.

I don't know why, but her frivolity annoyed me.

'Thank you, Henry,' I said. Then I got to my feet. 'Let's go home,' I said. 'I am tired.'

Angela looked at me in surprise. It was not usual for me to make any move on my own. I was too punctilious about letting her take precedence. However, she took it good-humouredly.

'I'm not surprised,' she said. 'I am exhausted myself. We aren't dining until nine—with any luck we will be able to have a rest before dinner.'

'No cocktail party?' I asked.

'Not this evening,' Angela answered. 'Douglas Ormonde said he might drop in and if he does, we can all have a drink in my bedroom.'

She said it casually enough, but I saw Henry's face darken. It wasn't the first time we had all met in Angela's bedroom for drinks. She would lie among her lace cushions, looking utterly lovely. There was really very little difference between her room and an ordinary sitting-room, save for the fact that it had a bed in it. Yet I knew that it annoyed Henry.

'Surely you can get dressed,' he had said to her once in my presence and she had laughed at him.

'Don't be so middle-class,' she had replied. 'It is typically Streatham to think that there must be something wrong in a bedroom.'

However, on this occasion Henry need not have worried, for when we got back to the house it was to find that already half a dozen people had arrived, whom Angela had forgotten all about. Leaving them laughing and chattering in the drawing-room, I crept away to my own room.

Alone, I pulled off my hat and flung it on the bed, then stood staring at myself in the looking glass, seeing not my own reflection, but the dark eyes and dark hair above the square-cut forehead of Sir Philip Chadleigh. I found I was whispering his name over and over again; there was a kind of magic in it and an echo of something I could not remember, could not recall.

What was it? Of what did his name remind me? I felt excited, thrillingly, tinglingly excited. I found myself counting the days, even the hours, until Tuesday, when I should see him again.

I had never felt anything like this before, never experienced such a feeling which I couldn't explain even to myself. I tried to remember his speech, the words he had used, but I could only remember the tone of his voice, a few eloquent gestures he had made and that swift movement when he had risen to correct the opposing speaker. Why had it made such an impression on me? Why, I asked myself?

I made no attempt to belittle the impression I had received; there was, I knew, no point in under-estimating what had occurred. Something tremendous had happened.

I bathed my face, changed my dress and went downstairs. After two hours in the smoky and noisy atmosphere, I was glad when everyone but Douglas Ormonde said good-bye. Henry shook hands with them in the hall and would have gone back again into the drawing-room, but I realised that Angela and Douglas wanted to be alone, and slipped my arm through his.

'You have got to come and dress,' I said. 'We are dining at nine o'clock and we mustn't be late. It is a frightfully smug party tonight—decorations and kid gloves.'

'Oh Lord!' Henry said with a groan. 'Not another of them.'

'I am afraid so,' I answered. 'Don't tell me you are weakening already—you aren't half way down the course. I am staying until July, you know.'

'As long as that?' Henry said with somewhat heavy facetiousness.

'And longer if you will have me,' I said walking upstairs with him, still holding on to his arm and thinking how tactful I was being to Angela.

'I shall have to marry you off,' Henry said. 'I can see it is my only chance of escape.'

'And why not?' I asked. 'If I can find a nice husband like you, I should be very content.'

Henry stopped abruptly on the landing.

'Lyn,' he said. 'Do you think I am a good husband?'

I answered him as seriously as he had asked the question.

'Yes, Henry. I think you are a very good husband.'

'Sometimes I think I am a damned fool,' he said.

Once again I felt that at any moment he might confide in me. And just now I felt it would be unwise. There was no time, nor had I any words of comfort with which I could possibly answer him. Instead I squeezed his hand, said:

'You aren't, and you know it,' then ran up the next flight of stairs to my own room.

I was in my bath when I heard my bedroom door open.

'Who is it?' I called out and a second later Angela came into my bathroom. She was looking very pale and there were tears in her eyes.

'Angela!' I said. 'What is the matter?'

'Oh, Lyn!' she said. 'What do you think has happened? I oughtn't to worry you with my troubles, but I must, because there's no one else I can tell. Douglas may have to go to Palestine. It isn't official yet, but they think it very likely that his regiment will be sent, with the next draft.'

50

'Oh, darling,' I said. 'I am sorry.'

'I can't bear it, Lyn, I can't really.' Angela sat down on the chair opposite the bath and buried her face in her hands. 'He's the only thing that makes my life worth living, that keeps me sane and prevents me committing suicide.'

'Angela!' I said horrified. 'Don't talk like that.'

'You don't know what my life is here,' she said. 'The misery of it and the awful deadly boredom. You have seen Henry—can't you imagine what it is like for me being with him, day after day, year after year?'

'He loves you,' I said.

'Oh, he does now,' Angela said scornfully.

'What do you mean by "now"?' I asked.

'Exactly what I say,' she said impatiently. 'When I first married him he was delighted to get a good bargain socially. He wanted an aristocratic wife, one who would look well at the end of his table and one whose social connections were beyond reproach. Well, he got that all right. He used to go about purring like a Cheshire cat that has just been given a bowl of cream.

'I was only nineteen, Lyn, the same age as you are now, but I was no fool. I used to watch Henry licking his lips over me and my title, talking about Father and Mother as though they were something in an exhibition. I suppose it was funny, if I hadn't been so desperately ashamed of it all. He looked up the family history, read all the records of Maysfield—and was always bringing them into the conversation some way or another. I used to wait for it—the sentences which began "My father-in-law, Lord Maysfield," or "An ancestor of my wife's" . . . "That reminds me of the Sherbrooke family" . . . it all made me sick. Then I made up my mind that I would enjoy my life; if Henry could get what he wanted, why shouldn't I have the same?

'It was inevitable, I suppose, that when other people began to take an interest in me and I in them, he realised that I had other attractions besides a whole page in Burke's Peerage. He began to see me as a woman, Lyn. So he fell in love with me. It is laughable, in a way, at least I have tried to laugh about it—but now, if Douglas goes away, I don't think I can go on.'

'What do you mean?' I asked in a whisper.

'I shall leave Henry,' Angela said firmly.

'You couldn't, you couldn't,' I said. 'Think of Mother and Father, think how upset they would be. Think of your children. Don't they mean anything to you, Angela?'

Her face softened for a moment.

'They were sweet as babies,' she said. 'But they are growing up awfully like Henry.'

I got out of my bath and wrapped myself in the big pink bath towel.

'Listen, Angela,' I said. 'You will think I am impertinent, but I don't mean to be. Have you ever tried explaining things to Henry? Have you ever talked to him and told him not to talk about you in the way you don't like, not to be snobby, not to boast about his money?'

'What's the use?' Angela answered. 'If I did, he would be rude to me. It is only by being as formal as possible that we manage to get along at all.'

'I think that's very silly,' I said firmly.

'Silly?' Angela echoed.

I nodded.

'Yes. You haven't tried to alter him in any way; you have just accepted him as he was brought up by that awful mother of his, and instead of remaking him, as it were, you have just sat down and resented him.'

'I suppose you are right,' Angela answered with a shrug of her shoulders. 'But all that is beside the point now. I love Douglas, Lyn. I want to marry him.'

'You can't,' I said firmly. 'You are married already.'

'Millions of people have divorces,' Angela retorted defiantly.

'And what's more,' I added, taking the bull by the horns, 'he isn't good enough for you.'

'Don't you like him?' she asked sharply.

'I like him all right,' I replied, 'but don't you see, Angela, that you are only in love with him because he is the very opposite to Henry? He's a gentleman, he is good-looking and he hasn't any brains at all.'

'How do you know?' Angela asked angrily.

'Don't be angry,' I said pleadingly. 'You asked me my opinion, Angela, and I am giving it to you, but can you quite honestly tell me any real interest you have in common? Tell me anything you have constantly discussed and argued about, except yourselves and, I suppose, love? Does Douglas read any books? Has he any really strong opinions about anything? If he has, I haven't heard them!'

I was guessing, of course. I wasn't certain of my facts, but I had seen enough of Douglas Ormonde to know that if he had brains he concealed them very effectively. Personally I thought him much more of a bore than Henry was ever likely to be, yet I could quite understand that Angela, carried away by his looks and charm of manner, was content for the moment with what she found on the surface. But I had to face this crisis somehow and instinctively I knew that the one way to help Angela was to make her feel superior to Douglas. It is extraordinary how easily most women can be flattered. I had learnt that even in a village, situated in the depths of the country, a piece of knowledge which stood me now in good stead.

'You are clever, Angela,' I went on. 'Clever and intelligent. Look at your appearance, at your house, at all the people you know, all the things you do. Henry's money helps, of course, but the taste is yours, the instinct for what is good, is yours. If it was only money, look at Henry's mother and compare her with you. You have made a life for yourself and taken up a certain position, however hard it has been. You can't chuck it all overboard now, not for Douglas Ormonde, at any rate. I, personally, would be very disappointed if you did.'

Angela dried her eyes and stared at me.

'Douglas may not read much,' she said. 'But I love him, Lyn, I do really.'

'Of course you do,' I said soothingly. 'But do you love him enough to marry him? That would be awfully different you know, Angela, to just having a good time with him on Henry's money.'

Angela started to her feet.

'You have no right to say that,' she said crossly. 'It makes Douglas sound such a cad.'

'Well, darling,' I said. 'You admitted that he hasn't got any money; why, the other evening you even had to borrow from me to pay for supper.'

I finished my bath and walked into my bedroom.

'My heart will be broken if he goes to Palestine,' Angela said firmly, but there was no hysterical note in her voice now and I felt she was acting a part, rather than really feeling it.

'Perhaps he won't have to go,' I said.

'I am afraid!' Angela answered.

She was looking in the glass as she spoke, patting away

53

the traces of tears from under her eyes with her powder puff. Suddenly she looked at the clock and gave a shrill cry.

'It is twenty to nine! I shall never be ready for dinner.'

Before I could say another word she had rushed out of the room, slamming the door behind her. I heard her running downstairs to her own bedroom. I gave a sigh of relief, for I felt that if Angela was determined to go to a party, the problem of divorce or suicide was certainly shelved for at least a few hours. I smirked at myself in the glass, rather pleased with the way I had handled the situation.

'Now is it the village Institute or the Girl Guides which has made me so tactful?' I asked my reflection.

And I decided it was just native cunning which had never been exploited before.

7

On Tuesday night before we went to dine at Chadleigh
House there was a terrible commotion over Douglas Ormonde. Angela had made up her mind that she wanted him
to come. It seems that if one is in love with someone, it is
impossible to be without them for a single moment, certainly not for a whole evening.

Angela managed, in some extraordinary way of her own,
to get Douglas invited to most places where she was going,
but not knowing Sir Philip well, there was no chance of his
coming with us to dinner. However, she insisted that he
should join us for the concert. As this was for charity it
should have been quite easy, except that it was by invitation
only, and although every guest had to pay five guineas,
there was no way of getting into Chadleigh House without
a card of invitation from the host himself.

Henry, for once, absolutely refused to do anything about
it. And he and Angela had what was really quite a scene.

'If you think I am going to ring up Chadleigh and say
that my wife won't come without a young man, I'm not,'
he said.

'And I'm not going to be alone the whole evening,'
Angela replied. 'Besides, as soon as the concert is over we
might go on to a night club or somewhere amusing.
Heaven knows the evening will be grim enough otherwise.'

'I thought you wanted to dine with Sir Philip,' Henry
said.

'I don't mind going to dinner,' Angela replied crossly. 'It
is quite a different thing to have no one to look after me
for the rest of the evening.'

'You have your loving husband,' Henry said sarcastically.

Angela did not reply. She only gave him a look of
positive dislike and walking across the room, picked up the
telephone.

'What are you going to do?' Henry asked.

'If you won't help me get my own way, I will find other methods,' she said darkly.

'I forbid you to ring up Chadleigh,' Henry said in a rage. 'I won't be made a fool of.'

'Who suggested I was doing anything of the sort?' she asked. 'Don't worry and thank you for being such a tremendous help! It is extraordinary how you try to frustrate me at every turn.'

'Damn the whole party!' Henry said suddenly, losing his temper. 'I have a good mind to ring up and say that none of us will go.'

With that he marched out of the room and slammed the door.

'Really,' Angela said, 'Henry should learn to control himself.'

'What are you going to do?' I asked, feeling a little apprehensive and not unsympathetic to Henry.

'Wait and see,' she said mysteriously.

She dialled a number, then waited.

'Hullo,' she said. 'Is that Chadleigh House? Can I speak to Sir Philip's secretary, please. No—not his political secretary, but to whoever is arranging the concert tonight. Miss Stanwick, is it? Oh, thank you.'

She waited a second or two.

'Hullo, is that Miss Stanwick speaking? This is Lady Angela Watson. I am so sorry to bother you, but I wonder if there is any possibility of my having another ticket for tonight's concert? Yes, I know you have been sold out for some time, but it is like this. A friend of mine who has arrived from Paris unexpectedly, is extremely interested in this particular charity as it is one he has supported for many years. So I thought as there was a chance of his giving a good donation, you might be able to squeeze an extra chair in somewhere, perhaps there might be even a cancellation at the last moment. Yes, yes, of course, I can understand your difficulty, but this is a rather exceptional case, isn't it? In fact, I would give him my seat if it wasn't that my husband and I have promised Sir Philip we would dine with him first. I mean, at this moment when it is so difficult to get money for anything, every penny counts. . . . You will do your best then? That is kind of you, Miss Stanwick. I can't thank you enough and I know the appeal committee will thank you too when they see the result of tonight's collection. The name? Captain Douglas Ormonde. He's only so sorry he didn't apply before, but as I said, he's been out of England. . . . You will ring me back? Oh, thank you so much. Good-bye.'

She put down the receiver.

'That,' she said in a satisfied voice, 'is going to cost Henry fifty pounds.'

'But Angela!' I said. 'Surely they will look up and see that Douglas has never given them a penny before.'

'If I know anything of charity organisers,' she answered, 'they are in too much of a whirl at this moment to think of anything except how much they are going to collect tonight. We shall have a ticket, wait and see.'

'But will Henry give fifty pounds?' I asked anxiously.

'I shan't ask him,' Angela said with a grin. 'I shall take it out of the housekeeping money, then have an overdraft at the end of the quarter.'

'I call that cheating,' I said half-seriously.

'Surely not if it is spent on a worthy cause?' Angela said. 'And what could be more worthy than this particular charity?'

'Why, what is it?' I asked.

'I haven't the slightest idea,' she replied lightly. Then humming a little tune, she walked out of the room, leaving me alone.

Needless to say, half an hour later a message came through from Chadleigh House to say that a ticket for Douglas had been dispatched to us by hand. I couldn't help being amused at Angela's methods. She had got her own way in spite of long odds against her. At the same time, I felt that mother would hardly have approved. There were so many things in this house which would have scandalised both father and mother. It was really quite hopeless my thinking about them, or the principles they had done their best to instil into me for nineteen years. Besides, at the moment, I was far too worried over the really pressing problem of what I was to wear tonight.

I had suddenly got a nausea against all my white frilly dresses with their blue sashes, rosebuds and white camellias. I felt I wanted to be sophisticated, grown-up, with a grace that would equal that which I had noticed in Sir Philip himself. How hopeless it all was, always wanting to be something one was not. There was nothing in my wardrobe which pleased me, or which fulfilled in any way the impression I wished to create. In the end I chose a dress of pale green chiffon.

Just as we were leaving for dinner, Henry presented me with a huge spray of mauve orchids, which I pinned on to my shoulder. Angela sniffed when she saw them.

'What a ridiculous choice for a young girl,' she grumbled. 'Why didn't you get her roses or camellias?'

'Only the best was good enough!' Henry replied.

'By which, of course, you mean the most expensive,' Angela said acidly. 'Regardless of what might be considered good taste.'

'But I am delighted with my orchids,' I said defiantly. 'I should have been furious if Henry had brought me roses or any of the sickly debutante flowers which I see all the girls wearing. Why, one of them last night even had a spray of lilies of the valley nodding on the very top of her head. But oh! How I wish I could wear your frock, Angela.'

Angela was in black sequins which fitted her like a second skin, glittered and shimmered as she moved.

'You will have to get much thinner, my girl!' she replied.

When we drove off to Chadleigh House, I think all three of us were a little excited. I personally was tense with anticipation, not so much because I was going to one of the smartest and most exclusive houses in London, but because I wanted more than anything in the world to see Sir Philip again.

During the days since we had last met, I had not only thought of him, but I had also learnt more about his family. I didn't dare tell Angela about my curiosity, in fact I was terrified anyway in case she would find out that I had bought a book on the Chadleigh family and another on the treasures of Longmoor Park. I hid them in my bedroom and read them first thing in the morning when I was called. There were illustrations in the book about Longmoor Park and I could see that Sir Philip was very much like his ancestors; there was a picture painted by Romney, which I gazed at for a long time; except for the clothes and hair, it might have been the present Philip Chadleigh.

We struggled into our gloves before we arrived at Chadleigh House; Angela was wearing a long black pair which came up about her elbow and she had arranged all her bracelets outside them, but I had a short Victorian pair, dyed the same colour as my dress, which fastened at my wrist with a diamanté button and an absurd frill of organdie.

When we left our furs in the big marble hall I felt a sudden chill of apprehension and fear before we mounted the huge double staircase, Angela leading the way. At the top of the stairs, Sir Philip was waiting.

'How are you, Lady Angela?' he said; holding out his hand to me he said, 'How do you do?' in what seemed to me a cold and distant voice. I felt abashed and chilled. I don't know why, but I had been looking forward to this meeting; now I knew how absurd it had been to hope, in spite of all logic and common sense, that he might have looked forward to it too.

'How are you, Watson,' he said to Henry. 'Glad to see you here.'

We moved away into the big drawing-room where other people were already grouped, talking and sipping cocktails, which were being handed round by footmen with powdered hair. Angela knew two or three people present and went away to talk to them, so that Henry and I were left alone.

'What do you think of the pictures?' he asked me.

I started when he spoke for I had been staring across the room at Sir Philip, shaking hands with late arrivals.

'Lovely,' I replied.

'Worth about a quarter of a million,' Henry said.

I forced myself to attend to my brother-in-law.

'What else ought I to admire?' I asked.

'The last relic of a dying age,' he said. Then when I looked at him inquiringly, he explained: 'I mean, here is one of the few private houses left where you can see this sort of show. But it is only a question of years, with added taxation, higher death duties, before Chadleigh House follows in the footsteps of all the rest. It will become a museum, I suppose, or a firm of caterers will take the place and let it out for parties.'

'Don't!' I said. 'It sounds awful!'

'But it is true,' Henry said and he said it with relish. I had the feeling that he resented the tradition behind Sir Philip Chadleigh. The Watson money made in beer couldn't buy what Sir Philip had inherited from his ancestors; not only the house, the pictures, or the tapestries, but the feeling of age, security and of conservatism; that was an indivisible part of our host. Even if his wealth disappeared, he would still have something which Henry could never acquire. Poor Henry, he had only money which, so far, had failed to bring him very much happiness. I was trying to find something consoling to say when Henry nudged me:

'Here come the Duke and Duchess,' he said.

I looked and saw appearing at the top of the staircase two of the youngest and most glamorous Royalties. Sir Philip brought them forward and everyone was introduced to them. I made my curtsey neatly and was quite proud of myself until Angela came up beside me and said in a whisper:

'Don't stare, Lyn! Really your eyes are popping out of your head.'

I was dashed. But then Angela so often had that effect on one. I felt that for both Henry and myself she was rather like the proverbial fly in the ointment. Yet we both loved her.

Dinner was rather a nightmare. I sat between two pompous old gentlemen who found very little to talk to me about. It was the first time I had eaten off gold plate and it was with the utmost difficulty I prevented my knife and fork from squeaking. I looked at Sir Philip quite often during dinner; although he was sitting far away from me at the head of the table. He looked very impressive with a lot of orders and decorations shining on his black coat.

I had a chance to study his face. He looked tired, I thought, and sometimes, when he was not talking, a little sad. I wondered what he thought about; I wondered if he was happy; I wondered if he had everything in the world he wanted. I thought it seemed funny that a bachelor should have all this state about him.

I had tried to learn a little about the man himself these past days. It was not difficult to get people to talk about him. Angela had only to say:

'We are dining at Chadleigh House on Tuesday—will you be going?' and the answer would come, 'With Philip? My dear, what fun for you. His parties are always amusing and I couldn't admire him more. Really, at times, I think he is the most fascinating man in London.'

But they said it insincerely, as though they did not really know Philip Chadleigh well, but were just trying to be impressive about him and make other people think that they were more intimate than they were.

When dinner was over and the ladies retired through to the drawing-room, I found there was one girl about my own age. She too was fair, in rather a mousy-coloured way, but with a sweet expression and a dress which, from long experience, I guessed had been made cheaply and not too recently.

She saw me looking at her, and crossed the room to sit beside me on a tapestry sofa.

'My name's Elizabeth Batley,' she said. 'I know you're Angela Watson's sister, although I am not sure of your name.'

'Lyn Sherbrooke,' I told her. 'Tell me who everyone is, if you know.'

'Oh, I know them all,' she said. 'Philip's a cousin of Mummy's and we always come to his parties.'

I then remembered that I had heard Angela speak of Lady Batley, who was in attendance on one of the Royal Duchesses.'

'Do you enjoy them?' I asked.

'Sometimes,' Elizabeth answered. 'But you see I am really in disgrace because I didn't get married at least five seasons ago, so everyone is frightfully bored carting me around.'

'How awful,' I said.

'Yes, isn't it,' she replied. 'I have got two sisters—one who came out last year and one this, so of course, it is terribly galling for them having an old hag still grabbing invitations.'

'Are they here tonight?' I asked.

'Good heavens no! They would be bored stiff,' she replied. 'It is rather an old party, isn't it, but then, of course, there is no reason why Philip should entertain the very young. He likes older people—clever ones—he's clever himself, very clever.'

There was something in the way she spoke of Sir Philip that made me jump to the conclusion that Elizabeth was in love with him. I had no grounds to go on, but I felt it, as Nanny would have said 'in my bones'.

Coffee was handed round. When we had drunk ours, Elizabeth said:

'Let's go up and powder our noses, shall we? I know the way.'

The older women were grouped together talking, and Angela was speaking to the Duchess, so that I could not interrupt her. We left the big drawing-room quietly and took the lift.

'We won't go where the maids are waiting,' Elizabeth said. 'There will be a crowd in there in a moment and we won't be able to get anywhere near the looking glasses. There's a small guest room up here, where I have often stayed. We will use that.'

She stopped the lift at the third floor and led the way into a charming little room, decorated all in pale blue damask. In the bathroom adjoining were towels, soap and powder, all ready laid out.

'It looks as though they are expecting a guest,' I said. 'Shan't we mess everything up if we use this room without anybody knowing?'

Elizabeth laughed.

'You needn't worry,' she said. 'It is one of Philip's peculiarities that every room in the house must be opened while he is in residence. He can't bear dust sheets and drawn blinds. He says it makes him depressed. Do you know him well?'

'I have only met him once,' I answered. 'At the House of Commons last Thursday, when he asked my sister and her husband to come and dine tonight.'

'I have never seen her here before,' Elizabeth said. 'Your brother-in-law is in the House, isn't he? I do like your dress,' she said changing the subject with disconcerting swiftness, which was obviously a habit of hers. 'I wish I had a decent one to wear, but every penny has had to be spent on the girls and I am lucky if I can get so much as a new hat.'

'Why don't you get a job?' I asked.

'Mother would faint with horror at the idea,' Elizabeth replied. 'She has lived too long with royalty to believe that there is any other possible career for a woman but marriage.'

'Why don't you marry?' I asked, with a curiosity that I could not prevent because I wanted to hear her answer.

Her expression altered. There came into her eyes a look of yearning and of desire. It was so obvious that I felt ashamed of having aroused it in her.

'I would give anything in the world to,' she said.

'Is there something to stop you?' I asked in a low voice, feeling that I was behaving badly, but unable to help myself.

62

'Something that is very difficult to fight,' Elizabeth replied. 'A ghost.'

'A ghost!' I echoed in surprise. 'What do you mean?'

'Let's talk of something else,' she said quickly. 'What lipstick do you use?' She took her own and applied it heavily to her mouth.

'No, do tell me,' I pleaded. 'I have only just met you, but somehow, I would like you to be happy. That sounds silly, doesn't it and sentimental, but I would really.'

She gave me a smile, which for the moment made her almost pretty.

'I like you, Lyn,' she said. 'It is a long time since I have had a friend who cared a damn one way or the other what happened to me.'

'But why a ghost?' I persisted. 'Is it someone who is dead?'

She nodded.

'But that is ridiculous,' I said. 'Surely you can make the man you love forget? Surely a wife who is alive is a far more difficult obstacle? You are here and the other woman's gone away for ever. Make him forget her. It ought to be easy.'

'I know he will never forget,' Elizabeth said.

And with a sort of clairvoyance I knew with absolute certainty that she was speaking of Philip Chadleigh.

8

I felt my curiosity like a kind of fever within me—I had to
go on, I had to know more. It was with difficulty I con-
trolled the words which sprang from my lips and which
threatened to overflow in an excess of questions which
would have annoyed Elizabeth and gained me nothing. A
sort of cunning which I did not know I had in myself came
to me. I knew the only way that it was possible for me to
obtain her confidence.

I got to my feet and walked across the room to where
she was looking into a mirror. I slipped an arm round her
shoulders and kissed her cheek.

'Here's good luck to you,' I said, 'and if you ever want
any help, call on me.'

She turned to me with that sudden half-radiant smile of
hers, which spent itself so quickly.

'You are a darling, Lyn,' she said. 'But I am a fool. Do
you know how old I am?'

'I haven't the slightest idea,' I replied.

'I am twenty-seven,' she said. 'Twenty-seven with no ac-
complishments, no money, and just a hopeless love for
someone who never even notices me. It makes every year
that passes seem more miserable and more hopeless.'

'I am sure you are making things much worse than they
are,' I accused her.

She gave a little laugh with no humour in it.

'Perhaps, but oh, Lyn, never love anyone who doesn't
love you. It is hell.'

'But why doesn't he love you?' I asked. 'Why can't you
make him?'

'I have told you,' she said. 'He will never look at another
woman.'

'I don't believe it,' I said stoutly. 'Men aren't made like
that, except in novels. One passionate love, which goes on
all through their lives, is quite fictitious.'

Inwardly I laughed at myself for my tone of conviction, for what did I know of men? Yet, at the same time Elizabeth's dramatic misery seemed to me overacted, and rather stupid.

'If only the family would give me a chance!' Elizabeth said dismally. 'How can I attract anyone looking like I do? I ought to go to a beauty specialist and to a good dressmaker. But Mother faints if I suggest such a thing and the girls keep telling me how selfish I am to want anything now, that I have had my opportunity and lost it.'

'If you want a thing hard enough, you'll get it,' I said, thinking of Angela.

'I can't,' Elizabeth said mournfully. 'I haven't got the guts, if you like to put it that way. I crumple up under opposition. I am sure you are a brave person, Lyn. I wish I was.'

'Well, can't you find someone else?' I suggested. 'Perhaps it would make him jealous.'

'My dear, he would never even notice! If I married a bus driver he would send me an expensive present and never think of me again.'

'It does sound a bit hopeless,' I admitted.

'It is,' Elizabeth answered. 'But there it is, and here am I in a permanent abyss of misery.'

I had to laugh. She had a tragic way of saying things which was so utterly out of keeping with her appearance.

'I shan't help you,' I said, 'if you give in so easily to defeat. Now listen, we will make a campaign together and something will happen. I know it will.'

She shook her head.

'You don't understand.'

'Well, I'm not likely to,' I answered almost crossly, 'if you keep talking in epigrams.'

She put out her hand and took mine.

'Come,' she said, 'I will show you something.'

We went out into the landing but instead of going downstairs or towards the lift, she led me through a heavy baize door. Behind it was obviously a suite of rooms and passing several doors, she opened one at the end of the passage. She switched on the light and we walked into a huge booklined room with a vast desk in one corner, littered with papers. Although it was summer there was a log fire burning on the hearth, which made the room seem cosy and inviting, and before it were two or three big comfortable armchairs of the type a man would prefer.

'What a lovely room,' I exclaimed, but Elizabeth gave me no time to admire our surroundings. She walked across the room, opened a narrow door which was concealed between two bookcases, and beckoned to me.

'I found this quite by accident,' she whispered. 'We will have to hurry in case we are missed.'

The door behind the bookcases led into another room where it was concealed by a curtain. We crept through it into a bedroom. Here again a log fire was burning. The room was very plainly furnished, only the curtains were of magnificent brocade, in contrast to the severity and plainness of the walls.

Elizabeth led me into the centre of the room.

'Look,' she said. 'That's her.'

I looked up; over the mantelpiece was the picture of a woman. I stared at it and suddenly felt as though all the blood was draining away from my head. Quite unaccountably my heart began to thump for I recognised the portrait. The head was painted against a background of dark hangings which seemed to make the arms and neck glow with strange brilliance. The face was oval and huge dark eyes stared back at me from beneath a low forehead. The dark hair was half-veiled and jewels sparkled here and there under a mesh of emerald green.

I recognised the picture; I knew it as intimately as I knew my own face. The fine pointed nose, the full red mouth and the grace of the long thin fingers which were just shown touching lace-covered breasts.

'That is the ghost!' Elizabeth said again dramatically.

I had forgotten she was with me; forgotten that she was there beside me as I looked at the picture. Now I started, gripping her arm with a force of which I was quite unaware until she gave an exclamation of pain.

'Who is she?' I asked.

I could not believe, even while I asked the question, that I did not know, that I could put no name to the picture—to the face that was so familiar.

'You are hurting me,' Elizabeth cried.

'Who is she?' I asked again.

A log shifting itself in the fire made us both start.

'Quick,' Elizabeth said. 'We mustn't be found here.'

66

I was too dazed to do anything but follow her, back again behind the curtain, through the small concealed door, into the book-lined sitting-room, to the landing where, before I could regain my breath, Elizabeth had pressed the button for the lift.

'I have got to know,' I said quickly. 'Tell me.'

Elizabeth stared at me in surprise.

'How queer you look, Lyn,' she said.

'Tell me,' I insisted.

'Her name was Nada,' she whispered. 'I can't tell you more now.'

Even as she spoke the lift door opened and there was a servant in attendance to take us down.

'The gentlemen have left the dining-room, miss,' he said. 'The company are proceeding to the concert hall.'

'Thank you,' Elizabeth replied. 'Take us down to the ballroom floor then. I expect we shall miss them in the drawing-room.'

She was right. The Duke and Duchess were being led to their places in the concert room, even as we came out of the lift. Following them was the rest of the dinner-party, while the other chairs in the big room were already packed with those who had come in for the concert.

I found my way to a seat beside Angela, who had managed by some mysterious way of her own, to get Douglas Ormonde beside her, so she was in a good temper.

'Where have you been all this time?' she asked, but pleasantly—I was afraid she might have been annoyed.

'With Elizabeth Batley,' I replied.

'Oh, that's good,' she answered. 'She's a nice girl,' and turning half round in her chair towards Douglas, she paid no more attention to me.

From where I was sitting I could see the back of Sir Philip's head. He was about six rows in front of me; he was bending towards the Duchess, talking to her and at times I could just see his profile. My thoughts were still too chaotic for me to do anything but wait for the subsiding of my pulse and my heart, which was still thumping. What did it mean? Who was she? Why did I know her face so well? Why had this strange emotion gripped me when I looked at her picture?

Nada. I had never heard the name except in some novel or Russian tale. Was she Russian, and if so, what connection could she possibly have with me? I touched my forehead and found that it was damp.

'It is ridiculous, madness,' I told myself. I was letting my imagination run away with me to such an extent that I might almost be insane. Yet, I knew that nothing could explain away such an extraordinary feeling, and that having seen it, I could never forget the portrait which hung over the mantelpiece in Philip Chadleigh's bedroom. The woman he had loved and who, presumably, loved him.

I heard nothing of the concert. The best singers in Europe sang in front of me. The applause rose and fell tumultuously. I sat as though I was in a dream, seeing only those dark eyes and the half-smile on that red mouth. As the concert came to an end with God Save the King, and everyone got to their feet, I stared round the audience for Elizabeth. I could not see her anywhere.

As soon as the Duke and Duchess had left the room escorted by Sir Philip and we had all meekly dropped our curtsies, there was a general rush for the doors. I saw that I had no chance of finding anyone in the general mêlée. By the time I had found Henry, I had lost Angela and Douglas. Whether intentionally or not I don't know, they disappeared into the crowd and I was alone with my brother-in-law.

'Do you want to go on anywhere?' he asked.

I shook my head.

'Right,' he said. 'We will go home, if that will suit you. I expect Angela will go in Douglas's car—it is no use waiting for them, anyway.'

We went into the hall to retrieve our coats. As we were waiting for them a footman came up to Henry.

'Mr. Watson?' he asked.

'Yes,' Henry replied.

'Sir Philip, sir, would be delighted if you and your party would have supper with him.'

Henry was about to refuse. I saw it in his face, but before he could form the words I put my hand on his arm.

'Please!' I said.

'You want to go?' he asked.

'Well, of course.'

'But what about Angela?'

'We can't do anything about her,' I replied, 'can we?'

'I suppose not,' Henry answered.

68

He turned to the footman.

'Tell Sir Philip that Lady Gwendolyn Sherbrooke and I will be delighted to have supper with him, but Lady Angela has already gone home.'

'Very good, sir. Sir Philip will be supping out. Perhaps you would follow me to the other entrance?'

I got hold of my ermine coat, which was one of Angela's that I had borrowed for the evening and Henry found his coat after some trouble. Then we were taken through a private way at the back of the marble staircase to another small hall. A butler and two footmen were in attendance and through the open door on to the street I could see a big grey Rolls.

We stood for a moment, when Sir Philip came hurrying down the staircase.

'I am sorry your wife's gone home, Watson,' he said to Henry.

'I don't know whether it is home or not,' Henry replied. 'But she had gone before we got your message.'

'Well, I suppose that you and I are sufficient chaperons for Lady Gwendolyn,' he said laughing. Then looking at me, 'Did you enjoy the concert?'

'Very much,' I replied.

Another man appeared at the top of the stairs.

'Come on David,' Sir Philip called to him. 'You're keeping us waiting. Do you know each other? Colonel Parker—Lady Gwendolyn Sherbrooke—Mr. Watson.'

Colonel Parker, who looked too young for his rank, shook hands with us and we got into the car.

'You get in front, David,' Sir Philip said to the Colonel. 'Then we three can sit at the back.'

I was in the centre with Sir Philip on my left and Henry on my right. The footman tucked the rug round us. Then we were off. I was sitting very close to Sir Philip. I could feel his arm against mine and I scarcely had to turn my head to see the strong lines of his face. I felt strangely, tremendously elated.

'What do you think of my house?' he asked casually.

I hesitated and he laughed.

'All right!' he said 'Tell the truth, I expect it from you.'

'It is rather overwhelming,' I said.

'I have often felt like that myself,' he answered. 'I remember as a small boy being terrified of all the pictures in the drawing-room. I felt they were all looking at me and saying, "Well, if this is what we have produced, we don't think much of it".'

I had a mad desire to ask him about another portrait, to tell him what I had seen in his bedroom and to find out about the one picture which he would see last thing at night and first thing in the morning. I wondered what he would say if he knew how interested I was in the dark-haired, beautiful Nada.

We arrived at a fashionable night-club, a bottle party which managed by some extraordinary means to keep its clientele exclusive.

'I telephoned for a table,' Sir Philip said and we were led instantly to a small alcove where we were more or less secluded.

Colonel Parker and Henry both found friends as they were passing through the room and while they stopped to talk, Sir Philip and I sat down at the table and he ordered champagne.

'Talk to me,' he commanded. 'I want to hear what you think about things.'

A little embarrassed, but obedient, I started to tell him about my season in London and how much I was enjoying myself. While I talked he did not look at me, but sat, drawing meaningless designs on the table cloth, with a burnt out match.

I watched him . . . then suddenly I had the queer idea that while he was listening to my voice, he was not trying to understand one word of what I was saying. I stopped.

Instantly he said:

'Go on, tell me more.'

I felt sure with an innermost conviction that he was not really listening and to test him I said one or two things which were quite nonsense, interspersing them among other sentences. He took no notice.

'You are not listening to me,' I said quickly.

'Yes I am,' he replied in a low voice. 'I am listening with far deeper interest than you will ever know.'

'Not to my words,' I said.

He gave me a quiet appraising glance, then he said:

'You are no fool, you know.'

'Why do you want me to talk if you are not really listening to me?' I asked urgently.

He looked embarrassed. He took up his match again.

'To be honest . . .' he started, then hesitated.

'It reminds you of someone!' I interposed.

'Why do you say that?' he asked sharply. 'And tell me now why you called me what you did in the House of Commons the other day.'

I didn't want to answer him. I didn't want to try and explain, even though I had no explanation. I looked round wildly. To my relief I saw Henry and Colonel Parker making their way through the crowded tables towards us.

9

For the first time in my life I enjoyed a feeling of power. I knew Sir Philip was longing to talk to me, was anxious to get me alone, away from Henry and Colonel Parker—I could sense that, although he was far too polite to say so, or show the irritation he felt when they sat down at the table, joking, laughing and making comments to me about the various people present.

It amused me to give them my full attention, to flatter Colonel Parker a little, so that he talked to me eagerly, and after a few moments suggested that we should dance.

'I think perhaps it wouldn't be fair when there are three men to one woman,' I said demurely, and I knew too that this decision of mine annoyed Sir Philip because if he had danced with me he could have continued the conversation which the others had interrupted.

I don't know why I suddenly became coquettish in this way. It was very unlike my usual behaviour, but then I was very far from being myself all the evening. From the moment I had met Sir Philip I felt that I had altered in some way, although altered was hardly the word. It was as though some part of my character, slumbering deep within me, had become wakened, and that same part had been roused tonight still further by the sight of Nada's picture.

But it was only when the evening was over, when Sir Philip and Colonel Parker had dropped Henry and me at home and when after saying good night to my brother-in-law, I was at last alone in my own room, that I could try and think coherently about the portrait.

I undressed and put on my dressing gown, then, pulling back the curtains, stood at the window, looking out over the great trees of the Square, reflected in the light of the moon. There was very little traffic, only the occasional purr of some car driving homewards from a party to disturb the quiet and the feeling of peace there was here, even in the heart of London. There were dark purple shadows, cool and mysterious, under the trees, which were hardly lightened by the street lamps, or the moonlight. There was the gentle rustle of leaves in the night breeze, and a faint almost indiscernible scent of flowers and growing things above the heat and stale air of the streets.

As I stood there I felt a calm and peace descend upon me; my agitation and the tumultuous emotions of the evening were soothed away. Yet I knew this was but a passing, superficial, narcotic, that something great and tumultuous was beating within me, something which I could not yet understand, but which was part of me and from which I could not escape.

Who was Nada? Why should I know her face? Why indeed did her portrait and everything about Sir Philip stir in me such strange feelings? Was I in love with him, I asked myself? It was quite impossible to answer that question, besides, how ridiculous in such circumstances it was to think of love at first sight. I was not an hysterical schoolgirl, however easily an outsider hearing my story might level the accusation against me. I knew too, that it was not only my heart that was involved in this; my mind, indeed my whole being, were linked in these new emotions.

I left the window and walked about the room. If only there was someone to whom I could turn, someone who would show me the way to an understanding of even a part of these strange problems—yet how could I explain myself to anyone?

I thought again of what Mother had said about my imagination and sternly I told myself that this was but an example of how I let it run away with me. I had promised I would keep it in check. This was certainly not in keeping with my promise. Yet how easy it was to say that such things were all imagination and deny an innermost conviction that they were far more fundamental.

'Forget it! Forget Sir Philip, the portrait and your ridiculous ideas!' I told myself, but I knew such a course was impossible for me. Besides, I had to admit to myself that I was looking forward to seeing Sir Philip again.

When we had got up to leave the Club he and I had walked ahead of the other two. As we reached the street and stood waiting for the commissionaire to bring up the car, Sir Philip said to me in a low voice:

'May I telephone you tomorrow?'

I only had time to answer 'But of course,' before the others joined us. He hardly spoke again during the drive home; when he said good night, I felt his hand cold as I touched it.

'Good night, Lady Gwendolyn,' he said formally and I knew that he was exercising some restraint upon himself, forcing upon himself an indifference which he did not really feel.

Is he too fighting against his interest in me? I asked myself, then dismissed the idea as being too fanciful. Just because I was aroused in some queer way about Sir Philip, there was no reason why I should have the same effect on him. Yet there was that remark about my voice. Could it be that Nada and I spoke alike; if so, how strange.

I hardly slept at all all night, but lay asking myself question after question which I could not answer. Only when the sun was already streaming through the uncurtained window and the household was awake, did I fall into a heavy slumber, to dream strange disjointed dreams of Elizabeth, Sir Philip and a portrait whose face I could never see in my dreams, but of which I was acutely conscious.

I had my breakfast brought to me about eleven o'clock. While I was pouring out my first cup of coffee, the telephone rang beside me. I picked up the receiver.

'Sir Philip Chadleigh, mi'lady,' the butler's voice said.

'Put him through,' I answered, trying to speak coolly.

There was a slight pause before I heard Sir Philip's 'Hullo.'

'Good morning,' I said lightly. 'I am only just awake. I hope you didn't try to get on to me before.'

'No, I didn't,' he replied. 'I am glad you have had such a good night.'

'Thank you for a very marvellous evening,' I said politely.

'Will you lunch with me today?' he asked.

I hesitated, not because I didn't want to lunch with him, but because I suddenly felt extraordinarily reluctant to tell Angela that he had asked me.

'If it isn't convenient,' he said, 'would you come down to Ranelagh with me and watch the polo? I could call for you about a quarter to three.'

'I think that would be better,' I answered. 'I am not quite

certain of Angela's plans, but don't bother to come here in case we are going out. I will come to your house.'

'You are quite certain that is all right?' he questioned. 'I can easily send the car for you.'

'No, I would rather come to you,' I answered.

'That's splendid then,' he said. 'Don't have to be back too early—there are two or three good teams playing and we may not want to get away.'

'All right,' I answered.

After a few conventional good-byes we rang off, and I lay back against my pillows, not attempting to eat my breakfast, but making plans. How could I avoid telling Angela, I wondered? There was every likelihood that she would be going out with Douglas during the afternoon, but I should have to account for my movements. I picked up the diary which was beside my bed, in which I had haphazardly jotted down a few of the more important engagements we had accepted for the next weeks. There were few inscriptions for today—a dance in the evening and dinner first with the hostess, nothing for luncheon, nothing at cocktail time!

Suddenly I had an idea. I picked up the telephone book and looked through the 'B's' until I found Lady Batley's name and address. I dialled the number then when the house answered, asked for 'Miss Elizabeth.' There was a long delay before she could be found, but finally she came to the telephone.

'Hullo,' I said, 'This is Lyn—Lyn Sherbrooke.'

'Hullo,' she said. 'What happened to you last night? I never saw you again after the crush of getting into the concert.'

'We all got lost, one way or another,' I replied.

'I was going to telephone you,' she said. 'Then I thought you might have so many engagements you wouldn't have time for me.'

'Nonsense!' I retorted. 'In fact, I've rung you up to suggest luncheon, if you are not going anywhere else.'

'That would be lovely,' Elizabeth said.

'But don't come here,' I went on hastily. 'We will go out—somewhere where we can talk—what about Gunters?'

'I would love it,' Elizabeth answered. 'What time—one-fifteen?'

75

'That will suit me,' I said. 'Don't be late because I have got to leave you about twenty minutes to three.'

I told Angela my first lie when I went down to her room ten minutes later.

'Elizabeth Batley has asked me to luncheon,' I announced. 'Is that all right? I couldn't see any other appointments in my engagement book.'

Angela looked relieved.

'That's perfectly all right,' she said. 'Douglas is coming here and I am going to Wimbledon with him afterwards to watch the tennis.'

'You didn't mind my accepting without asking you?' I asked, feeling hypocritical, at the same time anxious to keep Angela in a good temper.

'Of course not, popsy,' she said. 'I am glad you have made friends with the Batley girl—you couldn't have chosen better. Alice Batley gives herself dreadful airs, although they are as poor as church mice, but I must say she manages to get asked everywhere. Of course she has tried to marry Elizabeth off to Philip Chadleigh for years, everyone knows that.'

I turned my back to Angela so that she shouldn't see my face and fiddled with the things on her dressing table.

'Why doesn't he marry her?' I said casually. 'She seems awfully nice.'

'Oh! Philip Chadleigh is a confirmed bachelor,' she answered with a laugh. 'And a woman hater nowadays! A large number of women and ambitious mammas have come a tumble at that fence. By the way, I hear he asked us all out to supper, last night. I wonder if that was because of your beaux yeux or because of mine.'

'Yours, undoubtedly,' I said. 'He seemed awfully disappointed when Henry said you had gone home.'

'Do you really think he admires me?' Angela asked. 'I believe that girl he was mixed up with years ago was dark, and men always run to type.'

'Do they?' I questioned, feeling in some ridiculous way upset at the idea.

'Of course they do,' Angela said. 'Look at Douglas. He has never taken to blondes, and heaven knows, enough of them have run after him. I wonder, shall I ask Philip Chadleigh to dinner on the 7th—it is the sort of party that might amuse him. I am sorry I missed last night, it was just

76

bad luck that Douglas and I didn't meet you. We were undecided where to go, and in the end went to the Embassy. However,' she added consolingly, 'I expect he will ask me again—that is if he really wants me.'

I could not help being slightly amused, not only at my sister's complacency, but also the easy way her interest in another man could be aroused, if she thought that he found her attractive. I felt that her love for Douglas could not be so tremendous if she could still find time for other admirers.

'What time will you be back this evening?' I asked.

'Oh, about six,' Angela said. 'What are you going to do?'

'Elizabeth did say something about a cinema,' I said, hoping my voice wouldn't betray me, but Angela was not much interested.

'All right,' she said. 'You had better wear your white dress this evening. I will order you some fresh pink camellias for your hair—you must have a touch of colour with that dress, it is too white.'

She picked up the *Daily Sketch* and feeling that she was no longer interested in me or my business, I hurried thankfully away. When I got upstairs I stood looking in my wardrobe for some time. Tonight didn't matter very much; the urgent question was what to wear today. I wanted terribly to look nice for Sir Philip.

I must eventually have made the best of myself for Elizabeth was frightfully complimentary when I met her at Gunters.

'You are pretty, Lyn,' she said enviously. 'I wish I looked like you.'

I laughed.

'I have always wanted to look quite different,' I said. 'In fact, if you want to know, I have always had a sneaking desire to look like the picture your friend Philip Chadleigh has in his bedroom, dark, sinuous and sophisticated.'

'I certainly don't want to look like that woman,' Elizabeth said sharply.

'She must have been very attractive,' I said.

'She wouldn't look so attractive if she was alive now,' Elizabeth answered. 'Why, she would be quite old.'

'How old?' I asked.

'Over forty,' Elizabeth replied. 'After all, she died just after the war.'

'All that time ago?' I said. 'You must have got the story wrong, Elizabeth. He couldn't have been in love with her all these years.'

We had sat down by this time at a table in the window.

'Let's choose something to eat,' Elizabeth suggested. 'It is awfully nice of you to be interested, Lyn. Nobody else ever wants to hear about me and my troubles.'

Feeling a horrible hypocrite I ordered myself a dish I particularly disliked as a kind of penance. When the waitress had gone, I turned eagerly to Elizabeth.

'Go on,' I said.

'Well, of course, I knew nothing about it at the time,' Elizabeth began. 'I was much too young, but when I was about fourteen or fifteen I remember the family always saying "Philip must get over it soon; if only he would come home and open up the house again. It is too ridiculous to wander about the world in strange places. After all, he has his responsibilities".

'I think Mother's solicitude was not entirely impersonal, you see Philip has always been awfully kind to her. He is only a cousin, but he has always helped her because his father did, and when he was away there was no one to whom she could go with tales of illnesses and stories of overdue schooling fees.

'When I was about sixteen he did come back. There was terrific jubilation. They all said: "He has recovered now, surely he will marry, settle down and carry on the family in the old tradition." It was then I began to get curious as to why Philip had gone away and what had happened. Of course no one would tell me—you know how tiresome families are. They hummed and hawed, made excuses and told me to ask each other. Then in the end I found out what it was.'

Elizabeth paused.

'What was it?' I asked.

Elizabeth looked round as though she was frightened of being overheard.

'Nada,' she said, 'committed suicide because of him.'

'Because of him?' I questioned. 'What do you mean?'

'He wouldn't marry her,' Elizabeth said. 'She was madly in love with him and they had a row or something, anyway, she threw herself out of a window at Chadleigh House.'

78

'How awful!' I said.

'Can you imagine the scandal there must have been?' Elizabeth went on. 'And what was more, Philip was most terribly upset; he loved her.'

'But if he loved her,' I asked, 'why didn't he marry her?'

'He couldn't,' Elizabeth said. 'That is the awful part. She was half Indian.'

'Half Indian!'

I echoed the words, feeling that the whole story was so fantastic, far stranger than I had even anticipated. I would have suspected that Elizabeth had made it up had there not been such an obvious air of sincerity about her, and the unmistakable ring of truth in her voice.

'Half Indian!'

That accounted for the shape of those dark, mysterious eyes, for the perfect oval of the face, for the fullness of the mouth and that hint of something sinuous and seductive in the whole poise of the head and shoulders.

'Who was she? Tell me more about her,' I commanded.

'I couldn't really find out anything,' Elizabeth said. 'The family are frightfully cagey about it—they always mention her with bated breath, and a mixture of reserve and horror. I think she was an actress of some sort, but you see, they kept it from me, especially, because . . .' she hesitated.

'Because they wanted you to marry Sir Philip,' I added for her.

Elizabeth blushed.

'How did you guess?' she asked. 'When I came out he was frightfully kind to me. I suppose really it was because of Mother—but I was a fool, Lyn, I thought it was because he liked me personally—he gave a dance for me, and let Mother have a large sum of money for clothes both for her and me. Then, on top of everything else, he gave me a pearl necklace and bracelet, which had belonged to his mother.

'I suppose if I am honest, I knew, even at the time, it was just the kindness of a relation, but I was only too eager to put the same interpretation on his gifts as the family did. You can imagine how excited they were, so excited that I think they must have made it pretty clear to Philip what they were expecting from him. Anyway, after being absolutely charming to me for nearly three months, he suddenly ignored me. I was asked to Chadleigh House, of course, but not especially by him, and he never danced with me at the balls, or sought me out in any way. But by that time it was too late, Lyn. I was madly in love with him.'

Elizabeth's voice broke and there were tears in her eyes. Impulsively I put out my hand and took hers.

'I am so sorry,' I said. 'It must have been hell for you.'

'It was and still is,' she said miserably. 'You see, I suppose I am a bit like Philip himself—perhaps it runs in the family—to love once and once only. I just can't even begin to get interested in any one else. No other man seems to me to be worth while. I can only think of Philip and of him alone.'

10

'Listen to me, Elizabeth,' I said. 'You have got to stop this and be sensible.'

Elizabeth looked at me in surprise.

'I thought you were going to be friendly and understanding,' she said. Her mouth was trembling.

'I am both those things,' I said. 'But don't you see, that you are just ruining your chances of ever being happy? You are letting yourself get worse. Why, you must have been feeling like this for eight years, just giving in to your unhappiness, and getting more and more morbid. It is the last way to attract Sir Philip, or any other man, at least I should have thought so.'

'I suppose you are right,' Elizabeth said dismally. 'But how can I be anything else. Look at my clothes, look how bored everyone is with me. I am an old-maid-on-the-shelf—and the family never stop letting me know it.'

'Don't be browbeaten by them or anyone else,' I said hotly. 'After all, your sisters may be much younger than you, but don't tell me that they have got more brains. You have experience compared to their youth. Stand up to them, Elizabeth, and stand up to Sir Philip. He's not going to love you while you are wilting about the place, looking as though you had lost half-a-crown and found a three-penny bit!'

Elizabeth laughed.

'You do say the most ridiculous things,' she said, then her mouth drooped again. 'I am sure you are right, but you don't know how difficult it is."

'Oh yes I do,' I said. 'I've often felt lonely, unwanted and unattractive. And I get awfully depressed at times, but it doesn't do any good, I know that, and I really believe that courage is the thing that gets one anywhere.'

'Well, if you can suggest one thing that I can do, I will do it,' Elizabeth said.

I longed to say 'forget Sir Philip!' but I didn't dare. Instead I answered:

'You have got to plan your life entirely afresh. If your Mother won't let you take a job, at least she can't stop you working for some charity or other. Have you ever thought of that?'

'No,' Elizabeth answered. 'I just sit at home doing the odd jobs which nobody else will do.'

'Then just leave them undone,' I said savagely. 'I can quite see you are the type of person that is put upon. You are too nice, Elizabeth, and much too easily crushed. Make yourself proud, aggressive and arrogant and people will like you for it.'

'It is easy for you to say that,' Elizabeth retorted. 'Look at your face, then look at mine.'

'You would be much prettier if you made the best of yourself,' I said honestly.

'I have given up troubling,' Elizabeth confessed.

'That is more of the nonsense you have got to stop now,' I answered. 'We will make a plan, Elizabeth, about your new life. You have got to promise to keep it exactly.'

'I believe if I made myself look like Marlene Dietrich and Greta Garbo rolled into one,' Elizabeth said, 'Philip wouldn't notice me now. He has grown used to ignoring me. It is too late.'

'Well, Philip Chadleigh isn't the only man in the world,' I said, and before she could speak I added, 'And don't you dare say he's the only man in the world for you, because you haven't tried any of the others!'

'All right, I won't say so,' Elizabeth said meekly.

I talked to Elizabeth for some time about herself and we arranged to meet the following week; she was to come round to me one morning and I would make up her face and try some of my clothes on for her to see what sort of thing suited her the best. After that, very skilfully, I manoeuvred the conversation back to Nada.

'Couldn't you find out anything about her?' I asked. 'It seems extraordinary that nobody would tell you.'

'I think I hated her so much that I didn't want to know,' Elizabeth confessed. 'I had seen the picture, you see. I oughtn't to have, of course, but it was quite by accident.

'I went round to the house with a note from Mother, and I had to wait for an answer. They told me that Philip was busy but would come up to his study as soon as he had finished, if I would wait there. I sat down in front of the fire, when one of his dogs, who was lying on the sofa, had a sort of fit. I can see it now, gasping and rolling about. Of course I rang the bell, but the servants seemed to take a long time coming, so I opened the door into his bedroom, thinking perhaps that the valet or someone would be there. I had never been in Philip's bedroom before. Although I was worried about the dog I just had to glance about me and naturally I noticed the picture. I only had a moment to look at it before his valet came hurrying in response to my shouts. The next time that I got the opportunity, I went in and looked at it more carefully.

'How did you know who it was?' I asked.

'It was obvious, wasn't it?' Elizabeth said. 'I know most of Philip's relations. Besides, she looks half Indian, doesn't she?'

'I suppose she does,' I answered. 'But has Sir Philip never mentioned her to you?'

'He never talks to me about anything now,' Elizabeth answered. 'It must have been that the family frightened him. He used to be so nice those first months I came out. Then mother was always making excuses to leave us alone together and I began to see that he was equally determined the other way. He won, although the family blamed me.'

I felt terribly guilty when I left Elizabeth at twenty minutes to three.

'Where are you going?' she asked. 'Can't I come with you? I have got nothing to do.'

'I am sorry, dear, but I promised to meet Angela,' I lied. 'I am late as it is, so I must hurry.'

I got into a taxi and gave my home address. As soon as we were round the corner I opened the little window between me and the driver and told him to go to Chadleigh House. When I arrived, Philip's big Rolls Royce was standing outside the door. As soon as I got into the hall I was told that he was expecting me and was waiting in the library.

I was shown into a room that I had not previously seen on the ground floor. A huge magnificent room with masses of books in mahogany and glass cases and with four long windows looking on to the Park. Sir Philip was sitting in a chair reading when I was announced.

He jumped up and held out his hand in greeting.

'Surely you are the most punctual woman in the world,'

he said. 'I wasn't expecting you for at least another half hour.'

I knew he was only teasing me, but I felt embarrassed as though I had appeared too eager to reach him.

'I am sorry,' I said. 'I will remember to be fashionably late another time.'

As soon as I had spoken I wished I hadn't said that, because it inferred that there would be another time, that he would ask me again.

'Don't spoil a delightful virtue which is exceedingly rare,' he said. 'Sit down a moment and have a cigarette.'

'I don't smoke,' I answered.

'Another virtue!' he said. 'You are full of them! Have you any vices?'

'A great many, I am afraid,' I replied. 'But don't ask me to confess them. I would rather they were discovered slowly.'

He laughed.

'What do you think of this room?'

I looked round.

'It is magnificent,' I answered. 'But I would never dare to read quite an ordinary, frivolous novel here, would you?'

'That is why I have a sitting-room upstairs,' he said, 'where I usually sit. I would like to show it to you one day.'

I didn't tell him that I had seen it the night before.

'Where have you been lunching?' he asked curiously. 'Was it so important that you couldn't honour me?'

'I made a mistake,' I said slowly. 'The party that I thought I was going to, is tomorrow, so instead I have been with a friend of yours.'

'Who?' he asked.

'Elizabeth Batley,' I replied. 'Actually I met her here last night for the first time, but I like her so much.'

'She is a distant cousin,' he said. 'I am glad you like Elizabeth, she is a sweet girl.'

'She seems to me extraordinarily pathetic,' I said.

He looked at me sharply.

'Why do you say that?'

'She has a rotten time,' I replied. 'It seems to be the usual thing in London to brand any girl who has not got married by the time she is twenty-seven, as a complete old-maid. Everything is given up to Elizabeth's sisters, and she is pushed steadily into the background.'

'I can't think why she has never married,' he said, but while the words were spoken casually enough, I felt that he had a very good idea.

'Nor can I,' I replied. 'She would make a marvellous wife for any man, unselfish, considerate and very good-tempered.'

'You seem to have learnt a lot about her in a very short time,' Sir Philip said.

'It is not very difficult to learn things about Elizabeth,' I replied.

'Perhaps it is too easy,' Sir Philip suggested. 'Perhaps that is why she has never got married.'

'Are you suggesting that men only like mysterious women? Women they can't understand——the ones that "keep them guessing"?'

'There's a lot in it,' he admitted.

I felt strangely daring.

'And so you have always understood all the women you met too well?' I said.

I was frightened that I had been too personal, for I saw his face darken and he took up a cigarette and lit it before he answered. But when he spoke, his tone was as light as it had been before.

'Are you like all the others?' he asked. 'What is this conspiracy amongst every woman I know to force me into matrimony?'

'Is there one?' I asked with wide eyes.

Sir Philip laughed.

'If I say "yes", it is conceited; if I say "no", it is untrue,' he said. 'All right, Lyn, you win that point.'

It was the first time he had called me by my christian name and I wondered if he was aware of it. The night before he had always been very careful to say 'Lady Gwendolyn' formally.

'I am not trying to fence with you,' I said. 'I shouldn't dare.'

'Why not?' he asked. 'Don't tell me that you lack the courage to challenge anyone.'

I thought of my words to Elizabeth, less than an hour ago.

'Is it courage to rush in where angels fear to tread?' I asked.

'By which you mean?' he questioned.

'That the worst vice I have got is curiosity,' I replied. 'I like knowing things about people and it is generally far easier to ask them to tell you about themselves, than to go snooping round listening at keyholes or gossiping.'

Sir Philip smiled as he would have smiled at the precociousness of a child.

'So you want to know things about me?' he said.

'But of course!' I cried. 'You are a new person in a new world to me and, for all I hear, a very important one.'

He made a gesture as though such a statement was ridiculous.

'But it is true,' I said. 'And all sorts of legends have grown up about you.'

'Legends?' he questioned. 'What sort of legends?'

'That is just what I am not going to tell you,' I answered. 'That is why I would much rather you told me about yourself. Nothing is more boring than hearing about people second-hand. It is like being given clothes that have been worn by other people—they never seem to be entirely comfortable.'

'I think you are turning the tables on me,' Sir Philip said. 'Last night I asked you to tell me things about yourself and now you are cross-examining me.'

'It is obvious that,' I replied, 'we must work on a fifty-fifty basis.'

'Why not?' he asked. 'But before we start, shall we get into the car and drive down to Ranelagh?'

'Yes, let's,' I said and led the way out into the hall.

I was pleased when Sir Philip dismissed his chauffeur and took the wheel himself. He drove well and we quickly got through the traffic at Hyde Park Corner and into the less crowded side streets.

'Do you drive?' he asked me.

'Only a Morris,' I answered. 'But if you saw the old car you would realise that it was a feat of endurance. I ought really to be given a medal every time I take it out on the road.'

'I remember your mother when I was a boy,' he said later on. 'She was a very beautiful woman—is she still?'

'I think so,' I answered. 'And I think you would think so too. She has accepted old age as though it were a present and it becomes her.'

'You are very like her—you know that of course,' Sir

Philip said. 'But I expect you are tired of being called beautiful.'

'I'm not and nobody tells me that I am,' I replied. 'Anyway, I have never wanted to look like myself.'

'Why?' he asked.

I looked at him. His eyes were on the road ahead. I felt I wanted to speak the truth.

'Ever since I have been a child,' I said, 'I have wanted to be small and dark.'

'Like your sister, I suppose,' he said. 'Except she isn't small.'

'Not a bit like my sister,' I said firmly.

I had a very different idea in my mind. Then suddenly I knew; it was as though a cloud was brushed aside from my mind and I understood. It was Nada that I had wanted to be like. It was Nada's face that I had always imagined instead of my own. That was why the portrait was so familiar; that was why I recognised it in that first startled glance. Of course I knew the face! Hadn't it always been with me in my dreams; hadn't I always expected to see it reflected back at me every time I looked in the glass? The portrait of Nada was my idea of myself; how I had always wanted to look and what I had always expected to be.

11

I was so interested in my own thoughts that I now have no recollection of what we spoke about for the rest of the drive down to Ranelagh. I suppose we must have talked, although we may quite easily have sat silent, both staring ahead—Sir Philip looking at the road, I seeing nothing but that familiar face which hung on the walls of his bedroom.

It was a very hot brilliantly sunny day and the trees at Ranelagh seemed delightfully cool and inviting, after the roads and the traffic blocks, with the smell of petrol rising from the buses and cars. We walked slowly though the gardens towards the polo ground; when I saw the people massed in the stands, I said involuntarily:

'Oh! What a crowd!'

'Would you rather sit the other side of the field?' Sir Philip asked.

'Much rather,' I answered.

'Good!' he replied. Then, as we retraced our steps he said, 'I thought I was the only person in the world who hated crowds. Most women love them.'

'I shouldn't have thought that was true,' I answered.

'Oh, I mean London women,' he said. 'The sort that come down here wanting to show off their new frocks, or their new young man.'

I felt that from the way he spoke Sir Philip had often suffered from being shown off and I longed to say that the last idea I had in mind was to be seen with him, especially as I had lied to both Angela and Elizabeth.

We found two seats well apart from anyone else under a shady tree. We couldn't, perhaps, get such a good view of the field, but we could be cool and relax. I pulled off my hat and threw it down beside me on the grass. Sir Philip stretched out his legs and lit a cigarette.

'Talk to me,' he commanded.

'Why?' I answered. 'Because you want to hear the sound

of my voice, or because you want to hear what I have to say?'

'That's the first unkind thing I have heard you say,' he said.

'Why unkind?' I asked. 'The first part of my question is true, isn't it?'

'Perhaps,' he answered enigmatically

I waited. I felt that the moment had come when he was going to ask me about our first meeting in the House of Commons, but to my surprise, he suddenly threw away his cigarette.

'No,' he said as though I had asked a question, 'I have changed my mind, Lyn. And, what is more, I am going to change myself. I think perhaps the most damned silly thing any man can do is to live in the past. Don't you?'

'If it makes him dissatisfied with the present—yes.'

'I have tried to ignore the present,' he said. 'I see now that I have been making a fool of myself for a great many years.'

I said nothing.

The tension he was obviously feeling seemed to pass. He took out his cigarette case again; when he had lit his cigarette, he flicked away the match and smiled at me.

'Behold a man new born,' he said lightly

'How do you do?' I answered, trying to play up to his mood, deeply interested, but at the same time afraid that any unwary remark or word of mine might make him remember what strangers we were.

'Aren't you interested?' he asked, with a note of banter in his voice.

'Of course I am,' I answered. 'But if the past is to be forgotten, there is from this moment nothing to be curious about. We can only speculate on the future.'

He took off his hat to me with a sweeping gesture, then chucked it on the grass in front of him.

'Lady Gwendolyn Sherbrooke,' he said, 'I believe that you are a very intelligent young woman.'

'You are the second person who has told me that since I came to London,' I answered. 'I shall begin to believe it in time.'

'If you are as intelligent as I think you are,' he said, 'you have got a very good idea of it already. Well, I am in your hands—what do you suggest for me?'

'What do you want most out of life?' I asked, speaking quite seriously.

'If you had asked me that question half an hour ago,' he said, 'I should have told you that I wanted to put back the clock. Now, I find it difficult to reply. I have grown so used to having no ambitions, that I have forgotten how you begin to formulate them.'

'That's perfectly easy,' I said. 'You make your goal always a little higher than it is possible for you to reach. Therefore, if you fall short of it—which everyone does—you will still do very well indeed.'

'And keeping this conversation strictly personal,' he said, 'what do you suggest for me?'

'Well . . . Prime Minister?' I answered. 'I suppose there is nothing higher if you are in politics.'

'Why not propose that I become a dictator?' he asked mockingly.

'Because I don't think you would make a very good one,' I replied.

'That is frank enough,' he answered. 'And why?'

Thus challenged I realised it would be hard to tell him what I really thought. For I was disappointed in Sir Philip. I suppose my mind was still filled with the ideal childhood's hero buckling on his armour, girding on his sword, ready to journey out as a knight errant, to succour the weak and rescue the oppressed. There was, indeed, something about Sir Philip himself which made me think of King Arthur's Knights. He might so easily have sat for any of the illustrations in the book which I pored over when I was twelve. He had at times that same stern look in his eyes, and in repose an expression which made one think that he was looking beyond the present, seeking relentlessly the Holy Grail. Now in disillusionment I knew he was merely looking backwards. How extraordinary it was, I thought, that one woman should have held him all these years, should have retarded his progress, should have utterly stifled all his natural desires and what must have been his natural joys and inclinations.

'Well?' he interrupted me.

I realised I was sitting silent, making no effort to answer his last question.

'I am sorry,' I said. 'I was thinking about you.'

'And what were you thinking?' he asked.

'I don't think I want to tell you that yet,' I answered. 'It seems ridiculous to say I don't know you well enough, but that is what I mean. I am afraid of forming an opinion which may be too hasty.'

'Which means that so far it isn't a very good one,' he retorted.

'It is so difficult to say,' I answered. 'You see I have heard people talking and that made me imagine certain things about you, which I now find are wrong. I am not exactly disillusioned or disappointed, but I want to be quite certain that I am not making another mistake, before I replace my first impressions with others.'

'Why do you think about me at all?' he asked.

I blushed; I couldn't help it. His remark was so unexpected. Then I forced myself to answer him, keeping my head turned away, as though I was watching the polo players galloping up the field.

'I think a great many people do think about you,' I answered.

He sighed.

'If you only knew how I try to escape them,' he said. 'I went away once, for many years—I expect you have been told about that. I lived in India among other places, all alone in the mountains. I knew then that I hated people for their prying, inquisitive minds, which cannot leave anything alone, however sacred, however personal.'

'I think it is a form of fear,' I answered.

'Fear?' he questioned. 'Why fear?'

'Most people are afraid that someone will get to know or understand just a little more than they know themselves,' I replied. 'I don't mean in a gossipy, social way, I mean about real things—life, the truth, the evolution of mankind. They don't think of it like that, of course, but instinctively, in self-protection, they probe into everything, especially into the feelings and emotions of others.'

'Your theory is as good as any other,' he said. 'But if you ever had cause to hate humanity as I have, you would know that you would find no excuses for them, and that you would willingly see them boiled alive in their own vileness.'

He spoke so violently that I knew that the wounds that had been inflicted on him were not healed yet, however much he might wish to forget them, or desire to put all that was past behind him.

'We can't do without people,' I said gently. 'Although

men are naturally more independent than women, for what woman ever wants to be alone in the mountains, even for a little while? They are terrified of loneliness.'

'Men can feel lonely too, I assure you,' he said, and there was a great sadness in his voice.

'If men and women could escape the herd instinct,' I went on, 'surely the world would stop? Fear of loneliness is one of the strongest spurs to marriage humanity has yet invented.'

'You think marriage can prevent loneliness?' he asked. 'Surely one would be utterly alone if one was married to someone one didn't like?'

I thought of Angela before I answered. Then I said:

'I don't know. I think even in an unhappy marriage it is better to have someone to nag at than no one to talk to at all.'

Sir Philip laughed. Then he got to his feet.

'Come and have tea, my little philosopher,' he said. 'This is a rotten game, not worth watching.'

As neither of us had taken the slightest interest in the game, I felt this was rather unfair on the players. However, obediently I picked up my hat and followed him to the club-house, in front of which tables were laid under shady umbrellas.

We were both rather silent at tea. There seemed to be very little to say and I personally was remembering the conversation we had just had, reading a deeper meaning into every one of Sir Philip's remarks; wishing I knew more about him and about the events which had meant so much to him. Various acquaintances nodded to him as we had our tea, then, just as we were finishing, a rather over-dressed woman of about forty came hurrying up to us.

'Philip!' she said in exaggerated tones. 'Fancy seeing you here. But how delightful!'

'How do you do, Monica,' he said.

'I wish I had known you were coming this afternoon,' she said. 'I would have cadged a lift from you. I had to come down with those awful bores the Browne-Gores, because, of course, Mother has taken the car as usual. Won't you introduce me?'

'Do you know Lady Gwendolyn Sherbrooke?' he asked. 'Lady Monica Shawe.'

Lady Monica held out her hand and gave me a scrutinising glance, which I felt was full of curiosity and interest.

'Have you been watching the polo?' she asked. 'It was a marvellous game, wasn't it?'

'Yes, we were there for some time,' I said.

Without being invited, Lady Monica sat herself down at our table.

'Give me a cup of tea, Philip,' she said pleadingly, look-at him with large brown eyes. 'I am absolutely faint with heat and exhaustion.'

He was far too polite to show her anything but courteous consideration, yet, somehow, I felt that I already knew him well enough to guess that he wasn't particularly pleased at having an uninvited guest.

'Who are you?' Lady Monica said to me abruptly. 'Tell me about yourself. I know I ought to know, but Philip will tell you I am so scatter-brained that I always get behind with the news and muddle up the latest scandal so that the wrong person gets the blame.'

'I hope there is no scandal about me as yet,' I said. 'I am Angela Watson's sister.'

'Oh, my dear. Of course I didn't mean that,' Lady Monica gushed. 'There you are, you see, my tongue just runs away with me. Angela Watson! Of course I know your sister. I haven't seen her for years. You must give her my love and say I am longing to come and see her and that charming husband of hers.'

I promised to give Angela the message.

'Now, Philip,' Lady Monica went on, 'what have you been doing lately? I hear all sorts of rumours about you. But my dear, they are all such dull ones—you must be living an exemplary life!'

'I am,' he announced shortly.

Lady Monica gave a little squeal of laughter.

'Isn't he ridiculous?' she said, turning to me. 'There's Philip with everything in the world and all he does is to keep his nose to the political grindstone.'

'And not even a job to show for it,' he said dryly.

'Ah, but a little bird told me,' Lady Moncia said, 'that you refused one the other day.'

'Little birds have a habit of talking nonsense,' Sir Philip retorted.

'But this was a very big bird,' Lady Monica said. 'In fact, it was somebody really in the know.'

'Then you may be quite certain that what they knew was untrue,' Sir Philip answered.

A fresh pot of tea came for Lady Monica and a plate of iced and cream cakes, which she fell upon hungrily as though she had not seen food for some time.

'I am so lucky,' she said to me, 'nothing I eat makes any difference to my figure. What do you girls who have to bant say to that?'

I felt that at her age it hardly mattered whether one got fat or not, in fact, her thin scraggy neck and veined hands, which looked like talons, would have been much better had they been covered with a layer of fat. However, I murmured some polite congratulations, but by the time I had started to answer, she was talking of something else, chattering gaily in her nonsensical way about someone she had met on the polo ground and who had told her that war was imminent at any moment.

'I said to her,' Lady Monica said, 'that if war comes, I shall stay just where I am. If I am going to be killed, I shall be killed. That's sensible enough, don't you think so, Philip?'

'Oh, very,' he answered. 'Are you a fatalist, Lyn?'

I felt it was with a sense of relief that he turned to me, but before I could answer, Lady Monica said:

'Of course she is a fatalist. How can any sensible person be anything else? It is all written in the stars at the time one is born. I went to my pet astrologer last week. My dear, the man's a wonder. He said to me "you are passing through a period of financial stress, but by the end of the month, everything will be all right".'

'And was it?' I asked.

'We haven't reached the end of the month yet,' Lady Monica replied brightly, 'but, of course, he was absolutely right about the financial stress. I am always in the last stages of penury, aren't I, Philip?'

'Ever since I have known you,' he answered, 'which is many years . . .'

'Don't say it, don't say it,' Lady Monica screamed. 'It is terribly unlucky to mention age; your age is what you think you are. That is what a psychologist said to me the other day. "Don't think in terms of age," he said. My dear, I have been trying not to ever since.'

'Well, then, I will say since the time we played together as children,' Sir Philip said with a smile.

'That isn't fair either,' Lady Monica expostulated.

'Everyone knows how old you are, Philip, but I have had my age taken out of Debrett.'

'How did you manage that?' Philip asked.

'I went round to see the editor personally,' Lady Monica said. 'I wept on his shoulder and he promised. Of course I haven't seen the new edition yet, he might not have kept his word, but he was such a nice man, I feel I can trust him.'

Sir Philip looked at his watch.

'What about going back, Lyn?' he said to me.

'Oh, must you go?' Lady Monica asked.

'I am afraid we must,' Sir Philip answered.

'I suppose I must wait for the Browne-Gores,' Lady Monica said wistfully. 'It would be rude if I came with you.'

'I am afraid it would,' Sir Philip said gravely. 'Another time, Monica.'

'Oh, when?' she asked.

'I will telephone you,' he promised.

'Thank you a million times for my tea,' she said, pressing his hand. Then to me: 'Good-bye, Lady Gwendolyn, or what does Philip call you—Lyn? Such a pretty name. I should never use the other one, if I was you.'

'I don't,' I answered. 'Good-bye, Lady Monica.'

Philip and I walked briskly away. As soon as we were out of earshot, he slowed up his pace.

'Heavens! I am sorry to inflict you with Monica Shawe. She is one of the biggest bores in the world and not quite right in the head, poor thing. She forces herself on people whether they want her or not, and is quite impervious to hints.'

'Is she really mad?' I asked.

'Oh, not mad enough to be shut up,' he answered. 'But she flutters about any man she meets, finds it quite impossible to concentrate on any one subject for more than two minutes, and is crazy on fortune-tellers and astrologers.'

'It doesn't sound very mad to me,' I said. 'Not worse than many people who have nothing to do with their lives.'

'Oh, it is much worse than I've made out,' he answered. 'If you knew her family, you'd understand. They are far too decadent, I suppose. In fact, the perfect answer to those who ask that red blood and vitality should be injected into the aristocracy.'

'And you played together as children?' I asked.

'Yes. Her father's place adjoins my home,' he replied. 'I remember even on my fourth birthday disliking Monica. She always screamed and used to declare that we boys had pulled her hair and pinched her, when we hadn't even been near her. She wanted attention and was determined to get it.'

'In fact, she was really feminine,' I said.

'Of the worst type,' he answered.

We reached the car and got into it.

'I didn't mean to come away so soon,' he said. 'But we couldn't go on chattering indefinitely and Monica would have stuck to us like a leech. It would have been impossible to lose her.'

'Poor woman!' I said.

I saw her going through life, always unwanted, always being avoided, yet so anxious to make friends, so eager to be the center of attention. How awful to be like that, always anticipating that things were going to be better than they were, always disappointed.

We drove down the drive, but instead of turning right for London, Sir Philip said:

'Let's drive round Richmond Park. You aren't in a hurry to get back, are you?'

Rather guiltily I thought that Angela might wonder what had become of me, but nothing would have made me say so.

'Oh no,' I answered. 'Any time will do.'

In a few moments we were in the park, seeing the deer grazing by the side of the road, watching the picnickers enjoying their tea on the sunbaked grass, hearing the voices of the children as they chased each other round the trees. Sir Philip drove on until we were on a hill overlooking the Thames Valley. Here there was no one else about, and backing his car on to the grass, he switched off the engine. There was a sort of calm contentment in being there together, in hearing the chirping of the crickets in the grass, the sound of the birds in the trees behind us. . . .

I don't know why, but two lines of poetry came to my mind and with my eyes half closed I said them out loud.

'We are ever and always slaves of these,
Of suns that scorch and the winds that freeze.'

I felt Sir Philip become alert beside me.

'Why do you say that?' he said brusquely. 'Why do you suddenly say that to me?'

I was astonished and his voice startled me, so that I hesitated, then stammered my reply.

'I have no idea,' I answered. 'It just came to my mind.'

'But there must be some reason,' he said tersely with a fierce, almost hungry look in his eyes. Then, abruptly, he put his hand up to his face and sat back in his seat. 'Forget it,' he said roughly. 'I am talking nonsense.'

He started the car again, turned it on to the road, and exceeding every speed limit, drove furiously towards London, as though he were escaping from something.

Not another word was spoken between us until we reached my doorstep. When we said good-bye it was formally and with a restraint that I was too bewildered to try and understand.

12

A whole week passed before I saw Philip Chadleigh again, a week in which I admitted to myself that I was desperately unhappy and that I wanted to see him more than anyone else in the world.

What had happened, I asked myself again and again? Why should those two lines from a poem which I could not remember have made so much difference to a relationship which had been friendly and happy the whole long afternoon? How much would I have given to unsay them, but like Philip himself, I could not put back the clock; so there they were, a barrier between us, a barrier all the more impregnable because I didn't understand its erection.

I could only suppose it was Nada again. I felt now that I hated that ghost of Philip's, just as much as Elizabeth did. I saw Elizabeth once or twice, but I found she could tell me very little more about Sir Philip than I already knew. I did not hesitate to question her and she was simple enough to believe that my insatiable curiosity was because I wished to help her.

The dances and the parties to which I went every night and which before had seemed so amusing and so exciting, had lost much of their savour. The young men with whom I danced appeared to me stupid and while I suppose I talked gaily and looked my best, so that neither Angela nor anyone else realised what I was feeling, I knew that everything was changed.

'I am in love!' I told myself quite solemnly the morning after I had been at Ranelagh with Philip. I was not quite fool enough to believe that any girl would lie awake all night thinking of one man, or hear his words echo again and again in her ears, simply for the sake of friendship. No, I was in love. I admitted it to myself and the hopelessness of it made me feel at times as though the only thing to do was to go straight back to Maysfield and never come to London again. 'Perhaps I will forget him,' I thought, but I realised that that was unlikely. There was some link between me and Philip. What, I did not know, but there was some fundamental bond which time and distance would not alter.

Surely he must have liked me, I asked a thousand times, else why should he have bothered to seek me out the night after the concert, and again the very next day? And I knew that it was Nada—Nada standing between us, snatching him back to herself in that very moment when he had tried to escape.

'You are dead,' I said out loud. 'Dead and buried!' And I was a little afraid of my own words. I wondered if the dead really did live and if, even after death, they could play a part in the world, still keeping near to, and impressing their personality on those that were still alive.

Alone in my bedroom in the long hours of the night, I asked myself what I believed, and was horrified to find how little I had formulated for myself any creed or faith. I had accepted just what I was taught, giving lip service to the God of my fathers and that was all.

For the first time in my life I meditated on death and what came after. How often in the past had I been told to think about it, and it had eluded me as an unimportant event which came to all people and which, in time, would come to me but which was not yet of any urgency.

Now death was a vital thing to me. Was Nada still living? Was she still consciously holding on to Philip with those lovely thin fingers? Could she still keep him hers, even while her body was buried beneath the ground, her flesh returned to the earth from which it had sprung? What did it all mean? Death and Life? What was it, this moving, pulsating, living thing—soul, ego or personality—which arrived in a child the third month of conception to make a living entity; a creature apart from the parents who had conceived it, or who had brought it into being? What was life? And if there was such a thing as eternal life, could death have any reality?

It was all impossible to put into words, but I sought out of the tangle and jumble of phrases to find some meaning within myself. Was life a power, a kind of universal broadcasting house, to which each person could link himself as long as they had the right instrument, I asked myself? Was the body but an instrument, a thing as lifeless as metal and wood, unless connected with the right station, or were we just a part of evolution, a vegetable which had become animal, animal which became man? Was there nothing beyond our three score years and ten of consciousness, except the final development of a still better man and woman—perhaps of one person who would jointly fulfil the functions of both? What did I think? What did I feel? I didn't know myself.

I bought books once again; I had to lie to Angela pretending that I required the money for more stockings and gloves, but really hurrying round to Bumpus, seeking along their stacked shelves for books on Philosophy, Science and Religion. They told me so much, and yet held so little which struck an answering chord within myself.

'No one has ever yet gained faith from a book,' the Vicar had once said to me and I realised that what I lacked was faith. With it one could believe anything; without it —what evidence was there that anyone could rise from the dead, or indeed that life was anything but a dream, of which we were not even sure that we were the dreamers?

Night after night when I came back from parties I would lie in bed reading until the sun was shining through my windows and the milk cart with its noisy bottles was clinking its way through the Square.

I was almost in despair, not only because books gave me no solution to my problems, but because I wanted so terribly to see Philip. His silence hurt me as nothing had ever hurt me before.

One morning about half-past ten the telephone rang beside my bed. I was cross and resentful of the sound, for I had been awake nearly the whole night and was dozing now from sheer exhaustion.

'Hullo,' I said sleepily, 'Who is it?'

'Is that you, Lyn?' a voice said.

Instantly I was awake; my heart beating, both hands clutching the telephone nervously.

'Oh, it is you,' I said before I could stop myself.

'So you recognise my voice?' he said.

'It is surprising if I do,' I answered recovering myself a little. 'For I haven't heard it very often lately.'

As soon as I had spoken I would have given anything to recall the words, but as usual I had said what first came into my head, letting him know that I had missed him, that I had wanted to hear from him again.

'Where are you dining tonight?' he asked.

'Nowhere,' I answered. It was untrue, but I did not care.

'Come and dine with me,' he said. 'Not here, it is too hot in London, but at Longmoor, my house in the country. It will only take us an hour-and-a-half to get there. Will you come?'

'I would love to,' I answered.

'Good. I will call for you at seven o'clock,' he said. 'Don't dress up—the party will consist of ourselves, or would you rather you were chaperoned?'

'Oh, I want at least a hundred guests and a band,' I answered sarcastically.

Philip laughed.

'I will be ready at seven o'clock,' I promised. 'So don't be late. Good-bye.'

I put down the receiver then lay in bed with an exquisite feeling of happiness and excitement creeping over me. He wanted to see me again; he hadn't forgotten me after all. Perhaps the words which had divided us had not been so momentous as I had thought; perhaps, after all, the ghost of Nada had been dispelled, or had merely shrunk a little into abeyance.

'Go away!' I commanded her. 'Go away and stay away. You had him once, you can't have him now.'

It was all very well to say lightly to Phillip that I had no other engagement tonight, but while I was dressing I remembered perfectly well that Angela was taking me to a dance—another of those young girl affairs of which I had had pretty nearly a surfeit in the last few weeks. What was I going to say? Perhaps it would be better to tell the truth, or at least partially the truth, I decided, but when I went into Angela's room I was nervous, afraid that I should over-act my part, or do it so badly that she would be suspicious.

'You were late waking up this morning, darling,' I said drawing a bow at a venture.

'I suppose I was,' she answered. 'Anyway, I am still damnably tired.'

'They put Philip Chadleigh through to me as you were not called,' I said.

'Sir Philip?' Angela said sharply. 'Why, what did he want?'

'Nothing very exciting,' I said. 'He is taking a small party of young people down to Longmoor Park tonight and wanted me to join them. I think it is a party for Elizabeth.' I spoke cautiously, not daring to look at Angela as I did so, but walking across the room to her dressing-table, fiddling about with her gold dressing-table things and with the huge bunches of roses which were arranged on either side of the gilt mirror.

'Didn't he ask me?' Angela questioned.

'No. He said he wouldn't bore you with it,' I replied. 'It is only a very few of us and, I gather, practically a debutante affair.'

'Elizabeth Batley is no debutante,' Angela said.

I caught my breath sharply, realising I had overdone my story.

'Oh, but she is a cousin,' I answered. 'I suppose relations don't count, they are ageless.'

'Well, we have got a dance tonight,' Angela said.

'I know. I really didn't know what to do as you weren't awake. Then I thought that you and Henry would both want me to go to Sir Philip's as he is so important, so I accepted although we can always ring up and put him off.'

'Perhaps you had better go,' Angela said grudgingly. 'The Dawsons' dance won't be much of an affair, anyway, and I can write afterwards and say you were taken ill or something. Was Henry coming with us—I can't remember?'

'I don't think so,' I replied.

'Well, then Douglas and I can go out together,' Angela said brightening. 'That is perfect. You were quite right, Lyn, quite right to accept.'

'I am glad you are pleased,' I answered. 'I was very worried, I was really.'

That at least was truthful, but when finally I left Angela's room, I felt guilty and ashamed. It was awful to lie, especially to someone who had been as kind to me as Angela had. At the same time I knew I couldn't bear the buzz of excitement, the speculations and the innuendoes which would arise if for one moment, Angela, Henry or anyone else, thought that Sir Philip was interested in me. I could visualise only too well, what Elizabeth had suffered; how every time she returned to the house there were enquiring looks, the unspoken question on everyone's lips of—has he proposed? I couldn't bear it. I would rather never see Philip again but go away and try and forget him, try and forget the excitement and thrill which made me tingle when I thought of the evening before me.

Later in the day Angela asked me casually if Sir Philip was picking me up.

'I think he is sending the car,' I replied.

'If he's coming himself I would like to see him,' Angela said. 'What time are you going? Half-past seven? I could be back from my cocktail party by then.'

'That will be splendid,' I answered, evading a direct lie, but knowing at the same time that long before half-past seven we would be well on the road towards Longmoor.

I was ready much too early and I changed my dress three or four times before I was satisfied with my appearance. When seven o'clock struck I went downstairs, my coat over my arm, and waited—not in the hall where I was likely to be seen by the servants—but in the dining-room, from the windows of which I could see up and down the Square, and recognise Sir Philip's car before it arrived.

Everyone would be out to dinner that evening, so I knew there was no likelihood of the butler or footmen coming into the dining-room. I stood there among the Chippendale chairs with their satin seats, wishing that the minutes would pass quicker and that Sir Philip would arrive. Every second seemed an eternity, until I caught a glimpse of the big grey Rolls coming slowly up to the door. Before the chauffeur had time to get out, I had opened the front door and shut it behind me.

Philip himself opened the back door of the car and jumped out on to the pavement.

'Surely I'm not late?' he asked holding out his hand. 'How are you, Lyn?'

'Let's go,' I replied, rather flustered. 'I will tell you why when we have started.'

He handed me into the car and got in beside me.

'Well,' he said as we drove off. 'What have you been up to? You look like a conspirator.'

'I am,' I admitted. 'I ought to be getting ready for the most ghastly dance. Debs, post-debs and sub-debs—you know the type. Only by telling the most enormous amount of lies did I manage to come this evening.'

'You wanted to as much as that?' he asked.

Perhaps it was reaction; perhaps it was because I had never wanted to pretend with Philip, that I told the truth.

'Yes,' I said. 'I wanted to come very much '

'I am glad,' he answered. 'I should have been disappointed if you had refused.'

His words were warm but the tone of his voice somehow chilled me. He had become formal again. He had crept away into his reserve, eluding me, although at our first moment of meeting, I knew that he was genuinely glad to see me.

I felt a sudden depression, then gave myself a hard mental shake and forced myself to say lightly:

'I wouldn't miss seeing Longmoor for anything in the world. I have read all about the treasures there, the pictures and the tapestries. I don't know whether you can bear it, but you are going to do guide to me for hours this evening, until I have satisfied all my sight-seeing instincts.'

He laughed.

'So that is why you were so keen to come.'

'But of course!' I answered innocently. 'What did you think?'

'I am never quite sure what I do think when I am with you, Lyn,' he answered. 'Sometimes you seem your age, but other times you might be a sophisticated woman of fifty or sixty, guiding a young man through the perplexities of life.'

'Well, you are going to do the guiding tonight, I promise you.'

'Oh dear!' he said with a sigh. 'I ought to have suggested dining in a restaurant, I can quite see that.'

'Restaurants are full of people who hate their husbands and can't keep their servants,' I said. It was not my own remark—I had heard one of Angela's smart friends say it the week before, but it made Philip laugh, which I meant it to do.

'Did your sister mind your coming without a chaperone?' he asked.

'Not a bit.' I replied. 'You forget I am not really a debutante. Also she was delighted to get the evening off.'

'I felt rather guilty about not asking her,' he said. 'I thought you and I would have so much more to talk about if we were alone.'

'I hate parties,' I said.

'I can quite see you are going to be one of those problem children,' Philip said. 'What on earth will they do with a society beauty who doesn't like parties, who doesn't care for restaurants and who can't bear crowds?'

I was glad he had remembered that.

'I shall marry a curate, I expect, and settle down in some lonely parish where the congregation never exceeds half a dozen.'

'I think there's a better fate in store for you than that,' Philip said quite seriously.

'It will have to be marriage in one form or another,' I answered. 'I am neither trained nor educated for any other sort of existence. I don't believe I should even get a job as a mother's help.'

'In fact you are just an old-fashioned girl,' he said.

'Exactly,' I replied. 'The last rose of an Edwardian summer!'

Philip laughed.

'If you are not careful,' he said, 'you will turn into a wit, then you will have to have a salon and entertain people all day and all night too.'

'Then I will never open my mouth again!' I promised. 'I can imagine nothing I should hate more than that.'

'Would you really hate entertaining?' he asked.

I felt he had some reason for this question and I answered it quite seriously.

'Not if I was entertaining with a purpose,' I answered. 'What seems to me so senseless are the people who gather night after night at each other's houses, merely to drink and to talk about themselves and each other, what is the point of it all? It is nearly always the same collection who, as far as I can see, have invariably the same conversation.'

'And what would you call entertaining with a purpose?'

'Politically, commercially, charitably,' I replied. 'but not socially.'

'Who do you resemble in your family?' he asked suddenly.

'I look like my mother,' I answered, 'but otherwise I have no resemblance to anyone.'

'Then why are you as you are?' he asked.

'I have asked myself that frequently,' I replied, 'but I haven't yet found the answer.'

The time passed very quickly before we arrived at Longmoor Park. I could not believe that an hour and a half had elapsed before we drove through the huge iron gates, and up an avenue of giant oak trees, standing sentinel on either side of the drive. Then I leant forward and had my first glimpse of a perfect Queen Anne red-brick house, standing on the summit of a small hill, with lawns and terraces sloping away to a great lake of silver water.

13

It is difficult now to recapture my first impressions of Longmoor, but I think even in the first moments of our acquaintance it impressed me, in spite of all its splendours, treasures, and air of luxury, as being a warm, happy place, the kind of house one could easily live in and make a home.

I could understand why Philip was so proud of it, why at times his voice vibrated with emotion as he showed me round, especially when he took me into the rooms which had been his mother's and which were kept exactly as she had left them. One could sense that she had been a gracious, sympathetic, very loving person, and she must have had exquisite taste as well, for everything in her particular suite was perfect. From the pictures on the walls to the tiny china ornaments arranged on the shelves by her writing desk, each was of its type unique and irreplaceable—a connoisseur's piece.

'My parents were divinely happy together,' Sir Philip said. 'Of course you know the story of their death?'

I told him that I didn't—my interest quickened by two big portraits of his father and mother in both of which I could trace a likeness to their son, for while Philip had inherited the characteristic features of the Chadleighs, he had his mother's fine eyes, and the sensitive, yet firm, mouth which was very noticeable in her picture.

'Please tell me,' I added.

'My father had been ill for a long time,' Sir Philip began. 'He had been working far too hard, for although he was Prime Minister for a very short time, he had, nevertheless, held other posts in the Government and he was one of those people who work at anything they undertake to the point of exhaustion. He was an old man; he had fought in the Crimea War and had never entirely regained his health after the wounds that he received there. He felt that he could no longer go on giving his best to the people who had elected him, and having handed in his resignation, he had a final interview with the King, and came down here, a sick man accompanied only by my mother.

'They spent two or three quiet weeks sitting together in the garden, happy to be in the place which had always meant home to them and which they loved very dearly. Then one evening a messenger arrived from London. The Government had fallen! The party begged my father to return; they were in desperate straits, they needed him, if not in an official position, at least as a guide and counsellor. He hesitated, wondering what was his duty. My mother was very anxious; she realised that he had spent his strength far more than even he himself realised. She begged him not to go. Finally they decided that the question could be shelved until the morning, for it was then quite late. They invited the messenger to stay the night.

'In the morning my father said he had decided that his duty was to return. My mother was heartbroken; she had looked forward to his retirement; looked forward to the days that they might spend together here, without being constantly worried by the anxieties and tribulations of office.

'They went up to London, reopened the house and for nearly four years my father continued to work. He refused to fill any public place, but I believe his influence and his help were invaluable, to the country as well as to the party.

'It is amazing now to realise how he could stand it, but he refused to be conquered by his ill health. He forced himself to go on and on, although I believe that at times he suffered the most excruciating pain, and was in such agony that he could only sit, gripping the arms of his chair, unable to speak, the sweat pouring from his forehead. It was then my mother showed what real love means. She never grumbled or complained, never regretted the time that was being spent away from her, or the life that was gradually ending in the service of others. Whenever she could she was at his side, she spared him what she could, she ministered to him both night and day, never thinking of herself.

'The time came—as it was bound to come, although the doctors had predicted it would be far earlier—when my father collapsed entirely. I am told that it happened when many of the Cabinet were meeting in his house. He was speaking to them and the last words he used were: "For God and for this beloved England of ours." He fell forward in his chair unconscious, he never spoke again.

'Fortunately I was in London; relations and friends arrived from all over England, most of them expecting to find my mother prostrated with grief. To everyone's surprise, she was quite calm. I remember her now, dressed in black and rather pale, with her head held high, her clear voice quite unbroken as she discussed arrangements for the funeral—the hymns that were to be sung, the people who were to be invited.

'We stayed up until late that evening, everyone was amazed at her control; some of the relations, I feel, thinking it a little unnatural. When it was time to go to bed, we all went into the hall. She kissed me, then someone a little gushingly, perhaps, said, "Edith, you have been wonderful. You can rely on us to help you all we can in the future."

'She looked at us sadly for a moment, then she said, "Thank you, but I have nothing to live for now". She went upstairs.

'In the morning she too was dead, a quiet smile on her lips. She had passed peacefully in her sleep—the doctors could only describe it as "cessation of the heart"—but we all knew it was because her last words were so true, she had nothing left to live for.

'They were buried together and I think in some ways it was the happiest funeral I have ever attended. Although we mourned them we could not in any way wish things had turned out differently. My father had suffered so acutely those last years that one could only want him to have peace with his beloved wife beside him.'

There were tears in my eyes when Philip finished speaking.

'What a beautiful story,' I said in a low voice, and I added, 'How very wonderful to love like that.'

'They were lucky!'

There seemed to me there was a note of envy in Philip's voice. He turned away from the portraits and we walked through the picture gallery, looking at other portraits of Chadleigh ancestors, many of which I had already seen reproduced in the book I had bought on Longmoor Park.

We had dinner about a quarter past nine. When it was over we walked into the garden. There were lawns smooth as velvet and a smell of syringa and roses. It was very quiet, although occasionally the cry of a peacock in the shrubberies around the house broke the silence.

'I think your home is very beautiful,' I said looking back at it silhouetted against the darkening sky, the lights gleaming golden through uncurtained windows.

'So do I,' Philip replied. 'But I can't get here often enough. No,' he added quickly, 'that is not quite true. I come here with parties, but seldom by myself. It makes me feel lonely. This house is essentially a family place; all its history has been one of happiness, of devoted Chadleighs living in contentment with their families.'

I felt suddenly very brave.

'Why don't you get married?' I asked him.

I felt him stiffen beside me. There was a moment's tension while I knew my remark hung in the balance—whether it was taken as an impertinence, or whether he accepted it in a friendly spirit.

'Perhaps I am afraid,' he said at length.

'Of what?' I asked.

I expected him to say 'of being unhappy', but instead he answered:

'Of loving someone too much.'

I didn't answer. After a moment he went on.

'It has happened to me once. I expect you know that. Some kind friend will certainly have told you about my past, that is if you have been interested enough to listen.'

'Tell me yourself,' I said gently.

'No,' he said abruptly. 'It is something I don't want to talk about. I want to forget.'

'Have you ever talked about it?' I asked.

'No,' he said sharply. 'Why should I?'

'Sometimes it is the easiest way to forget,' I answered. 'Bottling things up inside one, being so reserved that one never seeks sympathy, often makes one's unhappiness more intense.'

'How do you know?' he asked.

I was nonplussed. I didn't know, but as far as Philip was concerned, I could have staked all I had that I was right. There were such a lot of little things about him of which I was quite sure. I don't know why I knew them, certainly not from experience of other men, but there they were, concrete factors in my mind, coming out in our conversations together with an assurance of which, had I paused to think, I should have been afraid.

'I feel certain,' I said slowly, 'that while you are trying to escape your own unhappiness, you have done all the things which, being made as you are, were bound to nurture and intensify it.'

'You can't know anything about me,' he said quite roughly. 'You are just imagining this.'

'I'm not,' I said earnestly. 'Honestly, I'm not. I just know—a woman's intuition, if you like to put it that way.'

'Well,' he said, 'you are wrong, quite wrong. The old theory that confession is good for the soul, may be all right for some people, but certainly not for mine. Anyway, as I have told you, all that is dead and done with. At Ranelagh I said I was going to turn over a new leaf; you don't think that I haven't got the strength to do so?'

'Have you?' I asked. 'Have things been better this last week—or worse?'

Once again it was brave of me to speak like that, but I knew now why Philip had not rung me up. He had been suffering. From the moment I had unwarily quoted poetry to him he had left me abruptly to go back to commune with his ghost, to torture himself with memories which would not fade, and he could not kill.

'Be quiet!' Philip commanded suddenly, there was a note of anger in his voice. 'I didn't come down here to talk about myself, or indeed about my past. I have told you that it is forgotten. It is also to be left alone.'

He took out his cigarette case and lit a cigarette. I watched him and I saw that his hand shook. For the first time I felt a little aloof, a little apart from him. I could watch him almost impartially. It was as though I was for the moment divorced from my own feelings, from my love, which made me at all times so acutely conscious of his nearness. I knew then that I could help him, that I had the strength and the power. I felt that he was like a man gripped by an illness, by some fever which would not let him rest, and in my hands was the antidote, the ultimate cure.

Suddenly he took the lighted cigarette out of his mouth and chucked it over the terrace into the garden beneath.

'I came here with a very definite purpose,' he said.

'What was it?' I asked.

'I wanted to ask you to marry me,' he said.

For a moment I felt that I could not have heard him

111

correctly. Then from a very long way off I heard my own voice ask:

'Why?'

He turned to face me.

'Lyn,' he said. 'This conversation was certainly not the prelude I should have chosen to a proposal of marriage. Before I asked you to come down here tonight, I felt that it must be here, in my own home, that you could judge whether you would be my wife. Yet there are many things that I can't explain to you, or rather, that I don't wish to. I would ask you to accept me exactly as I am, to leave many questions unasked, to let time solve many problems which won't be helped, and certainly not circumvented by facing them now. I am older than you, Lyn, but in many things I think we have the same interests.'

Again, as though it was the voice of a stranger, I heard myself say:

'You haven't answered my question. I asked you why you wanted to marry me.'

There was a moment's silence. I knew that Philip was staring at me in the twilight, striving to see my face, to look into my eyes. I turned away from him; I looked to where the green trees sloped down to the lake, to where, in the dusky sky, the first stars were appearing over the brow of a distant hill.

At length he spoke.

'I want a wife,' he said simply. 'I want a home and children.'

I felt neither pleased nor disappointed by his reply. I had known deep within myself that he would be honest, that he wouldn't tell me that he loved me when it was untrue. I clenched my hands together, feeling the rough cold stone of the terrace against my bare arms.

'I will try to bring you happiness,' I said.

He came nearer to me and took both my hands in his, then raised them to his lips.

'Thank you, Lyn,' he said and there was a gratitude in his voice which stirred me, which broke through the detachment I had been feeling, and which made me for the first time tremble with a feeling that was not fear, but rather a strange happiness I could not yet realise.

There seemed nothing else to say. Instinctively we both turned towards the house and after having iced drinks brought to us by the servants, I put on my coat and we walked towards the door. Philip said he would drive the car going back and he and I got in front, while the chauffeur sat behind. We did not leave down the drive which we had come by, instead we went another way, and having driven up a sharp incline, Philip turned the car so that we looked back on the house.

In its perfect setting of green and silver with its stone terraces and lovely proportions, it was almost breathtakingly beautiful.

'Your home as well as mine, Lyn,' he said gently.

I smiled at him, for I felt that no words could ever have told him what I thought, even had I been prepared to express them. We drove on to London, speaking very seldom and when we did, of conventional things. When we got home, Philip said:

'I will ring you up in the morning, and you must tell me when I can come round and see your sister.'

He walked to the front door with me as I searched in my bag for the latch key. The chauffeur was standing on the pavement by the car. When I turned to say good night, he took my hand formally.

'Good night, Lyn,' he said. 'Sleep well.'

'Good night, Philip,' I answered, and opening the door, went in.

I started to walk upstairs to bed, it was a rule of the house not to use the lift if Angela was in bed, for the noise sometimes woke her. When I reached the first floor to my surprise I heard voices in the drawing-room. I looked at the clock on the landing and saw that it was not yet twelve o'clock. I put my coat down on a chair and opened the door.

There were about half a dozen people grouped round the fireplace; Angela looking very lovely in blue satin, Douglas Ormonde with a large whisky and soda in his hand, several other men and women I did not know, and Henry in ordinary clothes, evidently just back from the House, smoking a big cigar.

'Hullo, darling,' Angela said. 'Did you have a good party? Lyn has been down to Longmoor Park—Philip Chadleigh's becoming quite a beau of hers.'

'Well, well, there may be more in this than meets the eye,' Henry said pompously. 'There's a story going round the House that the Prime Minister sent for Chadleigh and said to him, "Philip, I want you to be the next Viceroy of

India, but you have got to get yourself a wife". Chadleigh is supposed to have answered, "I know no one, sir, that I wish to marry," and the Prime Minister said, "Find someone, my dear Philip, find someone. I believe that surplus women are as plentiful as unemployed men".'

There was a roar of laughter at Henry's story. Suddenly, I don't know what came over me, but I felt furious. I hated them all—Angela smiling up at Douglas Ormonde; Douglas drinking Henry's whisky; Henry with his heavy manner, big cigar, and his obvious delight in having a story to tell; and the rest of them with their vacant faces and their over-fed, over-dressed bodies, anxious to hear anything about other people, so long as it was not too kind.

I turned towards the door.

'Philip Chadleigh won't have to look far,' I said in a cold voice. 'I have this evening promised to marry him.'

I had a quick impression of the embarrassment on their startled faces. Then I had left the room and was running up the stairs to lock myself in my own room, anxious just to be alone—absolutely alone.

14

When I woke in the morning, my anger had left me, but I felt nervous and a little apprehensive of what I had to face. Soon after I had got upstairs the night before, Angela had knocked on my door. I had not answered for a moment or two. Then I said:

'I am tired, Angela, and I don't want to talk tonight.'

'Let me come in for a moment,' she said.

I felt I could not bear it; that I could not, at that moment, make all the explanations which would be required of me or answer any of the questions which I knew she would be certain to ask.

'Please, Angela,' I pleaded. 'Let me tell you everything tomorrow.'

I guessed that she was annoyed, as well as disappointed. 'All right then!' she said at length. And I imagined her shrugging her thin expressive shoulders before she turned and went downstairs again.

I don't know why I had felt so enraged in the drawing-room; perhaps it was only reaction after the difficult evening I had spent and the many conflicting emotions I had experienced. My resentment did not die down for a long time. I lay in bed wishing that I could run away with Philip; that we could get married quite quietly, without any fuss or palaver, at some tiny village church, and that when we were on our honeymoon and out of reach of the world, we could announce that we were man and wife. How lovely that would be! But I knew it was impossible. My parents were to be considered, and Philip's position entailed a definite obligation from both of us.

It was only after a long while that gradually the full import of Henry's story began to sink into my mind. When it did so I did not doubt for a moment the significance of it, and I faced the truth quite frankly. That was why Philip wanted to marry me; I had known that there must be some reason!

I got out of bed and walked about the room. I have never found it easy to think while lying still, and to ease my mind, I have to make my body express the restlessness or indecision which is besetting me. More than once I thought it was a strange way to be spending the first night of my engagement. Most girls would have gone to bed thrilled and rapturous, content to have won the man they loved, believing that the future would bring a fulfillment of all they most desired.

But for me things were very different. I stood on the threshold of a new life, but what it held for me was very uncertain. I loved Philip. Of that I was quite sure; I loved him tremendously with a depth of feeling which was too great, too vast, for my comprehension. It was so intense that its strength seemed to come from some source of which, until now, I had been completely unaware. It was not newborn—this love of mine—it was no helpless babe I had to nurture, but a giant, my own superior, in force and power. I loved Philip—that was indisputable—but was it enough? Could my love hold him? Would it be strong enough to combat and vanquish the ghost of Nada?

Coming back in the car, I had wondered if it was entirely because of her and because he wished to forget all she had stood for in his life, that he had asked me to marry him. I had been prepared for that explanation; it was a reasonable and indeed a logical one, remembering all he had said and all he had inferred in our many conversations together. But now I knew the truth. It was because he needed a wife for political reasons, that we had become engaged. And I wondered if this excuse was easier for me to accept than the desire to escape from a dead woman.

It was three o'clock when finally I went to sleep and I did not wake until the sun, streaming in through the windows I had left uncurtained, roused me to the knowledge that a new day had started, a day during which much would be required of me.

On my breakfast tray there was a letter which had been sent round by hand, and I guessed before I opened it that it was from Philip. I had never seen his writing before, but somehow it seemed familiar, perhaps characteristic of him, upright, well-formed and yet expressing in a slight

116

illegibility a complex personality. The letter was not a long one.

This is just to tell you, Lyn, that you have made me very happy. I only pray that I can do the same for you and that in our life together we shall find both contentment and peace. Yours, Philip.

It was dated the night before and I guessed that he had sat down and written it as soon as he had reached home, leaving instructions that it was to be delivered first thing in the morning. I read it again and again. It was the first intimate thing of his that I had possessed.

'Our life together.' The words lingered in my mind and I vowed to myself there and then that if it were possible I would make our life full of contentment and peace, as he had wished.

There was so much that I did not understand, so much that frightened me, and yet so much that made me ecstatically happy. How many women, I thought, would give everything to be me at this moment, yet how few of them would realise that I was not setting out on an easy journey, but one that was fraught with dangers and difficulties.

I was still in bed holding Philip's letter in my hand when the door opened and Angela came in in her dressing-gown. It was so early that I looked at her in surprise, never having known her wake at such an hour since I first came to stay.

'Darling!' she said, sitting down on my bed and kissing me affectionately. 'I couldn't sleep a wink from sheer excitement. Tell me everything. What you said last night wasn't a joke, was it?'

I couldn't help smiling at her anxiety.

'No, it wasn't a joke,' I answered. 'I am going to marry Philip. He's coming to see you some time today.'

'Oh Lyn,' she cried. 'It is the most thrilling, marvellous thing I have ever heard. I can't believe it is true. Why, this is only the second time you have met him.'

'Not quite,' I answered. 'I spent an afternoon with him last week. I didn't tell you, but you mustn't be angry now.'

'Angry!' Angela exclaimed. 'My dear, don't you realise that you have pulled off the biggest triumph of the cen-

117

tury? No one could possibly be angry with you today, Lyn, or any day for that matter. Philip Chadleigh is the biggest catch in London. Henry is almost hysterical at your cleverness.'

'Don't talk like that,' I said sharply. 'I am marrying Philip because I love him.'

'But of course you are,' Angela said with a laugh. 'You would be a fool if you didn't. Apart from everything else, he's a very attractive man. You must be married from here, of course, and before the end of the season. We have just got time if we start shopping at once.'

I made up my mind at that moment that nothing would induce me to be married in London. I thought of the little village church at home where I had been christened, of the Vicar who had been my one friend, and of Maysfield, which I loved, in spite of my eagerness to leave it. I would be married at home, whatever anyone said or thought. But now was not the moment to argue.

'Angela,' I said anxiously. 'You won't be too gushing to Philip, will you? I don't want him to think that I have sprung at him like a hungry salmon.'

Angela laughed.

'I'm not as tactless as all that,' she said. 'In fact, I will tell him that I think he is very lucky to get you. He must be crazy about you anyway. Does he make love beautifully? I am sure he does.'

I felt a coldness creep over me at these questions and evaded them.

'I must write to mother,' I said. 'When you talk to Philip suggest that he writes to either father or mother, won't you? You know how old-fashioned they are and I am sure they will expect the conventional approach.'

'Well, you have certainly wiped my eye,' Angela said. 'The family thought I had made a good marriage, but I am just a Cinderella compared to you now!'

'I wish you wouldn't keep harping on Philip's importance,' I said irritably.

'Why not?' Angela said. 'After all, if he is Viceroy of India, you will be the youngest Vicereine there has ever been! I am sorry you had to hear that silly story of Henry's,' she added. 'It is sure to be untrue. I have never heard Henry repeat any rumour that wasn't.'

'You seem quite willing to believe part of it—that Philip may be Viceroy.'

118

'Oh, he has been talked of as a possible Viceroy for a long time,' Angela answered easily. 'Now, what about dates? Which day of the week would be best for a big wedding?'

'Hadn't we better talk to Philip first?' I said. 'He may have very definite ideas on the subject.'

'My dear girl,' Angela said seriously, 'if you take my advice, you will make it very clear from the beginning that you intend to have your own way in certain matters. After all, you are marrying a man older than yourself, just as I did, and they get pretty set in their ways, so if you are not careful, they treat you like a child, deciding things for you, without even the politeness of discussing whether you would like to do them or not. You must start as you mean to go on, and if Philip interferes about the wedding, tell him you won't marry him.'

'He might believe me!' I said laughing.

'Don't say it then,' Angela said in mock alarm. 'That would be a tragedy!'

She got up from the bed and was just going to turn away when a thought seemed to strike her. She put out her hand and took mine.

'All joking apart, Lyn darling,' she said tenderly, 'I do wish you every happiness. I want you to be terribly happy, far happier than I have ever been.'

'Thank you,' I said. 'But I wish you could be happy too, Angela. Perhaps one day you will find it where you least expect it.'

She shrugged her shoulders.

'I am discovering some pretty good substitutes for a happy marriage on the whole,' she said, 'so I suppose I mustn't gamble. Still, I suppose we all want to be loved by the people we love and to live with them happily ever after.'

Without waiting for an answer, she left me hurriedly, as if she was afraid of saying more.

'Poor Angela,' I thought, then I realised that I might almost say 'poor me'. After all, I was loving where I was not loved. It was dangerous, it was even in some ways foolhardy, but instinctively within me there were both hope and faith that somehow, in some way, things would come right.

I was half-dressed when the telephone rang. A few seconds later I was talking to Philip. He was a little uncertain of himself, I thought, and at first we just greeted each other politely, asking conventional, stupid questions about how we had slept.

'When am I going to see you?' he asked at length.

'When you like,' I replied.

'Will you lunch with me?'

'Of course.'

'What about your sister and her husband?' he enquired. 'I had better come round and see them this afternoon.'

'I am afraid you will have to,' I said. 'They are waiting, expectant, full of congratulations and good wishes. It is all rather overpowering.'

'Poor Lyn,' he said. 'But I suppose this is one of the occasions when we have both got to suffer our crowds gladly. Can you dine tonight too?'

'I suppose so,' I replied.

'Persuade your sister,' he said, 'that you must come alone tonight, as it may be for the last time.'

'For the last time?' I questioned.

'Well, the moment the engagement is in the papers,' he said, 'there's certain to be parties given for us by relations, colleagues, institutions, associations, and heaven knows what other horrors. Let's dine here tonight and talk, while we can.'

'I would like that,' I answered.

'In which case,' he said reluctantly, 'I expect I had better ask your sister and brother-in-law to luncheon.'

'Perhaps that would be best,' I replied. 'I am sure they would be able to come. Shall I say that we will all three come to Chadleigh House about half-past one, unless I ring you up in the meantime?'

'That would be fine,' he replied. 'I must rush now because I have got a committee at the House, but leave a message with my secretary if there is a change of plans. Good-bye and take care of yourself, Lyn, my dear.'

'I will,' I promised.

Angela and Henry were, of course, as I had expected, only too delighted to lunch with Philip. Angela fussed so much about her clothes and her appearance, that it might have been she who was going to get married rather than I. Henry, on the other hand, treated me with a new kind of tenderness and reverence, as though, overnight, I had become as fragile as Dresden china and as valuable as a piece of old Ming. I couldn't help being amused; at the same time it was rather sad to realise what a snob my brother-in-law was; he had so many good points that it was a pity that his upbringing should have left him so vulnerable in the matter of worldly importance.

After talking to Henry and Angela it was really rather a relief to sit down and write to mother and father. I knew they would be pleased that Philip was rich, but what would count far more was that he came of a decent family, was a gentleman, and someone whom they would consider a nice type of man to be my husband. It was such a very different way of looking at my engagement, and my letter to them was easy to write. I told them not only about Philip, but about his parents, his home, and his career.

'I am very happy,' I wrote at the end of my letter. I felt in many ways it was the truth, even though anxiety and apprehension underlay my joy.

The luncheon passed off quite easily, because Philip had been wise enough to ask two cousins and an aunt to meet us. One of his cousins was a Cabinet Minister, the other a well-known Admiral, while his aunt had apparently known Angela for some years. They were all very nice to me; they drank our health after luncheon and the cheery, if conventional, atmosphere made it easy for me to meet Philip again and to dispel any embarrassment either of us might have felt.

I managed to have a moment alone with him after luncheon and told him in a hasty whisper to suggest that we get married at Maysfield and not in London. To my relief he agreed instantly.

'The quieter the better,' he said. 'And I am sure your father and mother won't want to come up to London.'

'I am quite certain they won't,' I answered. 'But you will have to be diplomatic with Angela. You don't know how insistent she can be if she wants a thing.'

'I will do my very best,' he promised.

Sure enough, by the evening—in some miraculous way—Angela was asserting that it had always been her idea that I should be married from home.

'The garden will be perfect for a reception,' she said. 'And nothing is lovelier than a country wedding. You can walk from the church to the house, Lyn, with children scattering rose petals in front of you.'

I felt that if Angela was to arrange it, my wedding was

121

going to be highly theatrical, but I was too tactful to say anything yet. I knew that once I was back at Maysfield, father and mother would not allow Angela too much scope for her inventive imagination.

When the time came for me to go out to dinner, I was excited at the thought of dining alone with Philip. He sent his car for me and when I arrived at Chadleigh House, was waiting in the hall. We dined, not in the big dining-room where he had sat for luncheon, but in a much smaller room in which, Philip explained, he always had his meals when he was alone. It was octagonal in shape, with a perfect Adam ceiling, and a small oval dining-table, at which Philip sat beside me.

Being so near him, and looking at the gold cups and vases which decorated the polished table, at the hot-house flowers which matched the long thin candles, and at the big bunch of purple orchids which was lying waiting for me on my plate, made me feel I was living in a fairy tale. This couldn't be happening to me! Our conversation seemed to sparkle from our lips; we were both witty and amusing. We might have been actors in a play, divorced from reality, in an exquisite setting. The servants with their powdered hair moving silently round the room, handing us each course with white-gloved hands, the polished brilliance of their buttons twinkling in the light of the candles, the ruby-red curtains screening the windows, the fine paintings in their gilt frames, might all have been figments of a decorator's imagination.

'You're looking very lovely tonight, Lyn,' Philip said to me when we were alone with our coffee.

'Thank you,' I answered, wondering if he really meant it, or if my fairness left him unmoved when he thought of the small dark-haired figure which might have been there with him but for the circumstances of fate. The mere thought of Nada was enough to make me shiver.

'Are you cold?' he asked.

'A ghost walking over my grave,' I said without thinking of my words. Fortunately they meant nothing to him.

'Let's go upstairs,' he said. 'I would like to show you my own room. The view over the park is magnificent.'

One day, I thought to myself, I will tell him how Elizabeth showed me his room, but not now, not until we know each other so well that all barriers are down and we can be completely honest and frank with each other.

We went upstairs to the book-lined room with its comfy sofas and deep armchairs. There were big bowls of roses on all the tables and their fragrance mingled with the faint sweet smell of tobacco.

'This is the one room in the house that is truly mine,' Philip said. 'All the rest have been planned by my ancestors, altered very slightly by each succeeding generation, but left intrinsically the same. This I created; in fact, it was a bedroom until about ten years ago.'

'I like it,' I said. 'It is the sort of room I should have expected you to have.'

There were two or three fine pictures, but otherwise the room was in such perfect taste that it was difficult to notice anything in particular. It became the background for its owner—the frame of a portrait, as every individual room should be, unobtrusive in itself, never compelling attention from the centre attraction.

Philip went to one of the curtained windows and drew back the curtains. Outside dusk had only just fallen; everything was misty-blue, mysterious yet glowing, a twilight that one finds only in London when the sky is still undarkened and the street lights are lit. We looked over the trees of Hyde Park, to where the towers and chimneys of Knightsbridge were silhouetted against the blue, and away beyond we could just see the high masts of ships lying in the river awaiting the dawn tide.

'How lovely!' I exclaimed.

The roar of the traffic below us was like the sound of a distant sea. I felt that we were isolated here as though we were on an island, miles from anywhere, yet together, and in that moment I was nearer to Philip than I had ever been before.

As we had gone to the window he had switched out the lights in the room, so that I could see better. We were in darkness, standing shoulder to shoulder, yet hardly able to distinguish the expression on each other's face. I felt a thrill like a touch of fire rush through me; I was breathless and my body was tingling as though I was waiting for something tremendous to happen. Perhaps my excitement transmitted itself to Philip. Perhaps it was just inevitable, the propinquity of man and woman, that we turned towards each other. For a moment he stood looking down at me, before he swept me into his arms. He held me gently. Then as his lips touched mine, it was as though

123

some magnetic power consumed us both. It was like a flame burning, devouring, yet uniting us, one to the other.

His arms closed about me tight, until they were like bars of iron. I felt his kisses grow hard, almost savage in their intensity. He kissed my eyes, my neck, then my mouth again. The whole world seemed to reel about me. I drifted away from reality, I was in a haze of glory, in some strange heaven of wonderment and of thrilling ecstasy. I knew that Philip felt it too. I was linked to him—we were one person.

From a great distance away I heard his voice.

'Nada!' he said hoarsely, 'Nada!'

15

I can't remember the exact moment after I had become engaged to Philip when I decided that for my own peace of mind I must know all there was to know about Nada. I think, perhaps, it was very shortly after our engagement was announced that the idea was really born in me. So many people said in the course of their conversations 'it is splendid that Philip has got over that unfortunate episode in his youth,' or 'we never thought that Philip would get married after . . .' then they would stop and look embarrassed, while I knew quite well what they were about to say.

It seemed that nowhere could I escape from Philip's past. That night when he had first kissed me remained imprinted in my mind. I think that he had no idea whose name he had said in those moments of emotion. He had gone on making love to me, but when finally we drew apart and switched on the lights, he altered completely. It was as though those mad passionate kisses had never happened. He was cool, courteous and reserved, the man I knew, not the man who for one brief moment had identified in me the woman he really loved.

He never again lost control of himself—never attempted to kiss me save gently and quickly—kisses which left me unsatisfied and often emotionally unstirred. I would lie awake at night living again those brief moments of ecstasy, only to be chilled by the echo in my thoughts of his voice saying 'Nada—Nada.'

I realised that it was not going to be easy for me to find out about Nada. After all, she had been dead a great many years and it was obvious that no one who knew I was engaged to Philip, was likely to give me details about her, even if they knew them. I felt that Elizabeth had told me all she knew and there was nothing further to be gained from that quarter.

Lady Monica, whom I had seen once or twice lately, might be helpful because she was so stupid that she would not bother to choose her words, or realise how tactless it would be, under any circumstances, to talk about Philip's past to the girl to whom he was engaged. Fortunately she asked us both to luncheon a day that Philip had an official luncheon in the city. When I rang her up to tell her so, I said:

'May I come alone? But don't have anyone else, I want to talk to you alone. There is so much I want to hear about Philip—and you have known him for so long that you can warn me of all his faults and failings!'

As I expected, she was only too eager to be allowed to gossip, and when I got to the ugly, somewhat dingy, house in Lancaster Gate where she lived with her mother, I found that it was quite easy to lead her on to the story of Philip's sensational love affair.

'We were all afraid Philip would never marry,' she said. (I wondered how often I had heard the remark before?) 'He was so terribly upset when there was that hideous scandal, and of course the newspapers made it a "cause célèbre"! He went abroad—I expect people have told you that—and really, we believed at one time, that he would never come back, but would be buried in foreign soil, or go native, or something equally ridiculous.'

'Did you ever meet the lady in question?' I asked.

'I saw her dance,' Lady Monica answered.

'Dance?' I questioned. Had Nada been a dancer? I was intensely interested.

'Yes, she was a dancer, didn't you know? She appeared at the Adelphi, or was it the Coliseum—I can't remember. Anyway, she did queer native dances, of a type which I did not pretend to understand. Now ballet's an entirely different thing, how I love it! Have you seen Massine this season?'

'She was half-native, wasn't she?' I said, referring to Nada and determined that Lady Monica should not get away from the subject which I had come to discuss with her.

'Half or whole, I can't remember which,' she answered. 'She was very dark, and you can imagine what we all thought when Philip would go everywhere with her, just everywhere! He even had her at Chadleigh House and gave parties for her.'

Lady Monica spoke in such hushed tones of horror, that I realised a little of what the gossip and scandal must have been at the time.

'What was wrong with her apart from that?' I asked.

'What more could you want?' Lady Monica said. 'As my old father used to say, "One can stand for anything except a touch of the tar brush".'

'Was she beautiful?' I asked.

'I can't say I admired her,' Lady Monica replied. 'But a lot of men did. She appeared in London during the War, and had a sort of vogue, you know how women of that sort get taken up and, of course, everything had got very lax owing to the War. I believe she even got asked to parties where there were ladies—our own friends! That would have never been tolerated before 1914!'

'Did Philip meet her when he was on leave?'

'I don't know when he met her,' Lady Monica answered. 'But he certainly made a fool of himself over her—everyone talked about them. And when she was killed he behaved so foolishly. He shut up the house, went off abroad without even leaving an address, in fact he disappeared! I can't tell you how upset we all felt.'

'Why did she kill herself?'

'My dear, no one knows. Of course at the time everyone thought she was going to have a baby, but there was no mention of it at the inquest, and we would all have thought that he had chucked her, if he hadn't appeared to be absolutely broken-hearted. But then, Philip's a funny man, you never know what he might feel one way or another.'

'What was her name?' I asked.

'Now let me see,' Lady Monica said. 'Nadine? No, Nada. Nada Nelimkoff, or Medlikoff, it was something like that. I know we were all very amused that she had taken a Russian name when it was quite obvious that she was an Indian.'

'Perhaps it was her real name.'

Lady Monica laughed.

'My dear, how innocent you are! I don't believe actresses ever use their own names. They have to have something glamorous, something that will catch the public's eye.'

'Had she any family?' I asked.

'I haven't the slightest idea,' Lady Monica said. 'You don't suppose I bothered myself with such a woman do you? Of course we all refused to meet her or have anything to do with her. It was only after she was dead and there was such a scandal that my father and mother acknowledged they were even aware of her existence. Before they had closed their eyes. We were all very ashamed of Philip in those days.'

That was really all Lady Monica had to tell me, although she rambled on for some time, going over and over the same ground, speaking of everyone's shocked susceptibilities, of Philip's extraordinary unhappiness. One thing was useful—the knowledge that Nada was quite famous. It ought, I felt, to be easy for me to find out more, perhaps from some outsider altogether, who had been more interested in her than in Philip.

It was interesting to know that she had danced. That would explain the beautiful poise of her head upon her shoulders, of the delicate artistry of those long fingers and of a general air of elusive beauty, which seemed in the picture to come, not so much from her features, as from an inbodied grace which was quite indescribable. Often after my talk with Lady Monica, I would think of Nada, seeming to see her move, softly, sinuously, upon a stage, in time to strange music, every poise holding some hidden meaning as well as a superficial beauty.

Since I have been a child stories of India have attracted me, and I thought how she would have chosen the ceremonial and allegorical dances of the Hindu faith, perhaps moderating them and altering them for western appreciation, but keeping, as far as was possible, their traditional gestures and movements which have been handed down from one nautch girl to another for century upon century.

What a relief it must have been to come from the noise and horror of the trenches and to step into another atmosphere when Nada had danced! I could understand Philip with all his appreciation of beauty finding her a solace. She could bring him both forgetfulness and peace, if only for a little while. Perhaps that was how it had begun, then later he had found that she loved him even as he loved her.

How terribly he must have loved her! I could feel again those passionate burning kisses; the fierce strength in his arms; the throbbing beat of his heart beneath mine. I could not stir him like that. That was the Philip Nada had known; the Philip that perhaps I would never know, unless it was through lifting the veil which hid the past for a few moments.

One more question before I left Lady Monica's gave me another strand in the rope I was gradually twisting together, a rope which I believed might eventually save me from losing Philip's love.

'When,' I asked, 'did all this happen? How soon after the War?'

As usual, she found it difficult to concentrate.

'Now let me think,' she said. 'The War ended in 1918, didn't it? I remember so well I was working at the hospital when the news came. Well, Philip went about with the woman all that winter. Yes, I remember that distinctly, for in the spring they went down to Monte Carlo together. You can imagine how people talked about that! In fact, I believe that a lot of mother's friends cut him that summer and the following winter. It must have been, yes, it must have been 1920 when she died. I am almost certain it was. I can't remember exactly what time of the year, but I am quite certain it was 1920.'

I kissed her good-bye quite affectionately.

'I have enjoyed my luncheon,' I said.

'You must come again,' she said, 'and bring Philip with you. I always think it is such fun if one can get the men to come too, don't you?'

'Yes, of course,' I answered. 'Good-bye, Lady Monica and thank you.'

Back home I found Angela ready to discuss every detail of my trousseau. She was so excited and thrilled about it that it really might have been her own. Somehow I felt ashamed because I couldn't take more interest when she was going to such trouble, and costing poor Henry—who had offered to pay for it—so much money. I felt as though I wasn't sufficiently grateful or sufficiently interested.

We had already started to argue over the wedding dress. She wanted me to be a Winterhalter bride, with a huge crinoline of white tulle, but I felt such a dress would be completely out of place in the little village church. I wanted satin, as plainly cut as possible, with the traditional sheaf of lilies.

'But you can't have satin,' Angela said almost fiercely. 'Don't you understand, Lyn, that your wedding dress will be sketched and photographed for every paper in England? Your marriage is the most important of the season and I would really be ashamed if you had nothing better to show than dreary old white satin. Why, you might as well have it made by the village dressmaker.'

'All right,' I said. 'You choose what you like. Only do remember that the aisle is very narrow and, what's more, father and mother won't like it if I appear in fancy dress.'

'Leave it to me,' Angela said.

I said I would, simply because I was so tired of discussion and also because I didn't care. Already, indeed, I was beginning to dread my thoughts of the future. This marriage was going to mean very little unless the barriers between Philip and me were destroyed.

Two days before, Philip had told me confidentially that there was a chance of his being Viceroy of India.

'Would you mind?' he asked.

'I should be very proud,' I answered, pretending to be surprised, but at the same time finding that I was both hurt and miserable by the news I had anticipated. This was actual confirmation of Henry's story.

'The Prime Minister must be pleased!' I said involuntarily.

'What do you mean?' Philip asked quickly.

I realised that I had nearly given myself away.

'I heard that he was having difficulty in finding someone suitable,' I answered. 'Isn't that true?'

'I think it has been under discussion for some time,' Philip replied. I thought he looked at me suspiciously, but he said nothing more.

We were sitting in his own room at Chadleigh House. We had lunched together unexpectedly for our would-be hostess had contracted German measles from her children, and her luncheon party had been cancelled at the last moment.

'I shall have to go to the House,' Philip said looking at his watch. 'What are you doing this afternoon?'

'Nothing until half-past three,' I replied. 'Will it matter if I stay on here and look at the papers? It is too hot to kill time in any other way.'

'Of course, stay as long as you like,' he answered. 'We meet at dinner, don't we?'

'Yes,' I said. 'Angela has a party, don't you remember?'

'Of course,' he answered. 'For the French Ambassador. Didn't I warn you that we should have to put up with a lot of entertaining?'

'How right you were!' I said with a sigh. 'I suppose one day we shall dine together without a crowd of chattering friends as a chorus. I occasionally catch a glimpse of you miles away down the dinner-table, otherwise we mightn't be at the same party.'

'Engaged couples should be allowed to sit together,' he said. 'I can't think why there is this conspiracy to keep them apart.'

'To see they don't regret their promises before the knot is tightly tied.'

'Well, we certainly won't get the chance of boring each other,' he laughed. 'Good-bye, Lyn.' He kissed my cheek and walked towards the door. 'Ring if you want anything, won't you?'

'I will,' I answered. 'Good-bye, Philip, I enjoyed our quiet lunch.'

I waited for some time after he was gone, then putting down the *Tatler*, I started to walk round the room. The rows of beautifully bound, expensive books fascinated me. How often I had longed for a library like this! I inspected shelf after shelf and I was not surprised to find there were a great many works on India. I opened one or two and found they were mostly on philosophy and religion. Several of the sentences in each volume I looked at were underlined in pencil and I wondered with a quick stab of jealousy, whether Nada had marked them for him.

I had hoped that in our mutual interest in books we might, Philip and I, find a common bond, a corner stone perhaps for the building I was determined to erect, however insecure the foundations. But it was impossible to escape from Nada, her presence had begun to haunt me, even as she haunted Philip. But why, I asked, should the impression she had made in the short years of her life, be so ineradicable, when other people, far greater and far more necessary to the world, lay forgotten in their graves? Was she a more potent factor than they, or was there something particularly sensitive in us, some vibration which made us respond to her still, beyond the reasoning of logic or the confines of time?

I looked at the photograph of Philip's mother which stood on his desk—her face was gentle.

'Help me,' I whispered. 'Help me to bring him happiness! If Nada is not dead, neither are you. You both loved him, but he was yours first. Help me now—wherever you are, to give your son peace.'

It was a prayer. I turned from the desk to pick up my hat and gloves ready to leave. As I did so I noticed that two long shelves at the bottom of the bookcase beside the sofa were stacked with what were obviously photograph books. I got down on my knees and opened them one by one. Some of them were of recent date, others were mainly of views and temples and had obviously been taken by Philip on his travels. They were arranged more or less in years, and when finally I picked up the one that should have dated about 1919 to 1920 I felt excited. Perhaps here I should fine some clue to all I was seeking.

I opened the book. I looked at the first page in surprise, at the second, at the third! Finally I turned the pages over hastily, one after another. From every one photographs had been torn out roughly, some had even been cut and scraped away as though with a penknife. There were barely a dozen snapshots left and they were all of Philip himself, young, smiling and alone—at Longmoor, on the Riviera, in polo kit, at the wheel of his car.

Of the other photographs that should have been there there was left only an occasional corner of sky, or a jagged scrap, too tightly stuck to be moved, desolate in its isolation, and so defaced as to be quite unrecognisable.

What did it mean, I asked myself? Why had Philip done this, for I could not believe that any outsider would dare to despoil in such a manner his private albums?

I put the book back in its place and got to my feet. It was nearly half-past three. I must be going. Then I hesitated, half-ashamed of an impulse. Yet driven by a curiosity that was stronger than my sense of honour, I went across the room and opened the door between the bookcases, the one to which Elizabeth had beckoned me that first night.

The curtain concealed the bedroom. Again I hesitated before I pulled it back. But I was driven forward; I was unable to stop. I went into the room cautiously.

The blinds were half-drawn against the blazing afternoon sun; the room was dim. I tiptoed across it and looked over the mantelpiece. There was nothing there. Nada's picture had gone.

16

In the midst of all the excitement over the announcement of my engagement, in the mêlée of hospitality, the ceaseless arrival of letters and of telegrams of congratulations, and the fittings for my clothes which took place daily, I had not forgotten about Elizabeth, although I had not seen her.

I wrote to her the morning after I became engaged to Philip, explaining that I was going to marry him and asking her not to be too miserable about it, but to wish me happiness. I had back a conventional and restrained note which told me nothing, but which made me think she was hurt and upset, not only by the news of Philip's engagement, but by what she might consider as my treachery.

The morning before Philip and I had arranged to go down to Maysfield to see father and mother, I found that for once I had a few hours free in which Angela had not made any engagements with the dressmakers. So I seized the opportunity of telephoning Elizabeth. I gave my name to the butler with some trepidation wondering if, when she heard it, she would refuse to come to the telephone, but after a long wait—which was usual in the Batley household—I heard her voice.

'Hullo,' she said. 'Is that Lyn?'

'It is,' I answered. 'Are you furious with me for not ringing up before? But honestly, I haven't had a moment! Look here, are you dressed? I am sure you are; I am ashamed to say I am still in bed.'

'Yes, I am up.' Elizabeth answered. 'Why?'

'Will you come round in a taxi?' I said. 'Quickly, otherwise we shall have no time together. Come up to my bedroom and we will talk while I am dressing. I have got such a lot to tell you.'

There was a moment's pause and I felt that Elizabeth hesitated because she was anxious to refuse me.

'Please!' I said. 'I do want to see you.'

Elizabeth's soft-heartedness was not proof against my pleading.

'All right,' she said. 'I will come at once.'

Ten minutes later she was shown into my bedroom. I held out my arms to her and kissed her affectionately. Then I saw there were tears in her eyes.

'Don't,' I said. 'Don't be unhappy and don't be cross with me. There's so much more in this than you realise and so much I want to tell you. After all, Elizabeth, you are the only person to whom I can speak frankly.'

'Are you awfully happy?' she asked in a low voice.

'I am happy,' I answered. 'But, Elizabeth, Philip isn't in love with me any more than he is in love with you.'

She looked at me in startled surprise.

'Then why has he asked you to marry him?' she questioned.

'He is going to be Viceroy,' I answered. 'And for that position he has got to have a wife.'

I spoke absolutely frankly on purpose; I wanted to dispel any barriers that there were between us. I liked Elizabeth and I wanted her friendship and, most of all, I hated to hurt her. She was such a soft pathetic little creature. It was as cruel to make her suffer as deliberately to torture an animal. I felt the resentment she had been feeling against me relax, the tension in her face slacken. Impulsively she put out her hands in a gesture of sympathy.

'Oh, Lyn,' she said. 'Are you wise to marry him?'

'I love him,' I answered steadily.

She gave a little sob, got up from my bed and walked across the room. She was fighting for control, trying to stop the tears which welled into her eyes and overflowed down her pale cheeks.

'You have got to be my friend,' I said urgently. 'You have got to help me. There is so much I don't understand, so much that is frightening about the whole situation. There's no one else to whom I can turn, no one else with whom I can be completely honest about Philip.'

There was, I believe, a deep maternal instinct in Elizabeth which made it impossible for her ever to turn away from a cry for help, to refuse to succour anybody who she felt was weaker than herself. She wiped her eyes, came back to me, and pulling up a chair, she said softly:

'Tell me everything from the very beginning.'

I told her about my evening at Longmoor Park, how Philip had proposed to me and how I had accepted him. I told her too of how I had found the mutilated picture books, and discovered that the picture of Nada had gone from his bedroom.

'He is trying to forget her,' Elizabeth said.

'Of course he's trying!' I answered bitterly. 'But he is not succeeding.'

'What can you do?' Elizabeth asked.

'I don't know,' I replied, 'except face up to the truth. Admit that he loves her still and that I don't even begin to supplant her in his affections. But on one thing I am determined, Elizabeth; some way or another I will find out all about her. After all, how can I begin to cope with this extraordinary situation until I know all there is to know about them both?'

'But how can you find out?' Elizabeth asked.

'That is where you have got to help me,' I answered.

I told her of my conversation with Lady Monica.

'If you care for me at all, Elizabeth,' I went on, 'and if you still want Philip to be happy, you have got to try and understand my point of view. I can't marry him with this shadow, what you call a ghost, in the background. I want him terribly, but our marriage, as things are, would be a living hell.'

'Don't do it, Lyn,' Elizabeth said desperately. 'Run away, leave him, while there is still time.'

'I won't,' I answered. I said it almost savagely as though I had my back to the wall and was defying fearful opposition. 'I won't! I will stay and see things through and somehow, in some way, which I can't yet see, I shall win. But you must help me!'

'I will do everything I can,' Elizabeth replied. 'I will start today, as soon as I leave you. Perhaps now that there is no more chance of my marrying Philip the family will tell me more about Nada—that is if they know. But I don't believe that even during the years when he was with her, Philip confided in many people.'

'I am sure he didn't,' I said. 'But will you promise me to do your best.'

'Of course I will!'

She was so sweet that when I said good-bye I said again:

'I am sorry, Elizabeth. You do forgive me, don't you?'

'Of course,' she answered. 'Don't worry about me. I

135

shall be all right. What is more, I have taken your advice; I have found some work to do. I am helping at one of the Rose of England Clubs. You know the marvellous work they do among the unemployed and the children. There's one not very far from here which is run by a friend of mother's and I go there three afternoons a week.'

'That's splendid!' I said. 'Anything is better than sitting at home feeling miserable.'

'Anything,' Elizabeth echoed in heartfelt tones.

My talk with Elizabeth made me late for Philip and I kept him waiting nearly twenty minutes before finally I was dressed and my luggage taken down to the hall, ready to be put on to his car. He wasn't cross, as I was afraid he might be, but he teased me about my deterioration into bad habits.

'I thought your country upbringing would protect you,' he said gravely, 'but you've succumbed to slothfulness—that's the first step on the downward path!'

'Scene on the Road to Ruin!' I laughed. 'Sir Galahad warns the rustic maiden!'

'Alas, she wouldn't heed him!' Philip sighed, steering the car skilfully through the traffic in Oxford Street.

'Who knows?' I answered. 'Scientists tell us nothing is lost, another generation, perhaps another dimension, may pick up your words of wisdom from the ether and find them an inspiration.'

'Science hints at so much, yet gives us so little,' Philip said and I felt that he spoke regretfully.

'Is there anything else that can offer better food for thought?' I asked idly.

He answered me seriously.

'No, the Church should, but doesn't—perhaps it's our own fault. Are we really interested enough to seek for ourselves? And if we are, do we go the right way about it?'

I had no answer for him, but that Philip too was beset by unanswerable problems was vaguely a comfort to me. I felt less alone.

We arrived at Maysfield about teatime. Father and mother came out on to the doorstep to greet us as soon as we arrived, and I knew they had been waiting in the hall for the first sign of the car. They kissed me affectionately and I introduced Philip.

I couldn't help being proud, both of the man I was going to marry and of my parents. They all three looked so distinguished and there was a courteous ease and grace about their reception of each other which was very unlike the gauche, ponderous manner of Henry, or the careless indifference of many of the people I had met in Angela's house.

We had tea under the trees on the lawn and while I knew that old Grayson doddering about in his threadbare black coat, was a poor contrast to Philip's smart retinue of servants, nevertheless, I was not ashamed of him or anything to do with my home. We might not be rich, in fact we were hopelessly poor, but there was that same air of dignity, tradition and peace which I had noticed at Longmoor.

I don't think that ever before had I stood apart, as it were, from Maysfield and looked at it with the eyes of an outsider. I did so now for the first time. I saw what a lovely place it was, and how perfectly in keeping with its weather-beaten grey stone were its owners—my parents. Father couldn't have been anything but an English aristocrat with his high collar—the relic of Edwardian smartness—and his long grey moustache. Mother was dreadfully badly dressed, poor darling. Her grey and white crêpe de chine frock, which had been run up by the village dressmaker, fitted nowhere, and as usual, two or three inches of petticoat showed at the back when she walked. She had absentmindedly put on one of her grey stockings inside out and her shoes needed repairing, but were comfortable enough to be indispensable. Yet her appearance didn't seem to matter; nothing could alter her classical profile or destroy her air of serenity, or that indescribable something which would have proclaimed her a lady, even if one had found her naked in the middle of the Sahara Desert.

I saw at once that Philip liked both my parents, and that they were taken with him. In fact, the whole visit was an assured success from the moment he crossed the threshold at Maysfield, to tell mother in that charming voice of his, how kind it was of her to invite him.

I had written father and mother and told them what an exhausting time we had been having in London, and begged them not to invite a large crowd of people to meet us, especially on our first evening. So we four sat down to dinner alone and as cook for once had excelled herself, the food was nearly as good as the vintage port which father brought up from the cellar, which was saying a good deal.

I wore one of my new dresses and as I came down the

137

big oak stairs, I felt that its wide tulle skirts were made for a house like this, not for narrow lifts or London taxis. One day I would walk down the great carved staircase at Longmoor, my thoughts prompted me, and instantly I imagined myself there, perhaps entertaining Royalty—hostess to hundreds of guests. I don't know why, but for the first time I felt afraid. I thought of my conversation that very morning with Elizabeth. Had she been right when she had asked me not to marry Philip as things were at present? Was I deliberately planning for myself years of unhappiness?

At dinner and afterwards I found myself watching father and mother; how content they were together: how well they both seemed to understand each other. Often a little smile of understanding passed between them. In contrast I saw how utterly alien Philip and I were one from the other. There could be no secret smile of understanding, no unity which needed only a meeting of our eyes for reassurance, while between us stood his love for a woman who was dead and my unrequited love for him.

Father was talking politics; I got up quietly and walked through the open windows into the garden. I moved away from the house, over the soft green lawns, towards the lily pond. There was no moon, the skies were not yet dark. The pale dusk turned the whole place into a scene of romance and unreality. I could see the white waxen petals of the lilies riding on their great flat leaves, while every now and then there would be a soft splash as though some frog or fish moved gently in the still water. Everything was very still; I felt at that moment as though the world was hushed and waiting, pregnant with some tremendous revelation which would come to me personally.

When I turned and saw Philip coming towards me I was not surprised. I stood waiting for him, only my breath quickened a little. He drew near, and stood beside me for a moment without speaking. I knew then that I wanted his arms around me; I wanted his mouth on mine; to feel his kisses, passionate and overpowering as they had been that night when we had stood overlooking London from the window at Chadleigh House. Half-unconscious of what I did, I took a step towards him.

'Philip,' I said.

I stretched out my hand and laid it on his arm. I knew

then that I was trembling, that a burning, devouring fire was running in my veins.

'It is very lovely here,' he said.

'Do you think so?' My voice was very low, barely above a whisper. I stared up at him, my lips apart, feeling that he must know, must be aware of the emotion which was stirring me.

'Lyn!' he said harshly, so that his voice appeared loud and shattered the dreamlike quality of the world around us. 'Are you quite certain?'

'Certain?' I questioned stupidly.

'That you want to marry me?'

I felt myself shiver; I felt a chill, almost physical, dispel my warmth, my ecstasy.

'Why do you think I accepted you?' I asked.

He turned to look at me. I could see him trying to read my expression through the dusk. He did not answer, but I knew what he was thinking: I knew that he was trying to decide whether I had said yes to him because of his social position, because of the worldly advantages which so many girls had sought from him, or whether indeed, as he was half-afraid, I loved him. He had thought that I was young, that I was unsophisticated and that the advantages of such a marriage would outweigh and perhaps blind me to his own lack of enthusiasm. Now, for the first time, he was uncertain. He must know what I wanted from him; must be aware of the passion which had risen within me just a few seconds ago. Yet he was not quite sure, only hesitant, a little afraid, and half-ashamed of the bargain he was making.

'Why can I understand him so well?' I asked myself. Yet I did know his thoughts at times like these as though they were my own. My intuition saved me, checked my emotion, laid a restraining hand on the heat of my desires. I wanted to cry out, to throw myself into his arms, to plead with him for his love, to try to force from him all that which he could not give me, but instead, drawing myself gradually, but almost imperceptibly away from him, I said:

'Why are you so serious tonight? I am so happy to be here at home, Surely you aren't going to spoil it for me?'

My voice I knew was sane and sensible again. I fought against the tremulousness which was still so near the surface. I clenched my hands together so that my nails bit into the palms of my hands and the pain seemed to quell the throbbing of my pulses, to dispel that aching, hungry want within my breast. I wanted so much to touch him at that moment that I dared not look at him.

'It is cold out here. Shall we go indoors?' I asked.

I knew that he was relieved, at the same time still uneasy, still a little afraid of what he had sensed in me and so very nearly discovered.

'Tell me what you think of mother and father,' I chattered as we moved towards the house. 'I know one thing—you have made a complete conquest of them.'

'They are charming,' he said politely, but absentmindedly, as though he was thinking of something else.

'I only wish David was here to meet you too,' I went on. 'He is very like father, good-looking and tall. If I were a man I should hate to be short, wouldn't you?'

Talking nonsense and gradually in the process feeling the flush die away from my cheeks, my pulses beat calmly again, we came back through the drawing-room window. Mother looked up with a sweet smile. I knew she thought we had taken the opportunity of snatching a stolen kiss in the garden, of finding together that joy which all lovers know when they escape from the company of others for a few ecstatic moments.

'How little she knows the truth,' I thought bitterly.

I crossed to the piano. I do not play well because I have never been properly taught, but I can manage to stumble through a few classical pieces and improvise enough to make my music an unobtrusive background for conversation. I played for nearly half-an-hour, until it was time to go to bed. I didn't look at Philip, although I knew that once or twice he glanced at me with a puzzled expression on his face.

Mother got to her feet as the clock struck half-past ten.

'Are you children going to sit up and talk?' she asked.

I shook my head.

'I am terribly tired,' I said. 'Our gay London life has been getting me down. I am going to sleep all I can while I am here.'

'Quite right,' father said. 'And you, Philip, what are you going to do?'

'I will come to bed too,' Philip answered. 'As Lyn says, we've had an exhausting time lately, one party after another, all given so that I could show her off, but tiring all the same!'

We picked up our silver candlesticks in the hall, which are quite unnecessary now that Maysfield has electric light, but which are one of the traditions of the house and cannot be dispensed with.

'Good night, darling,' mother said as she kissed me at the door of my room. 'Sleep well. Father and I are delighted with your young man. He's charming and I feel you will be very happy with him.'

'I am sure I shall,' I answered brightly.

'We are both so very glad that you have found someone so quickly,' Mother said. 'I am afraid you have had a sad time this past year and you would find us very dull after such a wonderful visit to London.'

'I am not marrying because I don't want to come home,' I said smiling at her.

'Of course not,' she answered. 'But I am glad that things have happened as they have. Good night, dear child.'

When she had gone I took off my new dress and hung it up carefully. Then, when I could at last let myself relax, I threw myself face downwards on my bed and started to cry.

17

We got back to London late on Monday. We had meant to leave Maysfield early to be up in time for luncheon, but all our plans were altered because, to my disappointment, I found that the Vicar—my oldest and dearest friend—had arranged to preach at some distant parish on the Sunday, so that when I took Philip down to see him before the morning service, he was not there.

I was disappointed not only because I was so anxious for my friend to meet the man I was going to marry, but also because I felt, perhaps childishly, that someone who had helped me so much in the past and who had meant so much in my life, might help me now with the biggest and greatest difficulty I had ever encountered. So I insisted on our going to the Vicarage on Monday morning, and instead of starting at half-past nine, as we had intended, we left Maysfield village at midday and had our luncheon at a small wayside hotel, still many miles from London.

But as often happens with the things we plan and look forward to, the meeting between the Vicar and Philip was not the success I had meant it to be. The two men talked to each other politely enough, but it was obvious they had very little in common and I came away from the Vicarage feeling depressed and vaguely disappointed. I told myself I had expected too much, but perhaps a wider horizon had altered me so that I saw the Vicar, not as the great oracle I had always believed him to be, but merely as a gentle scholarly old man, striving to make the best of the trivialities around him.

Philip was in very good spirits as we drove up to London. I had been very careful, after that first night, to behave in an ordinary conventional manner and not once to let my true feelings disconcert or embarrass him. I saw now that my way was even more precarious than I at first thought it was; there was not only Philip's restraint to be considered, but also my love for him, a love which was growing deeper day by day with an intensity and passion which, at times, surprised me. It was as though I knew all that Philip could mean to me; all that he could give me, if he would. And in spite of common sense, every instinct in my body demanded his acquiescence, as though I was asking something of him with which I was already familiar.

Of course this was ridiculous, but at times I felt so close to Philip and had such an understanding of him, that it was difficult to believe that he could still remain aloof from me, or could be content with the almost platonic companionship, which was apparently his idea of how our engagement should be conducted. However, I was schooling myself well and for the first time I was glad that my looks didn't betray me. It is easy for the chocolate-box type of prettiness to appear joyous and unsophisticated, and my wide blue eyes betrayed no expression but a conventional pleasure in everything. Pink and white cheeks, fair hair, and limbs, which, as yet, appeared to retain still their baby plumpness, do not go with passion, with an agony of desire or with vivid imagination which seeks ecstasy.

It was not hard to fool Philip, but I wondered how long it would be before I broke down under the strain and revealed the truth.

We got back to find Angela exceedingly annoyed. We had sent her a wire early in the morning telling her we were delayed and the approximate time of our arrival.

Although she said little to Philip, as soon as he was gone, she started on me.

'Really, Lyn,' she said. 'You are inconsiderate. You knew perfectly well that I had arranged a thousand and one things for us to do today. However do you think we are going to be ready for your wedding if you go on like this? You had three fittings this afternoon; now every one of them has been missed, besides the hairdresser's appointment I had made for you.'

'I am sorry, Angela,' I started to say, but she would not listen.

'After all,' she went on, 'Henry and I are doing our best for you. I really feel inclined at times to tell you to go back to Maysfield and have your trousseau made there. If you don't care what you look like yourself, you at least might care for my sake. And what is more, remember if it hadn't been for me, you would never have met Philip.'

'I know, Angela,' I said soothingly. 'Please don't think I am ungrateful, because I'm not. I forgot about the fittings this afternoon, I did, really, but I will be up early tomorrow morning and get them all done before luncheon. I promise you—I will.'

'Well, we have got time to go to Molyneux now, at any rate,' Angela said. 'Leave your keys so that Bridget can unpack for you and we will go straight there.'

I had wanted to wash and change after the long motor drive, but meekly I did as I was told. We drove off to Molyneux, Angela still cross and reminding me again and again, in one way and another, who was paying for my trousseau and who was taking the trouble to choose it.

I decided at that moment that having too much money was as bad as having none, and I hoped that when I was married to Philip that I wouldn't get like Angela and Henry, weighed down with the stuff. Besides, the fuss and expense over my trousseau was rather farcical. As far as I could see, it wasn't going to matter to Philip one way or another what sort of clothes I wore. He wanted a wife, a wife he was going to have, and if she came to him in sackcloth and ashes it would be all the same, because her mere presence would ensure his career, which was his only important consideration.

I stood rather sullenly for the next hour or so trying on dress after dress. When finally we had finished I said:

'Oh, let's go and have a cup of tea, Angela. I am simply dying for one.'

'All right,' she said. 'But I have told the hairdresser to come to you at six o'clock. Of course it will be extra—they charge at least double when they go out—but I knew you wouldn't have time to go to the shop.'

'I am sorry,' I said again.

We got into the car and drove home. As we drew up at the door a footman came hurrying down the steps and I wondered vaguely to myself why he had been waiting for our return. I was soon to know for as soon as Angela got into the hall the butler came forward.

'I am afraid there is bad news, mi'lady. They rang up from the school to say that Master Gerald was ill and they were sending him to London in an ambulance. They

144

wanted to speak to you, but as I didn't know where you had gone, I got on to Mr. Watson at the House of Commons.'

'Master Gerald ill!' Angela exclaimed. 'Did they say what was the matter with him?'

'A mastoid I think it was, mi'lady.'

Angela gave a little cry. She turned and ran into the smoking-room. She picked up the telephone and dialled toll.

'Is Mr. Watson back?' she asked the butler who was hovering in the doorway.

'No, mi'lady,' he answered. 'But I understood Mr. Watson to say he will be coming here as soon as he had telephoned the school.'

Angela gave a number to the toll exchange then looked at the clock.

'Why isn't Henry back?' she asked me.

'He can't be long,' I said soothingly.

In a few seconds Angela had got through to the school and was talking to the headmaster. I saw her face get plainly whiter as she talked. I walked about, picking up the newspapers, but being unable to concentrate even on the headlines. I put them down again. Angela kept saying, 'yes . . . yes . . . I understand . . . yes . . .'

At last she threw down the receiver and faced me.

'He's got to be operated on at once,' she said. 'Oh, Lyn, it is too awful.'

I put my arms round her shoulders.

'Darling! How ghastly for you.'

'He's not strong. He has always been the weaker of the two.' She started to her feet, looking at the clock. 'Why doesn't Henry come?'

Even as she spoke I heard someone in the hall outside, but when the door opened, Douglas Ormonde was announced.

'Hullo,' he said brightly.

For the first time since I had come to the house Angela was not pleased to see him.

'I thought you were Henry,' she said angrily.

'What's the matter?' he asked.

'Gerald is ill,' she said abruptly. 'He is on his way up to London.'

'I am so sorry,' Douglas said. 'Isn't there anything I can do?'

'Of course there isn't,' Angela snapped at him. 'Don't be so idiotic.'

She was so crushing that I felt quite sorry for him and it was evident that he was surprised at her manner. There was nothing more to say; we all stood silent until we heard a taxi draw up at the door, and looking through the window I saw Henry get out.

'Here he is,' I said.

Angela ran across the room, opened the door and met her husband in the hall.

'Henry!' she said and reaching him, clasped both her hands on his arm in an appealing gesture, the first expression of intimacy I had ever seen her show to him.

'It is all right, my dear,' he said gently. 'I have arranged everything. Sir Howard Blake is going to operate as soon as he arrives. He will be at the Pembroke Nursing Home and you and I will go there right away.'

'It will be all right?' Angela asked, her voice trembled and I saw that she was very near to tears. It was so unlike my usual self-controlled, poised sister that I am afraid I stared.

'Of course it will be all right,' Henry said soothingly. 'Now don't worry, dear, but come along. The boy will be wanting to see you.'

I didn't want to intrude, but I stepped forward and Henry saw me.

'Yes, come too, Lyn,' he said. 'Angela may want you.' He ignored Douglas completely as though he was not there, and I think that Angela had really forgotten his existence.

We drove off to the nursing home in the car, which the butler had had the sense to keep waiting. When we arrived it was too soon for Gerald to have got up from the country, but the Matron greeted us and showed us into the waiting-room.

'I should think they would be at least another twenty minutes,' she said looking at the hanging watch she wore pinned to her chest. 'Would you like to look at his room?'

'Yes, please,' Angela said.

We went upstairs to a small but quite cheerful little bedroom, where Angela moved the chairs about, asked Matron if they could provide another screen, and told Henry to telephone Moyses Stevens for some flowers to be sent round.

This didn't take very long and very soon we were all back in the waiting-room, sitting on hard chairs, round an oval table on which was arranged a dismal green fern and several piles of *Punch* and *Country Life*.

'Surely they are taking a very long time,' Angela asked more than once.

'It is thirty-five miles,' Henry answered 'They won't want to drive too fast.'

'Of course not,' Angela said and I saw an expression of pain cross her face, as though she realised that bumping might make Gerald worse.

Finally, after what seemed a century of waiting, a nurse came in to say the ambulance had arrived but would we please wait a few moments while they got Gerald upstairs to his room. Through the open door as she was speaking, we caught a glimpse of a stretcher being carried in, with a very small blanket-covered body on it. There is something particularly pathetic about someone on a stretcher. I felt tears prick my eyes and Angela put out her hand and slipped it into Henry's. He said nothing, but I saw his fingers tightened over hers.

There was another long wait before they came to say that Sir Howard Blake was going to operate at once and would Mr. Watson and Lady Angela go up for just a minute. I was left alone. I turned over the pages of *Punch*, understanding neither the jokes nor the pictures, but listening all the time in a horrid nerve-racking suspense for Angela's and Henry's return. At last the door opened and they came back.

Angela was crying openly now, the tears were streaming down her face, she was making no effort to stop them. Henry had his arm round her and the moment she got into the room she sank into a chair and buried her face in her hands.

'It will be all right, darling,' Henry said. 'I promise you it will be all right. Sir Howard is the best man in London, there isn't anyone else to touch him.'

As I sat undecided what to do, he turned to me sharply.

'Get some water,' he said.

I hurried through the door into the passage and found a receptionist near the front door.

'Can I have some drinking water,' I asked

She fetched me a jug and a glass from a nearby pantry and I hurried back with it to Angela. Henry was sitting on the arm of her chair, doing his best to comfort her. He took the water from me.

'Try and drink this,' he said gently. 'It will do you good.'

She took a few sips, then put it down.

'I am sorry to be such a fool,' she said in a strangled voice. 'But if anything happens to him, Henry, I shall never forgive myself—never! I have been so casual about the children lately. I think this has been sent to punish me.'

'Nonsense!' Henry said, but I could see that he too was moved and his voice was hoarse.

'Do you remember when he was a baby,' Angela went on, 'how he used to run about with that funny little red train of his? Oh Henry, you do think it will be all right, don't you?' With another outburst of crying she turned and buried her face against his shoulder.

'Listen dear,' Henry said. 'You have got to control yourself. You will make yourself ill if you go on like this, then if he asks for you you won't be able to go to him, will you?'

His words obviously had an effect on Angela. Her crying lessened and after a moment she straightened herself, blew her nose violently and felt in the chair for her handbag.

'Here it is,' I said picking it up from the table where she had put it.

'Thank you, Lyn,' she said.

She opened the bag and looking in a small mirror, started feebly to pat away some of her tears with a powder puff.

'How much longer have we got to wait?' she asked after some minutes.

'You mustn't be too impatient,' Henry answered looking at his watch. 'We don't want to hurry them.'

The minutes ticked by. I sat watching the clock on the mantelpiece, feeling that there must be something as yet undiscovered about time from the point of the human element, for it is obviously impossible to divide day and night into equal portions as civilisation would have us believe. An hour when one is happy is gone in a flash, and is certainly not in any way the same as an hour spent in misery or anticipation.

We all started to our feet instinctively when the door opened and the Matron came in.

'I just wanted to tell you,' she said in her clear calm

148

voice, 'that everything is going along splendidly. Sir Howard will be at least another quarter of an hour, but I thought you would like to know that as far as we can tell at the moment, there are no complications.'

'Thank God!' Angela said, then, without any warning at all, she crumpled up in a dead faint.

Henry half caught her as she fell. He lifted her up and put her on a chair, with her feet resting on a stool. The Matron got some smelling salts and brandy. After about two or three minutes she was conscious again and quite all right, except that she seemed desperately weak and held on to Henry's hand as though she could not bear to be without support.

I don't think I have ever liked Henry so much as I did then. He was so extraordinarily tender and sweet to Angela, at the same time neither fussing her too much, nor being in any way inattentive. He seemed to strike exactly the right note of consideration and I felt if he would always behave like that, how much easier their marriage might be, and indeed how very much happier.

Angela seemed to appreciate him too, for more than once she said 'Thank you, Henry!' and smiled at him, a tremulous, heart-breakingly courageous smile.

The clock on the mantelpiece went on ticking and we all three kept stealing glances at it, until at last, when I had got to the point of feeling that any more waiting would drive me mad, they came down to say Gerald was back in his room, and we could go up and look at him if we liked. Jumping to her feet Angela led the way to the lift, which took us up to the second floor.

She was very pale but composed as she entered the sickroom. The blinds were lowered and there was a strong smell of ether, which I hate. After a moment our eyes grew used to the dim light, and we could see Gerald lying with his head bandaged and snoring in that funny peculiar way that people do snore, when they are still under an anaesthetic.

He looked terribly small and pathetic and for the first time I could understand a little of the protective love that a mother has for her child. Anything wrong with a child is literally a physical agony for the woman who has brought it into the world. Perhaps there is no greater torture than to stand by helpless and impotent, while part of one's own flesh and blood—a tiny, weak part—suffers pain. I knew then that maternal love manifesting itself in every strata of life, is one of the strongest forces in the world, and that in its strength it could, and doubtless eventually will, defy destruction, war, aggression and the cruelty of man.

Her head bowed, and her face turned from us, Angela stood looking at Gerald for some moments, then she bent down and dropped a kiss on his hand which lay outside the sheet.

I think Henry was frightened that she might faint again, or burst into tears, but she was splendid. She turned away from the bed quite bravely and walked out of the room.

'He won't be round for two or three hours,' Matron said. 'If you would like to come back at nine o'clock, I think he would like to see you then.'

'Thank you,' Angela said. 'And thank you for being so kind.'

'That's all right,' Matron said. 'These sudden operations are always a shock, aren't they? I know how you feel. If you take my advice, Lady Angela, you will go straight home and go to bed.'

'I will,' Angela answered.

'You will telephone us,' Henry said in a low voice, 'if by any chance . . .'

He did not have to finish the sentence.

'Of course, Mr. Watson,' Matron answered. 'But I don't think you need worry now. There is a doctor in the building and Sir Howard himself will be coming in again later.'

We drove home in silence. Angela seemed terribly tired and exhausted now it was all over. When we got back to the house Douglas was waiting for us in the hall.

'Is everything all right?' he asked anxiously.

But Angela had no words for him. It was Henry who answered, 'Everything, thank you,' as he helped Angela into the lift.

18

Angela came into my room before I was awake in the morning.

'Gerald had a good night,' she said, pulling back the curtains as she spoke, so that the sunlight pouring in through the windows, made me shade my eyes as I tried sleepily to realise what was happening.

'I am glad,' I said drowsily. 'Surely you are very early?'

'I couldn't sleep,' Angela confessed. 'And as soon as it was eight o'clock I got Henry to telephone the Home. Darling, I am so relieved, I have been so terribly worried.'

'I know you have,' I said. 'I am sorry for you, I am really, and for Henry too.'

'Poor Henry,' Angela said softly. 'He didn't sleep either. He was so quiet that I guessed he was awake—he snores terribly as a rule—so I went in and sat on his bed and, oh Lyn, I feel I have been a beast to him lately. I have, haven't I?'

'You haven't been very nice,' I admitted.

'I know,' Angela said honestly. 'But it has all been so difficult; you see I believed that I was terribly in love with Douglas. I thought it would be easy to go away with him, to leave Henry and the children and start a new life. Last night I realised how absurd my ideas were.

'Henry and I are going to try again and, what is more, I want to have a lot more children. In the night when I could not sleep I thought how terrible it would be to get old with nothing to look forward to, nothing to be interested in, except young men. I saw that if I wasn't careful I might become like Henry's mother. She's a nightmare, isn't she? And can you imagine the boredom of always running after men young enough to be one's own sons, who despise you? I was frightened when I thought about it, so I went in to Henry and talked to him. Things are going to be very different for both of us in the future. Shall

151

I tell you what we are going to do? I bet you will never guess!'

'I bet I do,' I answered. 'You are going to buy a house in the country.'

'You're right!' Angela exclaimed. 'How did you know?'

'Henry told me how much he wanted one,' I confessed.

'Of course we will keep this house on too,' Angela said, 'but we will have somewhere for the children to spend their holidays, and we can be quite near to London so that we can motor down for the night when it is hot in the summer, and our friends can come to us for luncheon or dinner at week-ends. Oh! I am so much happier now that I feel secure about the future! I suppose, really, at heart, I am suburban-minded.'

'No,' I said, 'I think you are just domesticated like we all are. After all, you can hardly call Father and Mother gadabouts, can you?'

'I have done all the gadding I am ever going to do,' Angela said. 'Last night I became really terrified when I thought how near I had been to making a fool of myself and how this might have happened to Gerald when I had already gone away with Douglas. I imagined myself the other side of the world, longing to get back, distraught with anxiety, perhaps unable to do anything, perhaps even prevented by law from seeing my children. Oh, dear, I love them so; I can't think why I didn't realise it before.'

She looked quite white and shaken with the intensity of her feeling. I put out my hand and took hers.

'Don't upset yourself,' I said. 'It is all right now and I feel sure that Henry understands. We all get moments of madness—everybody does.'

'How do you know?' Angela asked with a smile that would have been superior and amused, if she had not been feeling so tender and gentle at the moment.

I laughed.

'I do know,' I said. 'Although you will say I have had no experience. Perhaps it is reading too much, or else it is just an intuition which comes to me about people. You see I was right about Douglas, wasn't I? I told you he wasn't good enough for you.'

'Poor Douglas,' Angela said. 'But he will get over it—he's young, and I expect really, he will be rather relieved. It would have ruined his army career to have run away with a married woman.'

'Besides finding her much more expensive than polo ponies,' I said grinning.

'Don't be horrid,' Angela said. 'You don't know how economical and clever I could be if I tried.'

'I doubt it and I am glad for your sake that Henry is rich! At the same time, darling, quite honestly I like him most awfully.'

'Strangely enough so do I!' Angela said half laughing—half serious.

'And he loves you so much. It would make him very happy if you could love him too.'

Angela squeezed my hand, then got up from the bed.

'I am going to try,' she said, 'both to love him and to make him happy. You wait and see, Lyn, I shall get fat and domesticated and by the time we have got a nursery full of children, Henry and I will be a model Darby and Joan.'

There came a knock at my door.

'Come in,' I said, thinking it was the maid come to call me. To my surprise Henry put his head round the door.

'Is Angela here?' he asked, then before I could answer, 'Oh, there you are, darling. I was worried as you were not in your room.'

'Come in,' Angela said. 'I was just telling Lyn the good news about Gerald. I was telling her, too, lots of the things we have planned to do in the future.'

Henry was wearing a dark blue dressing-gown over his blue pyjamas. His hair was ruffled and he was smiling a new kind of proud happy smile which made him look younger and almost boyish.

'You see I have found a job, Lyn,' he said to me. 'I shall be my own estate agent. I might even try farming in a small way.'

'I am absolutely thrilled about everything,' I said to him. 'But don't forget to get me married off in the meantime, will you?'

'We aren't likely to forget that,' Henry said. 'You are going to have the best present that Cartier can provide— that I promise you, whatever it costs!'

Instead of being annoyed at Henry's reference to money, Angela crossed the room and linked her arm through his.

'We will give her a cow in diamonds,' she said laughing. 'Suggestive of domestic bliss.'

Henry smiled down at his wife. There was something intensely pathetic in his pride and in the love which showed so obviously in his face.

I was almost afraid for him that this happiness might not last—that once Gerald was well again, Angela might forget. And yet I felt that perhaps my sister had been more serious than she had sounded when she said she meant to try and love Henry. Angela was not in reality emotional enough to enjoy for any length of time an illicit love affair. She would not really be happy throwing the conventions away for passion, or exchanging security for a clandestine liaison. I felt with the same sort of clairvoyant intuition that had come to me on other occasions, that Angela would settle down and that if she was not overwhelmingly in love with Henry, at least she would be content with him, and that in the years to come, her children would mean much more to her than they had ever done before.

The clock on my mantelpiece gave a silver chime to say it was half-past eight. Angela looked at it, then said:

'It is so long since I have been up so early, I can't think what I am going to do with myself until my first appointment.'

'Which is to be at the nursing home at eleven o'clock,' Henry said.

'Yes, I know,' Angela answered. 'You are coming with me, aren't you?'

'Of course, darling,' he replied.

'Well, until then I had better go and struggle with my letters and the list of invitations which are to be sent out for Lyn's wedding,' Angela said.

'Don't talk about letters!' I said with a grimace. 'I had over thirty last night and all of them from perfect strangers to me. They have either known mother since she was a child, or have been life-long friends of yours.'

'Ah well,' Angela said, 'that is the penalty for making a successful marriage. More fools know Tom Fool than Tom Fool knows!'

'If I have got to write to them all over again when they send presents, I shall go mad. I wish I could have my letters typed.'

'Can you imagine what father would say if you did?' Angela laughed. 'Don't be so lazy, Lyn. If you say the same thing to each one of them it oughtn't to take long.'

'Oh, I assure you nobody gets anything original,' I answered. 'But I felt humbled after I had seen Philip's pile last week—there must have been nearly a hundred by one post alone.'

'You may be thankful you are nineteen instead of over forty,' Henry said. 'One's acquaintance grows heavier year by year.'

'Henry is obviously warning you against a second marriage,' Angela said, 'and perhaps he is right. Let the first love be the last love. . . .' She smiled up at her husband as she spoke. He whispered something in her ear which made her laugh. Saying goodbye to me, they went downstairs.

I lay for some time after they had gone, thinking about them—glad things had altered so much for the better. It was as though a volcanic eruption had shaken them out of the rut of indifference into which they had been sinking deeper and deeper. Perhaps that was what everyone needed, an eruption now and then to shake them into a realisation of what was of fundamental importance. Perhaps that was what Philip needed, something sensational in his life, which would show him that his feelings for Nada should be of secondary importance to living and of being loved. I sighed and felt sad. Every day my wedding was coming nearer. . . .

I was reading my morning post of congratulations and good wishes and opening the usual large collection of circulars inviting me to visit various shops for my trousseau, when the telephone rang. Elizabeth greeted me in mysterious and excited tones.

'Are you alone?' she asked.

'Yes, quite,' I answered.

'Can anybody listen in on this telephone, or overhear what we say?'

'I don't think so,' I replied. 'At least the butler could if he wanted to, but I think it is very unlikely—the servants are all busy at this time of the morning.'

'I have got news for you,' Elizabeth said.

'What is it?'

'I have found out about Nada's mother; her name is Mrs. Melinkoff and Sir Philip pays her a pension, at least he did until two or three years ago. I couldn't find out where she lives, or anything like that, but I think she was on the stage too, at one time.'

'Oh, Elizabeth! How clever of you,' I said. 'How did you manage to learn all that?'

'Well, I got some of it from mother and some from my

155

uncle. He was here to dinner last night and I managed to get them talking about Philip. I wish I could have found out more, but quite honestly, I think that is all they know.'

'You are a darling,' I said firmly. 'Thank you a hundred times for all the trouble you are taking. What have you been doing?'

'I went down to the club yesterday,' Elizabeth answered. 'It was really most awfully interesting.'

'I am so glad,' I said and told her about Gerald's illness adding, 'he's out of danger, but I don't know what I am doing for the next two or three days, because everything is upset, but as soon as things are normal again, we must meet.'

'In the meantime I will keep on with my espionage,' Elizabeth said, 'and ring you up if there is any news—but I'm not hopeful.'

When she had rung off I picked up the telephone book and went through the 'M's', but I was disappointed; there was no sign of any Melinkoff, however I spelt it. I was putting it back on the shelf beside my bed when suddenly an idea came to me.

The previous week when Philip and I had been lunching at the Ritz with a relative of his who had given a huge party for us, an old man had come up to us in the lounge and said:

'You must allow me to congratulate you, Sir Philip.'

He had a funny wrinkled face and white hair and he wore an old-fashioned morning coat heavily braided. In his buttonhole was a bright yellow carnation.

'Why, Mr. Grossman,' Philip exclaimed. 'I haven't seen you for a long time. How are you?'

'Very well, thank you,' he replied, 'but not as young as I was, alas!'

Philip turned to me.

'Lyn,' he said, 'this is Mr. Israel Grossman, the most important person in the whole theatrical world and one whose position has never been challenged!'

'Oh, I wouldn't go so far as to say that, Sir Philip,' Mr. Grossman said, but obviously pleased and flattered at the compliment. Then he turned to me. 'I am very pleased to meet you, my dear,' he said. 'You are a very lucky young lady, if you will forgive me saying so. Sir Philip is a great gentleman.'

We talked for a few minutes longer, before he said good-
bye, and as soon as he was out of earshot I said to Philip:

'Who is he?'

'Israel Grossman,' he answered, 'is the biggest theatrical
agent in England. He has been going for so many years
now that nobody can remember when he wasn't drawing a
fat percentage on every known star, or making his own
terms with the managers. He is a law unto himself and he
fears no one. He was sitting like the proverbial spider in his
curious ramshackle offices of the Haymarket long before
the War. When I first knew him, which must have been in
1918, he looked exactly as he does now. We thought he
was an old man in those days. When he dies London will
have lost yet another landmark, for you can see him at
every first night and he is almost a side-show on his own at
the Theatrical Garden Party.'

I had never thought any more about Israel Grossman
until this moment. Now when I remembered the conversation, I realised that of course he might have been Nada's
agent, and there was just a chance, a slender chance, but
certainly one worth taking, that through him I might find
her mother's address. I picked up the other volume of the
telephone book and started to look through the 'G's' for
Israel Grossman.

I found it and dialled the number. When I heard a voice
say 'Hullo,' I had a moment of panic as to what I should
say. Then something seemed to guide me and I heard my
voice say calmly:

'May I speak to Mr. Grossman's private secretary?'

'I will see if she is in,' someone said. 'What name please?'

For a moment I hesitated, then my eye caught sight of a
letter from mother lying open by my side.

'Miss Maysfield,' I said.

Some minutes elapsed while I sat quaking at the end of
the telephone. Eventually the sharp, efficient tones of a
woman's voice said:

'Miss Joyce speaking. What can I do for you?'

'I am sorry to bother you,' I said, 'but I wonder if you
would be good enough to tell me if Mr. Grossman has
anywhere on his records the address of Nada Melinkoff's
mother? He will know who I mean—the dancer who died
many years ago. Mr. Grossman was her agent, I believe.'

'Nada Melinkoff?' the secretary said. 'Yes, I think I

157

know to whom you refer. I should imagine it is unlikely
that Mr. Grossman has the address of her relatives, but I
will find out. Will he know who is speaking?'

'I am afraid he doesn't know me,' I said firmly, 'but I
am very anxious, for personal reasons, to get into touch
with someone who is closely related to Nada Melinkoff.'

'Hold on, please.'

Again I had to wait, wondering anxiously if my story
sounded truthful and if Israel Grossman would have any
information to give me.

'Hullo, are you there?'

'Yes,' I answered quickly.

'I have asked Mr. Grossman,' Miss Joyce said. 'He says
the last time he heard from Madame Melinkoff she was
living at 502 St. Catherine Street, W.C.2. This was some
years ago and he is afraid he cannot help you further.'

'Thank you very much,' I answered. 'I am very grateful
to you.'

I rang off quickly, my heart beating fast. At last here
was something concrete; here was a hope of getting nearer
to the mystery which was keeping Philip and me apart—a
mystery which I meant to solve whatever it cost me in the
effort.

19

It was nearly two days before I had an opportunity to be on my own so that I could visit Madame Melinkoff.

Angela, now that she was happy with Henry and determined to turn over a new leaf, had decided to see very little of Douglas Ormonde, and their afternoons alone together had definitely come to an end. Therefore, when she was not at the nursing home, she spent most of the day with me.

Gerald had to be kept very quiet after his operation, and for the first two days Angela saw him for only a few moments in the morning and again at tea-time. Shopping, of course, took up the bulk of our time, but there were luncheons and tea-parties to be fitted in, and invariably a well-planned afternoon would be upset by a last minute invitation from some relative or friend who could not be refused.

However, on Thursday afternoon my chance came. I was at Worth's being pinned into several sports suits, which had been chosen especially for my honeymoon, when Angela looked at the clock and said:

'Darling, will you mind if I leave you? I told Gerald I would give him his tea and after that I have promised to go on for an hour or so to see a very old friend of mine who has just lost her husband. I would offer to take you, but I don't think she wants to see anyone, and it will be very gloomy, anyway.'

'Don't worry about me,' I replied. 'I will go home when they have finished here.'

'All right,' Angela said. 'I will get back as soon as I can.'

As soon as she had gone I refused quite firmly, in spite of protests by the vendeuse, to fit things more.

'I am tired,' I said. 'I will come back tomorrow or the next day. We have got a party tonight and I want to rest.'

I hurried into my own clothes, snatched up my hat and bag, and without waiting for the lift—which I think rather

159

surprised them in the shop—ran down the stairs and told the commissionaire to get me a taxi. I gave him the address in St. Catherine Street, then sat back, literally panting from hurry and excitement.

It took nearly a quarter of an hour to reach St. Catherine Street; the traffic was bad and we got mixed up with a crowd of lorries coming from Covent Garden.

Finally we arrived and having paid the taxi off, I found myself facing a huge block of flats. They were the old-fashioned tessellated Victorian type, with an uncarpeted stone staircase running up the centre of the building. On every landing there were the entrances to three flats, their doors, half of frosted glass, identical in every particular. In the hall a list of names was painted on a board and I found that Madame Melinkoff lived at the very top of the building. There was no lift, and I climbed slowly up the stairs, getting hotter and hotter in the process and thinking wildly of what I had planned to say.

I had had plenty of time to think about this visit during the past few days, in fact it had hardly ever been out of my thoughts. But now that the moment was upon me it didn't seem so easy as I had anticipated.

In a few moments I was standing in front of flat No. 30. I paused for breath. Then, with a feeling that for better or for worse I had committed myself, I pressed the small electric bell over the letter box. It made a queer buzzing sound which startled me. I waited. Just as I was beginning to be afraid that no one was at home the door opened slowly. A little woman, leaning on a stick, stood looking at me.

'Yes?' she questioned.

'Is Madame Melinkoff at home?' I asked.

'I am Madame Melinkoff,' she replied.

'Oh!' I exclaimed and for a moment could think of nothing else to say.

'You wanted to see me?' she asked evidently surprised, either at my appearance, or my silence.

'If you could spare me a few moments,' I stammered.

'Come in.'

I did as I was told, stepping into a narrow passage in which there was barely room for the two of us. She closed the door behind her, then led the way into a tiny square sitting-room, filled with a miscellaneous collection of things which were quite bewildering at first sight.

There were brass and silver pots and trays; ornaments of

quartz, jade and soapstone; innumerable cushions covered in Indian silk, and brightly coloured scarves and cloths laid over small tables which were loaded with nick-nacks of all sorts—figures, boxes, bells, ashtrays and many pieces of carved ivory. Photographs were everywhere—on the walls, on the tables and arranged in rows on the mantelpiece. Men, women and children, either alone or in groups, all were signed and all seemed to be flashing the same toothy smile from their cardboard background.

'Stage stars,' I thought to myself, as I sat down on the small armchair that Madame Melinkoff indicated to me. She seated herself opposite to me, and waited for me to speak.

Now I had time to look at her I saw that she was older than I had thought. Her hair was quite white and her eyes were surrounded by a network of wrinkles, but the ravages of time could not destroy an impression of prettiness and I knew that Madame Melinkoff must in her youth have been very attractive. She seemed weak and fragile, but she held herself erect and it was easy to see that she had once had a lovely figure.

I had no time to choose my words; instead I blurted out the truth.

'I hope you will forgive my intruding on you like this,' I said nervously, 'but I have wanted so very much to meet you.'

'That is kind of you,' she said. 'Will you tell me why?'

'I wanted you to tell me about your daughter, Nada,' I said.

Her face softened and there came an expression of great sadness into her eyes.

'My daughter Nada!' she said softly. 'Why do you want to know about her? Did you know her? No, you are too young, that is absurd of me.'

I hesitated, then I felt that perhaps the only way to gain what I wanted was to be absolutely frank.

'My name is Gwendolyn Sherbrooke,' I said, 'I am going to marry Sir Philip Chadleigh.'

Madame Melinkoff stiffened. She stared at me.

'Has he sent you here?' she asked.

I shook my head.

'Sir Philip has no idea that I was coming to see you,' I answered. 'I will be frank with you, Madame Melinkoff. I have heard about your daughter, but not from my fiancé.

Won't you tell me about her? You see, he loved her so much—it is hard to marry a man knowing nothing about the woman who has played a tremendous part in his life.'

'Sir Philip has been very kind to me,' Madame Melinkoff said.

'He is not happy,' I said, 'but I want to make him so.'

She looked away from me, her thin sensitive hands clasping the ivory head of her walking-stick.

'It is difficult to know what to say to you.'

'Not really,' I said eagerly. 'I want you to tell me about your daughter. You can make her real for me, you can make me understand how attractive she was, so that I can know just how much Philip lost when she died.'

'Died!' Madame Melinkoff echoed in a sharp voice. 'She killed herself.'

'Yes, I know,' I said. 'I have heard that too. Why did she kill herself? Was she unhappy?'

'How could she be unhappy?' Madame Melinkoff asked harshly. 'She had everything. The world was at her feet. She was a star. The theatre was packed night after night; they were turning people away from the box office; her salary was mounting every year; she had motors, jewels, a lovely house. Why should she have been unhappy?'

'That is what I want to know,' I murmured. 'I don't understand.'

'Nor do I,' Madame Melinkoff's voice broke.

On an impulse I got up from my chair and went and knelt by her side.

'Please help me,' I pleaded. 'Only you can help me. There is no one else whom I can ask, no one who will talk to me.'

There was a moment of tension, then very slowly she put out her hand and touched my shoulder.

I pulled off my hat, but remained kneeling there, looking up into her face. I felt in that moment she had accepted me; there was an understanding between us and she would not turn me away.

'Poor child,' she said. 'So you are suffering too! It comes to all of us sooner or later.'

'Help me,' I whispered.

'Do you really want to hear about Nada,' she asked.

'I do,' I answered. 'I promise you it is not for selfish reasons. Unless I can gain the confidence of the man I am going to marry, there can be no happiness for either of us.'

'Philip loved her so much,' she said.

'And she loved him?' I questioned.

'She loved him,' Madame Melinkoff repeated. 'There were a great many men who wanted to be part of Nada's life, men who loved her passionately, often crazily, but from the moment she saw Philip, there was no one else. Many times I have said to her, "He is just a man like all the rest! Why does he mean so much to you? Why do you feel about him as you do?" and always she had the same answer. She would look at me with those big dark eyes of hers and she would say, "He is part of me, I can't live without him. You don't understand, but I promise you it is true. He is part of me and I am part of him".'

I felt myself shiver at the words. Were they prophetic for all time? It certainly seemed so.

'Tell me more,' I pleaded. 'Tell me everything. How your daughter started? Why she went on the stage? Was she Russian?' I asked the last question tentatively.

'Russian?' Madame Melinkoff said. 'Oh no! Nada's father was an Indian. Surely you have been told that? He was a prince, a prince of the Rajput. He was dark and very handsome. Nada was exactly like him. He had the same wonderful eyes with which he could hold spellbound all those who looked into them. He held me—the daughter of white parents, the daughter of a people who thought that all Indians were outcasts, a black race to be despised, to be used as slaves, too inferior for any consideration.'

'You ran away with him?' I asked.

'I loved him,' Madame Melinkoff answered simply. 'We were travelling in India because my father had been given a job as accountant to a Forestry Trust in one of the Northern Provinces. I was young at the time, not quite eighteen. I can see myself now, so sure of myself, so confident of the future. I was pretty, I had a good voice and I could dance—elegant skirt dances which were just then becoming the rage in England and which were considered very dashing. I would sometimes entertain my father's guests, although I think the majority of people in India thought it rather a regrettable accomplishment for a young girl.

'I met my Prince. I am not going to tell you about that, it is so long ago and, after all, it is about Nada you want to

163

hear, not about me. I had six marvellous months; six months of my life which I have never regretted, not even when I paid for them dearly in the years that followed.

'Nada was born in a mission settlement, where I was treated by the missionary and his wife as something unclean and disgusting. As soon as I was strong enough to travel, I took my baby and started for home. Luckily I had a little money, not much but enough, and I also had some jewellery which my Prince had given me. When I got back to England I realised that I was as much an outcast as any "untouchable". My relations would have nothing to do with me and although Nada was a lovely child, it was obvious at a first glance that she was of mixed parentage.

'I nearly starved; at times I almost gave in to despair and threw myself and my baby into the river. At last when I was absolutely desperate, my face and my dancing stood me in good stead. I got a job on the stage. It was only in the chorus, but gradually, very gradually, I progressed from the back row to the second row, the second row to the front. I got my first few lines to say, then a tiny solo part of my own.

'It all sounds so easy now as I am telling it to you, but I assure you, my child, that I have passed over many years of hard work in those few words. Men were kind to me, but it is very seldom that women extend their charity to those of their own sex who are pretty and in trouble.'

'But the Prince!' I asked. 'Why did he let you suffer so terribly? Why did you leave him?'

'My dear, I was only a passing interlude in his life. He forgot me, as I expect he forgot hundreds of other women with whom he spent a few happy leisure hours.

'Nada was ten when I married. He was a Russian and, as you can guess, his name was Melinkoff. He was a jeweller who loved beautiful things and I think that he valued me because he genuinely believed that I was the most beautiful gem in his collection.

'He adopted Nada as his own and gave her his name. The child was lovely, an exquisite creature, who would have captivated everyone who saw her, had it not been for the instinctive recoil of a white skin from one which is darker. Already she was planning a stage career, not only in imitation of me, but because the first note of music would find her on her toes, poised like a bird ready for flight.

'It was shortly after my marriage that for the second time in my life I went back to India. My husband had several commissions to execute among the Rajahs and we took Nada with us. We were there for far longer than we had intended—nearly eight years in all, travelling around from place to place, while my husband continued his trade, not only selling, but sending his purchases of jewels back to his firm in England.

'All this time Nada was absorbing the life, the music and, to some extent, the culture of her own country. She loved India; for her it was a homecoming and she expanded in the warm sun like a flower. She developed too a passion for the temples; often she would run away and I would be distracted until she was found, trying to take part in a Hindoo ceremony, or following a religious procession through the streets.

'When she was fifteen, against our wishes and in spite of continual opposition from her step-father, she insisted on learning the Nautch dances. But three years later when we came back to England we found that she had known better than we had what was best for herself. She was an instant success. I took her to Israel Grossman, whom I had known in my own theatrical days. After one audition he booked her for a big revue that was coming on at the London Pavilion. She went from there to a show in which she was the star.

'The War was on, men home on leave; they fought amongst themselves for the privilege of taking her out to supper when the show was over. I was afraid she would lose both her head and her heart, but no, she flirted with them all; she made them happy, but they meant nothing to her personally until she met Philip Chadleigh.

'Then for the first time Nada learnt the meaning of love as I had learnt it many years before from her father!'

Madame Melinkoff paused and put her hand over her eyes. I waited for some moments, then at length I said gently:

'But why didn't he marry her?'

'I prayed that he would,' Madame Melinkoff said. 'Yet, I suppose in my heart of hearts I knew it was impossible. I understood, for I had suffered too deeply not to understand the horror of the white races for those of coloured blood. Philip had his family, his position—and more important, his children—to consider. If Nada hoped to be his

165

wife, she never said so. But once when I found her exhausted after a long performance, I said, "You are tired, Why go out? Why not have a quiet evening at home?" And she answered, "I have no home. How can any woman call a flat where she sleeps and eats alone a home? A home must hold two people, two people who love each other".

'After that I wondered, but she did not give me her confidence. I think any criticism of Philip would have seemed to her a sacrilege. She grew thin as though her passion was consuming her, yet whenever he appeared she glowed like a flame. Philip had only to come into the room and she would spring up, vital, alive, seemingly as fresh as though the moment before she had not lain limp with closed eyes. They would go out together, I don't know where, perhaps to dance, perhaps to sit in his magnificent house, of which she often spoke to me, but which I never saw.

'The end came quite unexpectedly and without any warning. I was waiting that evening for my husband; it was a warm night and I had cold supper ready for him on the table. There was a knock at the door. I went to it, thinking he had forgotten his latchkey. Outside I found Philip's secretary; I knew him very slightly. He told me what had happened.

'They had taken Nada to her own flat; she lay on the silver bed of which she had been so proud, cold and still. The fall had not damaged her face. The back of her head had struck the pavement and she had broken her neck. Nada, my beautiful Nada, whose dancing had been the talk of all London, had broken her neck!'

There was a moment of poignant silence. Then I saw that Madame Melinkoff was crying.

20

Words cannot exactly explain the effect Madame Melinkoff's tears had upon me, but I felt as though I also was racked with sorrow. I would have done anything at that moment or made any sacrifice to help her.

'Don't, please don't!' I said. 'I didn't want to upset you, I only wanted to learn the truth.'

For a few moments she held a handkerchief to her eyes, then in the same quiet tones she continued to speak.

'At the time I thought that my life too was ended. Nada had meant so much to me. I had been so ambitious for her, so eager to see her make a success of her life, to find happiness as I failed to do.'

Seeing my look of surprise, she said:

'My husband was kind to me, but I cannot tell you all the insults I had to bear. People before the war were by no means as broadminded or as tolerant as they are today. I suffered terribly; the scars have never healed. I was snubbed, I was subjected to ribald jokes, to ridicule and to more humiliation than I would have cared to tell anyone. Perhaps I deserved it all; perhaps it was wrong of me to leave my parents and to throw over all the traditions to which I had been brought up. Yet, even in my most miserable times of despair, I used to look at Nada and think it had been worth it. Even after my marriage I felt I could never escape from the scandal I had created. I grew hypersensitive, expecting rebuffs from every woman I met, afraid of kindness, suspicious of any interest taken in me in case it should turn to cruelty.

'In some lesser degree, Nada suffered too, but only when she was a child. The children at the school she went to in England laughed at her, and, of course, their mothers made every effort to prevent them becoming friends with a child who was half-black. In India things were different.

167

She was forced, of course, to go to schools kept for Eurasians and better class natives, but they were kindly people and when we were travelling I saw to her education myself, although I was not very skilled in such matters.

'My husband adored her and it made no difference to him that every white person with whom we made friends looked at his step-child in disgust. In wartime things were better; the Indians were fighting for us and they were cheered as loudly as our own troops, and of course, from the moment that Nada became a star, nobody worried about anything except her personal success. She went to parties, she lunched and had supper with people who, in other circumstances, would have had her turned out into the streets by their servants. I used to laugh when I read her invitations—not always without bitterness.'

'It seems hard to believe,' I murmured, 'that there were such prejudices about people of another colour.'

'There still is,' Madame Melinkoff said. 'You don't come across it much here in London, but East of Suez . . .' She stopped. 'Don't get me on to such a controversial subject. I know how angry it makes me, and many years ago I swore to myself that I would never discuss it again.'

'Have you got any photographs of your daughter?' I asked, rather timidly, hoping she wouldn't think I was presuming too far.

'But of course!' she replied. 'I will show them to you.'

With the help of her stick she got to her feet. There was a huge portfolio lying in a place of honour on a table spread with a gauzy Indian shawl studded with a silver border. She opened the covers and inside I saw neatly stacked dozens of photographs of all shapes and sizes. One by one she held them out to me.

My first glance of that lovely oval face gave me again the same sense of shock and familiarity I had experienced when I had first seen Nada's picture hanging over Philip's mantelpiece. I gazed eagerly at every detail of her features. In many of the photographs she was dressed in the clothes she had worn on the stage—the full, heavily embroidered skirts, tight bodices, carved and jewelled native bracelets and necklets which I knew must have given a musical jingle each time she moved.

There could not have been a photographer in London who had not tried to make a beautiful study of Nada Melinkoff. She was very photogenic but there was, too, a strange mysterious elusiveness about her, which made every photograph seem as though it just missed something, as if the camera stopped at the very moment of revelation, so that the full personality of the sitter was not perfectly reflected.

'Here we were taken together,' Madame Melinkoff said passing me another photograph. 'It was taken for ourselves, just as a joke, after I had helped Nada at one of her sittings. But the newspapers published it. I was sorry—the contrast between my fairness and Nada's hair and eyes are very obvious.'

The pictures showed mother and daughter sitting one on each arm of a big carved oak chair. Both were wearing hobble skirts, pinched-in waists and the lacy cravats which had been so fashionable at one period of the War. The clothes were amusing, but their faces were arresting. Madame Melinkoff's hair was waved and curled until it formed a halo round her sweet almost childish face. Nada's head was smooth, classical in its severity. Her hair, parted in the middle, was drawn back to reveal her perfectly shaped forehead. Her long earrings accentuated the exquisite shape of her face. She looked strange in western dress, but was undeniably lovely, and nothing could destroy the glory of her eyes which appeared to hold in their depths all the mystery of the East.

'How pretty you were,' I said to Madame Melinkoff.

'Very different from what I am now,' she answered. 'From my appearance you would think I was a very old woman, wouldn't you?'

Any answer I could make honestly would have been embarrassing. I had thought she was very old, but now, doing a quick addition in my head, I realised that she could not be more than sixty.

'Nothing ages one so much as pain,' Madame Melinkoff said. 'But that is another story, of course. Soon after Nada's death my husband died of pneumonia. I nursed him for nearly two months and when finally the end came I was utterly exhausted. Physically I was worn out; mentally I had come to the end of my strength, the two people I loved most had gone—I only wanted to die. I developed rheumatic-fever; for several months they thought nothing would save me. My heart was affected, there were other complications too, far too long and too dull to bother you with.

169

'I longed to die. It was agony for me to linger on in a world which was destitute of love, holding for me only loneliness and heartbreak. It was Philip who made me live. Not him personally, but the money he paid for the doctors and the nurses who looked after me. And when finally I could take up some semblance of living again, I found that he had settled on me a definite income which would keep me from want for the rest of my life.'

'Do you ever see him?' I asked.

Madame Melinkoff shook her head.

'I think it would be too painful for both of us,' she said.

'Did you like him?' I questioned.

'It is difficult to tell,' Madame Melinkoff said with an expressive gesture. 'When Nada was alive I was jealous of him, yes jealous of the love which, until he had come into her life, had been whole-heartedly mine. Then later I hated him with a bitter resentful hatred, for I felt it was his fault she had died. Even now I doubt the coroner's verdict.'

'What was it?' I asked, my voice was low.

'Suicide while of insane mind,' Madame Melinkoff answered. 'It is laughable. How could Nada have been insane? Nada, with her brilliant intelligence, her sensitiveness and understanding. No, no that couldn't have been the truth! It was something else, something dramatic if you like, something which we shall never understand, but certainly not insanity.'

'Was Philip with her?' I asked. 'What did he say at the inquest?'

'He was so desperately upset,' Madame Melinkoff answered, 'that he was difficult to understand. At first he alleged that she had gone through the window and sat on the narrow parapet to look at the view, but he broke down when he was questioned, and admitted that she had said something about throwing herself over. That was enough. The coroner was the type of man who liked to humiliate those in high places, a socialist, I suppose, of the most resentful type. Anyway he seized on that admission and made it appear quite obvious that Nada's liaison with Philip had been an unhappy one, which ended in suicide.

'All the facts of the case were, of course, against her: —a half-caste and a man who belonged to one of the oldest families in England! There was no question that she had been infatuated with him for a long time. It was proved that Philip had given her valuable presents, that they had stayed abroad together and had been constantly in each other's company. It was all terrible, horrible! There were posters in the streets; headlines in all the newspapers; reporters ringing up day and night, badgering me for interviews, for photographs, offering me hundreds of pounds if I would write my own life story for the Sunday papers.'

'How beastly!' I said.

'As soon as the inquest was over I went away. My husband took me abroad, but even there, in my utter misery and unhappiness, I was haunted by people continually asking me if I was any relation, asking question after question, probing, enquiring, spying with every type of curiosity, from the sympathetic to those who enjoyed sensuously a sensational story of illicit love.'

Madame Melinkoff's voice broke.

'Don't talk about it,' I begged. 'Don't tell me any more. I know that it hurts you to remember these things. Oh, I'm sorry, so desperately sorry for you.'

I looked down at the pile of photographs. On top there was a large head of Nada smiling enigmatically into the camera, her eyes half-veiled by dark eyelashes, her long thin hands clasped under her chin.

'Why did she kill herself for Philip?' I asked myself. Why indeed should this lovely creature have wanted to die? I felt certain that everything she had done had been because she was swayed by emotion, by a deep consuming love. Yet, could she have been so utterly unbalanced as to die for that love? It was hers, it had given her great happiness. Surely her mother who had known her so well, who loved her so deeply would have known if there had been anything desperate in her mind before that moment at Chadleigh House? If there had been nothing, what could have passed between her and Philip? Did he know? Had he hidden all these years the secret within himself, a secret which not even the probing questions of the coroner had been able to discover?

I shut the portfolio. I could not bear to look any longer at that face which moved me so strangely, which, as it looked back at me from the cardboard on which it was printed, aroused question after question in my mind, questions to which I could find no answer.

I glanced at my watch and realised that I had been with Madame Melinkoff for an hour and a half.

'I must go,' I said, 'otherwise I shall be missed.'

'When are you to be married, dear child?' she asked.

'At the end of July,' I answered. 'I think about the 22nd.'

She took one of my hands in both of hers.

'I hope you will find happiness,' she said. 'Never be afraid of happiness. And make the most of it when it comes to you. Sometimes it lasts a very little time.'

'It is because I want it so much that I came here today,' I said. 'You understand that I didn't come to be inquisitive, but only because I am afraid of the future—afraid because your daughter Nada is still so terribly alive in Philip's memory.'

'It is cruel of me,' Madame Melinkoff replied, 'but I am glad. She loved him so much.'

'And he loves her still,' I said sadly.

She looked at me with her tired eyes.

'Are you sure,' she asked, 'that you are doing the right thing?'

'I don't know,' I answered. 'It is a question I often ask myself. I can only hope and pray that I shall find an answer before the 22nd of July.'

I stood looking down at her, then I stooped and kissed her. It was an action that I should never have done had I had time to consider. I am always shy of being too gushing or too demonstrative. But it was an impulse which I could not check and I think Madame Melinkoff was touched.

'Thank you, dear child,' she said. 'I shall think of you very often.'

'May I come and see you again?' I asked.

'Of course,' she replied. 'Come soon, for I don't think I shall be here for very long.'

'You are moving?' I asked.

She shook her head and a faint smile came to her lips.

'The doctors are surprised that I am still alive,' she said gently. 'I feel that at last my hold on this world is slipping. For so long I have wanted to find peace and rest and now I believe that they are not very far distant from me.'

'I will come again,' I said in a low voice, 'and soon.'

She showed me to the front door, limping as she walked. On the landing we said good-bye again, with a touch of restraint, then I ran quickly down the stone stairs, my feet clattering and echoing up the well of the building as I did so.

I had a lot to think about on my drive home, so much

indeed that it was with quite a start that I realised the taxi had pulled up at the house. I paid the driver off and hurried in to find that I was back before Angela. Henry was alone in the drawing-room.

'How is Gerald?' I asked.

'Much better,' he said smiling. 'I took him some toys this afternoon. He was well enough to look at them and in a day or two he will be sitting up and playing with them.'

'What sort of toys?' I asked, anxious to make conversation.

'Oh, model aeroplanes, engines, and all sorts of scientific puzzles that you and I couldn't possibly do,' Henry answered. 'By, Jove, it quite frightens me to realise how clever the children of today are. Angela and I will have to look to our laurels, or they will write us off as a couple of nitwits.'

He spoke with such pride and satisfaction that I thought to myself that in a few years Henry would find as much to boast about in his sons as he had in the past over his money. He was the type who had to justify an inferiority complex by having something that was superior to everyone else. If Angela only could love him, I thought to myself! What he wants is to be flattered, to be made a fuss of, then he would be pleased with himself, not merely proud of what he possessed.

I tried to do a little of the good work myself.

'I shouldn't be too modest, Henry,' I said. 'If the children have got any brains they get them from you, certainly not from our side of the family. Father's a darling, but I think his business capacity would always work out on the debit side, judging by our present income, and I imagine from results that our forbears were just as inefficient where money was concerned.'

'I always had a head for figures,' Henry said. 'There's nothing much in that, you know.'

'I think it is brilliant,' I said solemnly. 'In fact, I am genuinely impressed.'

'Oh well, all you will have to do in the future is to add up your dress allowance,' Henry laughed. 'Philip will manage the rest for you, although from what I have seen of the intended marriage settlement, you will need at least ten fingers on your hands to do that.'

'Is there going to be a marriage settlement?' I asked. 'It is the first I have heard about it.'

'But of course there is, my dear girl,' Henry said in shocked tones. 'Good heavens, we have got to safeguard your interests! Philip may be very generous and charming now, but it doesn't follow that he will always go on being so. You have got to think of the future, both for yourself and your children.'

I turned away and walked towards the table in the drawing-room where the papers are laid out. I somehow couldn't speak lightly, or even talk to anyone about the possibility of Philip and myself having children. That was an aspect of our marriage I had not yet considered, yet I felt that he wanted them and would be pleased to have them. It would be the right thing, just as he wanted and needed the right type of wife to hold the position of Lady Chadleigh.

Would our children, I wondered to myself, even mean as much to us as Nada had meant to Madame Melinkoff? And would any child of mine bring me in the future such happiness and such an absolute sense of loss?

21

It was the sort of day on which everything goes wrong. I awoke to find the rain teeming down and knew that that meant an alteration of all my plans. I had promised to lunch with Philip and go down to Ranelagh and we had also arranged to dine that night at a party that was being given in one of the big gardens in Holland Park. A floor had been laid on the lawn and the whole party from start to finish, was to be held out of doors.

I was waiting for Philip to telephone me when Henry came up with the news that Angela had a sore throat, and had decided to stay in bed.

'She thinks you had better not go near her,' he said. 'She often gets these throats and they are slightly infectious. I have sent for the doctor, but I know exactly what he will say. "Stay in bed and keep warm".'

I was sorry and wrote a little note to Angela to say so, which Henry took down to her. That meant the end of our morning engagements, because Angela had wanted to come with me to buy some hats. She would be annoyed if I chose them without her. So I was left with nothing to do until luncheon time.

Worse was yet to come.

Philip telephoned me to say that the Prime Minister had asked him to lunch at Downing Street and he felt bound to go.

'I couldn't very well refuse,' he said. 'So forgive me, Lyn, and I will pick you up as soon as I can afterwards, although I am afraid I may be late. There's a lot going on these days and I can't very well shirk my responsibilities.'

'No, of course not,' I agreed. 'I should be furious if you did. I want you to be very successful, Philip.'

I spoke shyly for he had no idea how ambitious I was for him. I longed to help him and to play my part, even if it were a very subsidiary one, in making him a great man worthy of his great traditions. I knew that the Prime Minister thought highly of him and that people spoke of his having a wonderful career in front of him, but I wanted more than that. I wanted Philip to stand for all that was best and truest in democracy, to represent not only the views of his party, but the will of the people; to make himself the champion of England's honour, integrity and ideals.

Philip seldom mentioned his work to me, but from one or two remarks he let drop, I knew how close to his heart was the government of our Empire and the necessity for making the bonds between our Dominions and Colonies closer and more real. Already I had begun to study conditions in India, hoping that when Philip did confide in me, my ignorance would not be too abysmal. But I had not told him this and now he seemed surprised and a little touched by my remark.

'Thank you, Lyn,' he said. 'If you help me things will be easier. I'm glad you understand that work comes first.'

'Naturally,' I answered. 'But what about tonight?'

'I expect they will hold the party indoors,' Philip answered. 'It won't be so amusing, but that can't be helped. However, we will wait and see, they are certain to let us know before the day is out.'

Feeling rather flat I got up leisurely, lingering over my bath and spending more time than usual creaming my face and polishing my nails. I sent down a message to the chef that I should be in to luncheon and hoped that Henry would be too, although I was doubtful—he was so very seldom home at lunchtime.

I found that Henry was not returning, but Mrs. Watson had come up to London for the day to see Gerald. She arrived at one o'clock with her young man, Peter Browning, in attendance. She looked more fantastic than usual. Her hair had recently been dyed a new and even more vivid shade of red-gold and perched on her head she wore a ridiculous, if fashionable hat, trimmed with two doves and draped with a veil festooned with white plush spots, the size of a pigeon's eggs.

'Dearest Lyn,' she gushed at me. 'How divine to see you. I never thought we should be so honoured. What has happened to your young man? Don't tell me that he has deserted you already!'

'He is lunching with the Prime Minister,' I said shortly.

176

'How thrilling!' Mrs. Watson cooed. 'You must feel so excited to be moving among such smart people these days. Rather a change from your quiet country life at Maysfield, isn't it?'

'By the way, many congratulations,' Peter Browning said to me, holding out a limp and rather hot hand.

'That's quite the wrong thing to say,' Mrs. Watson screamed before I could answer. 'You must only congratulate a man, never a woman, not even Lyn who has made the catch of the season.'

Her vulgarity, and quite obvious envy made me feel sick. I was as cold and distant as I could be and when luncheon was announced, said that I wanted to be as quick as possible as I had an appointment early in the afternoon.

'I am sure you won't give us three guesses as to whom it is with,' Mrs. Watson said coyly.

'The dressmaker,' I answered.

'There now, how unromantic!' she said. 'I am sure if I was Sir Philip I should want to be with you every moment of the day.'

'It is disappointing that Henry couldn't come back for luncheon,' I said trying to change the subject.

'I wanted to see him,' Mrs. Watson said. 'What is all this I hear about a house in the country? A little bird told me they were looking for one. Now, what does that portend, I wonder?'

'They thought it would be nice for the children's holidays,' I answered.

'It is a long time since so much interest was taken in the children,' Mrs. Watson said. Then as the servants left the room for a moment she bent forward and asked in a lower voice: 'Has there been a row?'

'A row?' I questioned raising my eyebrows. 'What about?'

'Douglas Ormonde, of course,' she whispered.

'I am afraid I don't know what you are taking about,' I said taking great pleasure in putting on a supercilious voice.

'Of course you do!' Mrs. Watson said crossly. 'Don't be so silly, Lyn. Do tell me, I want to know.'

'I am sure you do,' I answered. 'I should ask Angela.'

Mrs. Watson was furious.

'Some people,' she remarked to Peter Browning, 'adjust themselves very easily to a new position in life.'

I knew that I ought to be angry at this. Instead I burst out laughing. She looked so comic saying it, rather like a disgruntled cockatoo. As soon as I could I escaped from the dining-room and before I was out of earshot I heard Mrs. Watson start to complain about me in a querulous tone.

'I don't care,' I thought. 'She is an awful woman. I am only sorry for Angela having such a terrible mother-in-law!' One good thing about Philip was that although he had a great many relations, none of them was likely to interfere with me. I was glad; I felt that our marriage was going to be quite difficult enough without artificial complications.

I went upstairs to my own room, not because I was going out, but because I dared not stay downstairs after having told Mrs. Watson I had an engagement. It was still raining; the trees were dripping and the gardens in the Square looked sodden and depressing. I switched on the electric fire in my bedroom, more with the desire to make the room cheerful, than because I really felt cold. I went to the drawer where I kept various oddments and got out the book on Longmoor which contained the picture of Philip's ancestor, which was so much like him.

It was funny, I thought, that I had no photograph of Philip. I had somehow not liked to ask him for one. He had a photograph of me—one of the many which had been taken free by well-known photographers. It was a conventional studio portrait and personally I did not like it very much, but he chose it out of several others, and it was placed on his writing desk in a large silver frame. 'Not yet,' I thought to myself, 'has he allowed me in any way to invade the sanctuary of his bedroom.' That was still inviolate to the memory of Nada, for even if her portrait had gone—and how many times I wondered where he had put it—the blank space on the wall must have been quite easily filled for him in his mind's eye.

I opened my book and Philip's face stared back at me from the high collar and frilled shirt of the Georgian period. How handsome he was, yet it seemed to me that this Sir Philip Chadleigh at whom I was looking, had a softer and more gentle expression than the modern Philip, whom I loved so hopelessly.

There was, indeed, a hardness in Philip's face—I could not deny it. Perhaps it came from the tenseness of the control that he always kept upon himself, and the reserve which I had never yet been able to penetrate. Or perhaps it came from the pain he had suffered and which I believed he was still suffering.

I sat crouched in front of the fire, wondering first about Philip Chadleigh of 1939, then about the Philip of 1727. Had women loved him too? Had there been a tragedy in his life, or had he easily found contentment, happiness and joy? I wondered if to experience great happiness one must always be miserable first. It seemed sometimes as though the full depths of human capacity for emotion were not fully aroused until it had known both pain and suffering.

'If only Philip could put the past behind, could go forward with confidence, how great he could be,' I thought. Good would come out of evil, the love he had given to Nada would not be lost but transmitted into an undying force to be used for the well-being of others, and in the service of humanity. And I believed now that I would be content to leave to her the inspiration, the incentive, if I could but bring to him a sense of calm and peace. I loved Philip so much that at times my love was maternal, flowing out to him in generosity—in a protective tenderness which asked nothing for myself.

I must have grown a little drowsy for I was half asleep when the telephone rang. It startled me, so that the book fell from my lap and crashed on to the floor. I picked up the receiver.

'Sir Philip Chadleigh, m'lady.'

'Thank you,' I said. 'Hullo, Philip.'

'Hullo, Lyn. I have got away at last. Shall I come and fetch you or would you like to come round here? It is still raining so we could go to a cinema if you like.'

'That would be fun,' I answered. I could not bear to spend several long hours alone with Philip in his house. They were such a strain those times when I longed so much for some response to my feelings for him, but when I must tutor myself to a coolness, almost to indifference.

'I have got a paper in front of me,' he said. 'If you will tell me what you would like to see, I will telephone for seats.'

We chose a film after some discussion.

'All right, the Plaza,' he said. 'I will be with you in ten minutes. Au revoir until then.'

I went to the wardrobe to get out a black hat and a stole

of silver foxes which Angela had given me the other day as a present. The hat was an amusing trifle of ribbon and lace and I knew, when I had put it on my head, and powdered my nose, that I was looking my best. I sprayed a little scent over my furs and picked up my gloves. As I did so I noticed on the floor the book on Longmoor. I picked it up and opening the drawer at the bottom of my dressing-table, put it away. As I did so I saw pushed at the back, another book, half hidden by some letters and old invitation cards which I had thrown there carelessly, meaning to sort them out and destroy those which were no longer needed.

I pulled the book out, wondering what it would be. Not until I held it in my hands did its shabby red cover with battered edges remind me of how it had come into my possession. It was the book I had borrowed from the Vicar the morning before I came to London, the book I had snatched up on hearing voices in the hall, and which I had not looked at again from that day to this. The title was half-obliterated and I guessed that at some time the book must have either been left out in the rain, or read carelessly by someone in their bath.

I opened it. On the title page I read *The Evidence of Reincarnation.*

'What a funny book to choose,' was my first thought. Then the word seemed to reverberate in my mind. Reincarnation—that meant living again, returning to the world in a different body. Slowly, so slowly and gradually that I could trace the thoughts formulating in my mind, as though they were being fitted in there by one like a puzzle shape, came the idea of Nada and myself linked together, of our being one. 'It's absurd!' I said out loud, 'but . . .'

I visualised the whole sequence as I stood there, staring down at the book I held in my hand. At first it seemed so fanciful, that I regarded it half humorously. Then the deeper significance began to overwhelm me.

I shut the book and sitting down at my dressing-table, stared at my own face in the glass. Could such things be? Was that why I had recognised Nada's face? Had her portrait been of me? Was it my face, my own, the one I had known for twenty-two years, but which I had lost through death?

I stared at myself until my eyes hurt and I shut them to know the relief of darkness. I tried to steady the half-frightened, excited state of my mind. 'But why shouldn't it be true?' I asked myself. Wouldn't that explain so many things—the first moment when I saw Philip, the similarity of my voice with that of Nada's, the desire I felt for Philip which, at times, frightened me by its intensity; Nada's portrait and my recognition of it; the sympathy and understanding which I had felt for Madame Melinkoff?

Then common sense told me how ridiculous I was! Such things were but a few isolated incidents to which an over imaginative brain had given an exaggerated importance. What else could I remember of that past life, if it had been mine? Nothing at all! I could not even dance, so where was the talent in which Nada had excelled? I had always wanted to be small and dark, but so many people admire the opposite to themselves. Where too had I read that our brains are photographic, seeing something so quickly the first time that the impression is subconscious and when one looks again it appears already familiar?

'No, no!' I thought. 'I must not be ridiculous, I must keep myself strongly in control. I must not try to solve the problem of my love for Philip and his for Nada, by such easy methods.'

Determinedly I got to my feet, picked up my things again and went downstairs. I had not been in the drawing-room more than two minutes before Philip was announced. He greeted me with an affectionate kiss.

'You are ready?' he asked. 'I am sorry to hear your sister is in bed. I have sent her some flowers. I hope she likes them.'

'She will be thrilled,' I answered. 'I don't think there is much wrong with her, but a sore throat is always depressing.'

'Poor Angela, I am sorry for her,' he said. 'I'm sure she hates being laid up, but keep away from her. I couldn't bear you to be ill. You have always looked to me the embodiment of good health and good spirits.'

'Touch wood!' I said lightly. 'Don't tempt Fate.'

'Are you superstitious?' he teased.

'Sometimes,' I admitted. 'Aren't you?'

'I am a fatalist.'

'I think you tell yourself you are,' I said seriously, not thinking before I spoke, saying the first thing which came into my head.

'Why do you say that?' he asked.

'When things go wrong for people,' I answered, 'or they

feel that certain things might have been prevented happening, they ease their conscience by saying what must be—must be.'

Only as I finished my remark did I realise all that it implied and quickly before I could see Philip's expression or know if I had hurt him, I turned towards the door.

'Come on,' I said. 'We shall miss the big film, or arrive in the middle of it, which is worse.'

He followed me without comment. Only as we got into the car and drove off towards the cinema did he say:

'You are a strange person, Lyn. I want to get to know you better.'

'You might be disappointed,' I answered, but I felt glad, nevertheless, that he was interested.

22

I was particularly touched at the number of letters that I received from old servants. It is extraordinary how sometimes their affection for their employers lingers long after they have left their service—employers who, I am sure in many cases, forget them, from the moment they pack their bags and leave the house.

Mother, of course, has a genius for keeping in touch with people; housemaids that she has not seen for over twenty-five years receive presents from her every Christmas, and there are few people born on the estate whom she doesn't keep up with, whether they are in the colonies or merely away in some town.

I had letters from dozens of men and women who once had worked at Maysfield, many of whom I couldn't remember. But they spoke of my childhood days and enclosed a small present, often made by themselves, which touched me at times nearly to tears, because I knew to what trouble they had been in their efforts to please.

Among my letters one morning was one signed 'Ethel Henderson'. I had lain awake all night reading *The Evidences of Reincarnation* and was finding it difficult at nine o'clock in the morning to concentrate. I poured myself out a cup of black coffee and having thrown all the letters with the half-penny stamps on the floor, forced myself to attend to the letter I had already half-read without grasping its meaning. The notepaper was the cheap lined sort, the writing was round and uneducated, and I thought it must be from another ex-employee I had forgotten, until a single sentence sent me alert and interested back to the beginning again. It began:

Dear Lady Gwendolyn. I feel that I must write and wish you every happiness in your coming marriage. I know that you will not remember my name, even your mother may

*have forgotten it, but I was the nurse who assisted at
bringing you into the world, just nineteen years ago this
month. I have given up maternity work for a long time
now, and I am living near London. It would give me great
pleasure if there was a chance of seeing you at any time,
but if this would take up too much of your time I shall
quite understand. I have so often thought of your family
and noted with interest your sister's photographs in the society papers. Please remember me to your dear mother.*

*That you may have very many years of happiness with
Sir Philip Chadleigh, and that you will have strong and
beautiful children, is the wish of yours very sincerely,
Ethel Henderson.*

'I would like to see her,' I thought and taking up a piece
of paper, I dashed off a quick note asking her to call about
tea-time the following Friday.

I had a great many other letters to answer that morning,
and more than once when I started a letter, I found I was
writing rubbish and had to tear up what I had written and
begin again.

I had read every word of *The Evidences of Reincarnation.* The book was logical and full of what appeared to be
irrefutable arguments, but it was difficult for me to approach it with a clear mind. All the time I was trying to
apply to myself the examples quoted, seeking the personal
touch, longing to be convinced, yet afraid of being
credulous. Could I seriously contend that I was Nada? I
asked myself not once but a thousand times. The idea persisted within me, and more convincing to myself than anything else, was the deep love that I felt for Philip, which
had certainly not been fostered there by any passion or
tenderness on his part. I was sure it had not grown into
being; but had been there from the first moment of our acquaintance, a dormant quality within myself. But that, I
knew, was not evidence. I must have deeper and more
stronger proof.

I was torn by conflicting arguments, almost distraught,
until I could not bear the idea of being alone. I felt I must
talk to someone, certainly not about this most secret idea
within me, but about myself and Philip and, above all, my
coming marriage. There was no one to whom I could turn
but Elizabeth, but when I telephoned her at noon, she told

me that it was impossible for her to see me until the evening.

'But that's hopeless,' I said. 'I am dining out with Philip, he's taking me to some dinner party or other. I can't remember who is giving it, but I think it is one of his friends from the House.'

'I'm sorry, Lyn,' she said, 'but I'm just going to the Club. In fact I had actually opened the front door when I heard the telephone. I help give the children their luncheon on Tuesdays and look after them, their mothers come for them at five o'clock. After that we have a kind of social, you know the sort of thing—tea and buns and the most frightful amateur entertainment. They have even persuaded me to sing.'

'I had no idea you were so talented,' I teased her.

'Oh, you would be surprised!' she laughed. 'In fact, I am often surprised at myself.'

There was no doubt that Elizabeth sounded happier, and brighter and more alive than she had been for some time.

'Well, I won't tempt you from your duty,' I said. 'I will ring you up tomorrow morning and perhaps we can meet some other time this week.'

'Yes, please do, Lyn,' she said. 'I'm sorry about today. You know I want to see you, don't you?'

After we had rung off I sat looking moodily at the pile of letters that I ought to answer, wondering what I should do with myself. Suddenly I thought of what I would like to do. I would like to see Nada's grave.

I remembered when I was with Madame Melinkoff that among the photographs stacked together in her portfolio, was the snapshot of a tombstone.

'Is this your daughter's?' I had asked.

She had taken the photograph from me hastily.

'Philip sent it to me,' she said. 'I have never been to see it. I hate the idea of cemeteries. I wanted my darling to be buried alone, but I could not have my wish.'

She was so obviously disinclined to talk about it, that I had turned quickly to another photograph. Now I wished that I had not been so hasty. I knew why the desire was strong within me to look at Nada's grave—I was curious with a morbid urge to see the spot where, if what I half-believed was true, my first body lay. A body long crumpled into dust, but once mine and loved by Philip.

185

I walked downstairs to where Angela's secretary was typing in a small study which looked out on to the courtyard at the back of the house, a room never used by anyone else.

'Miss Jenkins,' I said, 'what is the biggest cemetery in London?'

She looked up at me with bright intelligent eyes.

'What a funny question, Lady Gwendolyn,' she said. 'I suppose Highgate Cemetery is the largest, but I really am not sure.'

'Has it been the largest for some years?' I asked. 'I mean, I don't want an absolutely modern one, which has just become popular, but where someone was likely to have been buried say twenty years ago.'

She consulted one of the reference books which were placed by her desk on a low shelf.

'Highgate certainly seems to be the largest,' she said, 'so I imagine it was started before the others. Of course, there is Kensal Green and St. Marylebone.'

'Thank you so much, Miss Jenkins,' I said. 'You are helpful.'

I was in the hall borrowing a pound from the butler—a habit we all had when we were short of change—when a message was brought me by one of the footmen to say that Sir Philip could be free about a quarter to four and he hoped that I would meet him somewhere.

'Tell Sir Philip I will go to Chadleigh House after luncheon and wait for him,' I said.

'Will you be in to luncheon today, m'lady?' the butler asked.

'No, I don't want any. Tell Lady Angela when she comes in I'll be back after tea.'

I felt any food would choke me. For the last week or so it had been an effort to eat, and Angela and Henry had teased me at meals, saying that at last they had hopes of seeing me with a fashionable figure.

At first I thought my abstinence must be due to love, for there is an old tradition that one is not hungry when one is emotional. But I think really it was the anxiety and the suspense of not being able to make up my mind about myself. In the last weeks I had been in a continual state of tension. Now I wondered were at last the gates of knowledge beginning to open for me? I felt at times that I was beginning to learn a little, to understand a microscopic part of what was happening to me, but always such optimism was followed by a depression which left me uncertain of everything.

I sat arguing with myself in the taxi I took to Highgate. It was far easier to pooh-pooh my own imagination, to laugh at my fancies, to tell myself that I was merely hysterical and that the wish was father to the thought, than to believe in rebirth. Because I loved Philip I naturally wanted to usurp the position that another woman already held in his heart. How childish I thought were my efforts to justify my jealousy. But I could not entirely quench my faith in my own intuition. I was groping blindly with an irrepressible hope towards a light of which, at present, I had seen but the faintest glimmer.

When I reached the cemetery I asked the taxi to wait for me; it was extravagant, but I felt I could not risk being stranded. There was something terrifying in the acre upon acre of tombstones. I could understand why Madame Melinkoff had not wanted to see her daughter's grave. For a moment I wished that I had not come. I hesitated at the gate and debated whether I should turn round and go away. 'This is morbid,' I told myself. 'What am I going to gain by going in.'

I forced myself, however, to visit the office and to find out where the grave was placed. Then, having received instructions, I walked for nearly ten minutes, along the well-kept paths lined with marble crosses, angels, urns and all the extraordinary fantasies with which people decorate the last resting places of those they have loved.

'When I come to die,' I decided, 'I shall be cremated and my ashes shall be scattered over an ordinary field. I should feel imprisoned in a place like this.' Then I laughed at my own fears. If I was Nada, there was no question of imprisonment! What did it matter to a discarded body if the spirit were free?

I reached the place to which I had been directed. I looked down a long line of graves. Then one, a perfectly plain tombstone caught my eye. It was different to the others because instead of being white, it was carved from an unusual stone of emerald green and the lettering was not black but silver, chiselled so deeply that at first glance it was hard to read. There were no flowers on the grave, which in its simplicity seemed to stand aloof from the others.

I drew nearer and bent down to read the slab.

In loving memory of Nada Melinkoff who departed this life on June 29th, 1920. May she rest in peace.

That was all. For a moment I stared at the words. Something about them seemed familiar, something which for a moment eluded me. I read the date again—June 29th was my birthday! It took several seconds for the full realisation of what I read to come to me. When it did I felt as though someone had struck me a blow. Nada had died the day I was born.

It was not difficult to realise in a flash that all my imaginings had been ridiculous. Five months before Nada had committed suicide I had been alive and kicking in my mother's womb. I could not by any stretch of fantasy pretend that the soul was not identical with the vital force of living. I was at least five months older than Nada.

I think I laughed out loud; to my surprise tears were pouring down my face. I stood before that green grave, trying vainly to control the sobs which shook me. I suppose it was a familiar sight, for the people moving about in the cemetery; I heard two or three pass me by, but I imagine they never even gave me a second glance. I turned and ran until I was outside the gate where my taxi was waiting for me.

'Drive to the West End,' I commanded.

It was some minutes before I wiped the last traces of tears from my eyes and began to repair the damage done to my face. I powdered my nose, then pulling off my shady hat, sat back with closed eyes.

What a fool I had been! What an idiot I had made of myself! This would teach me not to let my imagination run away with me. I offered up a prayer of thankfulness that I had not said anything to Philip; I saw how utterly fantastic my ideas had been. The mere coincidence of two voices being alike—that was really the sum total of any argument to back up my theory. That I had used out of the blue a few sentences which had once been spoken by a dead woman was of no significance, coincidence will always astound statisticians. I was desperately ashamed and ready to vow once again that I would keep my imagination in check. I would also, I hoped bitterly, be able to sleep with a peaceful mind, instead of lying awake, bothering myself over problems which never existed save in my own insanity.

I leant forward and told the taxi driver to stop at a tea shop in Baker Street. When he found one I paid him off and going in, forced myself to eat lunch—poached eggs, salad, rolls and butter and coffee. After I had finished, I spent a long time in the ladies' room freshening myself up, putting on my hat at a becoming angle and destroying with powder and lipstick, the last traces of my emotional outburst.

It was nearly three o'clock by that time and I walked briskly down Baker Street and through Portman Square towards Park Lane; I reached Philip's house just as a church clock chimed the quarter past.

He was waiting for me in the library downstairs.

'I have got bad news, Lyn,' he said.

'What is it?' I asked.

'An old aunt of mine,' he said, 'whom you haven't yet met who lives at Holland Park, has commanded us to go to a garden party she is giving this afternoon. I made every possible excuse, but to no avail. She insisted and I couldn't say we were both engaged. So I had to accept. Do you forgive me?'

'Of course I do,' I answered.

In a way I felt glad. Somehow I was not in the mood for a *tête à tête* with Philip. Our talks at such times had a personal significance for which, at the moment, I felt unprepared.

'You know,' he said as we got into the car, 'you are getting more of a stranger to me every day. I never see you for more than a snatched minute or so, either driving to or from a party.'

I was pleased with the compliment.

'Never mind,' I said jokingly. 'You may have far too much of me in the future.'

'I don't think that is likely,' he answered. 'Are you afraid?'

I shook my head.

'I have a feeling,' I said, 'that we shall never see too much of each other. Your job will keep you too busy and if your relations' warnings are to be believed, I shan't be exactly idle.'

'Poor Lyn!' he said, 'You are quite certain you wouldn't like to run away before it is too late, to go back to the peace of Maysfield and dream your days away in the garden?'

'I have given up dreaming,' I said sharply before I could stop myself.

He raised his eyebrows.

'Since when?' he asked.

'When I came to London,' I answered, 'I promised Mother that I wouldn't let my imagination run away with me. It is a long story, too shaming to tell anyone, but it has escaped me a little lately. Now at last I have got it to heel.'

'I like your imagination,' Philip said. 'Don't be too harsh with it.'

'I didn't think you knew I had one,' I said in surprise.

'No one could be with you for long,' Philip answered, 'without realising that you are always looking on far horizons that we mere mortals cannot see.'

I was so astonished at his remark that I turned round to look at him.

'Are you teasing me?' I asked.

'No, I mean it,' he said. 'What a funny child you are, Lyn. You are so perceptive where other people are concerned and so surprised if anyone noticed the smallest thing about you.'

'I suppose it is because I am not used to being noticed,' I answered humbly, but I was thrilled and rather excited at the thought.

I had an impulse to slip my hand into his, to ask him to tell me more, to tell me what he really thought about me. But I was afraid, afraid of the chill which might come to his voice, of the mask of restraint which might fall quickly over his face. 'Be careful,' I told myself. 'He is beginning to like you, beginning to take an interest in you. For heaven's sake go slow, don't frighten him!' The moment passed and we talked of other things until we arrived at the garden party.

We spent the usual dreary two hours talking to people I had never seen before, who were brought up continuously either by Philip or his aunt, to make my acquaintance. I drank some iced coffee which left me with a cold chilly spot in the centre of my tummy, and just as I was beginning to feel my legs and head were aching and that my smile was cracking my face, Philip signalled to me.

'Dare we escape?' he asked. 'I have just seen my aunt go into the house. Now is our opportunity.'

'For heaven's sake let's take it,' I said. 'I am exhausted.'

We crept out to the car like two children playing truant from school.

'Let's go home and have a real cup of tea,' Philip said, pulling down a small seat in the car for me to put my feet on.

'Shall we have to go to parties like that when we are married?' I asked.

'Hundreds of them,' he answered, 'and far worse!'

'Then the engagement is off,' I groaned.

'Too bad you can't give me back the ring,' he said.

I looked down at my ringless finger and laughed.

'It has been the subject of much comment amongst my relations.'

'I know,' he answered. 'I haven't really been neglectful. I have been having something made up for you. I believe we shall find it at the house when we get back.'

'It is sad that I must refuse it,' I said regretfully; at the same time I was excited.

I had wondered many times why Philip had been so long in giving me a ring, a fact of which Angela never ceased to remind me.

'So far, not so good,' she had said the night before. 'You have been engaged nearly a fortnight, Lyn, and a few orchids are all you have to show for it. You can't put them in the safe and keep them.'

'What do you expect me to do?' I had asked crossly. 'Demand diamonds?'

'Well, you might hint gently,' she suggested. 'I expect it has slipped his memory.'

I was so excited by the time we got to Chadleigh House that I could hardly wait for tea to be brought to us in Philip's sitting-room and for the butler and footmen to leave the room. When they had gone Philip tantalised me still further by insisting that I should pour out tea. Then he went to the drawer of his desk and opened it.

'How do you like receiving presents?' he asked. 'Do you catch them, or do you shut your eyes and guess?'

'Don't be a pig,' I answered. 'You know I am simply longing to see what you have got for me.'

'Very well then,' he said, 'here it is.'

Hurriedly I opened the big flat case that he handed to

191

me. The lid flew back, inside, lying on white velvet, was a wide bracelet, clips and a ring of emeralds and diamonds.

'Oh, Philip!' I exclaimed.

'Do you like them?' he asked.

'They're lovely,' I cried. 'I have never seen anything so wonderful.'

I clasped the bracelet round my wrist and slipped the ring on my finger, quite forgetting that conventionally Philip should have put it on for me.

'You are too young for ear-rings, as yet, Lyn,' he said. 'In a few years I will give you a pair to match. I have had the emeralds for some time—I bought them when I was in India and Cartier made them up for me. I think they suit you.'

'They would suit anyone,' I answered. 'They are the most wonderful stones I have ever seen.'

They were very dark, yet there was that deep flashing fire in their depths which can be found in the heart of all very beautiful stones. The emerald in the ring was nearly the size of a postage stamp and diamonds massed down the side of it encircled my whole finger. It flashed and glittered as I held it up to the windows and the sunshine caught it.

'I love them, Philip, I do really,' I said and walked towards him, holding up my face to be kissed.

He bent towards me and just for a moment his lips touched mine. As usual, at his merest touch I felt myself thrill. I would have given up all the emeralds in the world at that moment to be able to fling my arms round his neck, to hold him close and tell him how much I loved him. Instead I contented myself with a low-voiced 'thank you,' and turned away.

'When we are married,' he said, 'I will give you my mother's jewels. Most of them will have to be reset, but the stones are very fine. They are family heirlooms, of course, and at the moment are safely housed in the bank.'

'I don't think I could ever want anything more than these,' I said, looking down at my own emeralds.

Philip smiled.

'You will change your mind,' he said. 'In a few years you will be saying, "What, only emeralds? My dear Philip, you can't imagine that they are sufficient! I require rubies, sapphires, pearls and diamonds".'

'Wait and see,' I answered. 'I'm easily satisfied.'

It was nearly six o'clock when I left Chadleigh House

and Philip said he would take me home. As the car drove up Park Lane we saw two or three fire-engines coming towards us. They were not ringing their bells, but proceeding slowly as though they were going home.

Philip wound down the communicating window between us and the chauffeur.

'Has there been a fire, Hodgkins?' he asked.

'I think there must have been, Sir Philip,' the man answered. 'Three or four engines passed about an hour ago, just after you and her ladyship had gone into the house.'

'I wish I had known,' I said. 'I would love to see a big fire, it must be a magnificent sight.'

'I wonder where it was?' Philip said curiously.

He turned the window up again and we talked until we reached home.

'Come in for a moment and see Angela,' I said. 'I have been out all day and she may be annoyed with me. You will put her in a good temper.'

'All right,' he said. 'But I can't stay long. I have got a man coming to see me before I dress for dinner.'

As it happened, Angela for once hardly had anything to say to Philip. She was so filled with admiration for my jewellery that she could talk of nothing else.

'They are the most marvellous emeralds I have ever seen,' she kept saying. 'Really, Lyn, you are a lucky girl.'

'I thought that emeralds were supposed to be unlucky,' Henry said—trying to tease me, but obviously impressed by Philip's gift.

'That is a superstition,' Philip answered, 'which is entirely based on the fact that, like opals, emeralds chip very easily. If you drop an emerald on a hard substance, it is quite easy to cause a bad flaw.'

'How awful,' I said, looking at my ring in alarm. 'I shall be terrified of knocking it against something.'

'You will have to have a silver dress in your trousseau,' Angela said ruminatively. 'Shimmering silver with green shoes, and perhaps a touch of green at the waist.'

'I can see the conversation is going to get very feminine,' Philip said with a smile. 'Will you forgive me if I leave you? As Lyn knows, I have got an appointment before dinner.'

'I will come and see you off,' I said.

I walked downstairs with him towards the car. Outside

there was a policeman talking to the chauffeur. He saluted as Philip came out. The chauffeur opened the door of the car.

'The constable tells me, Sir Philip, that the fire was in Andover Street. A very bad one it was. It was at the Rose of England Clubhouse; several people were injured.'

I gave a cry of horror and clutched Philip's arm.

'Elizabeth!' I said. 'Elizabeth was there!'

'What do you mean?' he asked.

'Elizabeth Batley,' I explained. 'She is working at the Club. She told me this morning that she was going there.'

We stood staring at each other for a moment, then Philip slipped his arm through mine.

'We will telephone,' he said firmly, 'but I am sure it is all right.'

We walked back into the house and into Henry's sitting-room, which opened off the hall. Philip looked quickly through the telephone book then dialled a number.

'I'm ringing Elizabeth's home,' he said, 'they are certain to have news of her.' He held on for several minutes, there was no answer.

'One minute,' I said, and opening the door of the study, I ran through the hall and back into the street. The constable was still outside. 'Do you know,' I asked him, 'where the injured people have been taken? What would be the most likely hospital?'

He thought for a moment.

'I should think they would go to St. Anthony's Hospital, miss. It is not far from Andover Street. Yes, that would be it, St. Anthony's Hospital, Kitchener Square.'

I rushed back to Philip.

'Try St. Anthony's Hospital,' I said. 'The policeman thinks that anyone who was injured would have been taken there.'

I waited with impatience while he found the number and got through to the hospital.

'This is Sir Philip Chadleigh speaking,' he said. 'Would you be kind enough to give me the names of any patients brought to you from the fire which took place in Andover Street? You will enquire? . . . Thank you very much. . . . I will hold on.'

'Did they say that the injured people had been taken there?' I asked.

He shook his head.

'They are never very informative,' he answered.

I walked up and down the room; I felt I could not keep still.

'Don't panic, Lyn,' Philip said, his voice very kind. 'After all, it is a hundred to one against anything having happened to Elizabeth, even if she was there.'

'I feel worried about her,' I answered. 'I can't help it.'

'Yes, hullo,' he was speaking into the telephone again. 'Yes . . . yes . . . what's that name? . . . will you repeat it? Batley . . . you are quite certain that the name is Elizabeth Batley? You have got in touch with her relatives? Thank you very much. I am a relative. I shall come round immediately. Perhaps you would inform the matron that I am on my way? Yes. . . . Sir Philip Chadleigh. Thank you very much.'

'She is hurt?' I said breathlessly.

'She is in the hospital,' he answered. 'We will go there at once.'

23

St. Anthony's Hospital is a small congested-looking building from the outside, whose height seems out of proportion
to the other houses in the square, but inside there is calm
and peace which even I, in my agitated, distressed state,
could feel. It is managed by nuns and the Mother Superior,
who received us in her own room, is a little old woman,
wrinkled and bowed with age, but who, nevertheless, has
the most beautiful and gentle expression I have ever seen in
my life.

'Sit down,' she said to Philip and myself, and taking a
high-backed refectory chair, faced us. 'You have come
about Elizabeth Batley? I have just been speaking to her
mother, who is unfortunately in the country.'

'Will you tell us what has happened?' Philip asked. 'You
see we knew nothing until a few moments ago when we
heard that there had been a fire at the Rose of England
Club in Andover Street. Miss Batley had told my fiancée
that she would be there this afternoon, and naturally we
were alarmed.'

'I don't know how the fire started,' the Mother Superior
said. 'But I think it was in the basement of the building.
The Club, as you know, consists of a few rooms at the very
top. It was an old building and the fire-escapes were completely inadequate. Most of the children were got out
before the fire-engines arrived, but several older people
who had been assisting the evacuation were trapped on one
of the lower floors. Among them was Miss Batley, and
before she could be rescued, the ceiling above her fell in.'

'She is not dead?' I asked. My voice came through dry
lips and was barely audible.

'She is not dead,' the Mother Superior replied, 'but she is
severely injured. I think you would rather know the truth,
so I must tell you that she is in a critical condition. Timber
fell on her, pinning her beneath it and crushing the lower

part of her body. Her legs were badly burnt, also her hands.'

'What do the doctors think?' Philip asked.

'The specialists are with her now,' the Mother Superior replied. 'Our own house surgeon realised that he could do very little for her and we telephoned at once to Mr. Gossett and Sir Randolph Newton.'

'I know them both,' Philip answered. 'She couldn't be in better hands.'

'I had met Miss Batley once before,' the Mother Superior went on. 'The Rose of England is not a Catholic organisation, but many of the children who go there from the district around here are of our Faith. She brought me a patient only a week ago, a small boy who had had an accident while playing in the streets. I thought then that she was a girl of character and courage. What she has done today has proved it.'

'She will live?' I asked.

The Mother Superior got to her feet and looked at me very kindly.

'My dear,' she answered, 'that is in the hands of a far greater Doctor than any we can provide.'

She touched my shoulder, then moving towards the door said, 'If you will excuse me, I will find out if there is any news.'

She left us alone and instinctively I turned towards Philip, holding out my hands. He took them in his and held them tightly. Neither of us said a word, there seemed to be nothing to say. We could only sit and wait. I was praying with all my heart that Elizabeth might live.

We were sitting side by side, hand in hand, when the Mother Superior returned. We got to our feet.

'Sir Randolph Newton would like to speak to you, Sir Philip,' she said.

He went towards the door.

'Please let me come with you, I want to hear too,' I pleaded.

I saw his eyes meet those of the Mother Superior's. Gently she shook her head.

'I will come back in a moment,' he said, turning to me. 'I think it would be better if I went alone, if you don't mind.'

I walked to the window, which looked out on to another wing of the hospital. There were many curtainless windows. What was behind them, I wondered? How many people suffering; how many holding precariously on to life, on the verge of slipping away into the unknown?

I was suddenly afraid of it all—of the suffering, of this closeness to death, afraid also of the news about Elizabeth, which I knew instinctively was bad, so bad that they were telling Philip before they told me. I was standing waiting for him when a few minutes later he crossed the room to my side.

'Lyn,' he said, looking down at me. 'You have got to be very brave.'

'I know,' I answered. 'Is she dead?'

'She is dying,' he said tersely. 'Nothing can save her. The whole of the lower part of her body is crushed. There's not even a chance of an operation.'

I stood quite still, feeling a strange calmness. I felt it couldn't be true, it was too terrible, too frightful to comprehend, that Elizabeth, whom I had spoken to that very morning, was going to die.

'She is conscious,' Philip went on. 'How long she will remain so, they don't know. They hope she will still be alive when her mother arrives, but they rather doubt it. Would you like to see her?'

'Can I?' I asked eagerly.

'If you would like to,' he answered. 'Sir Randolph says it doesn't matter one way or the other, and as she is out of pain, there is no reason why you shouldn't.'

'I would like to go to her,' I said.

'You are all right?' he asked.

I put my hand in his. It was cold, but I knew it was quite steady.

'I am quite all right,' I replied.

We went up in the lift with the Mother Superior, who was waiting for us in the hall. I felt as though I was in a dream. An extraordinary detachment had come to me. I wanted to pinch myself, to say 'Wake up, realise what is happening. Elizabeth is dying! You are taking it too calmly, don't you care?'

We walked along several passages. Through the open doors of the wards I could see women and children in coloured bed-jackets sitting up in bed. Some of them were laughing and chattering, while from one room there came the cry of a tiny baby. The Mother Superior opened a door

198

at the end of a long passage. She beckoned me. I went in alone.

I had to pass round the corner of a screen before I could see Elizabeth. The blinds were half lowered and the room was in twilight. After a second or so my eyes grew accustomed to the dimness. I could see Elizabeth lying in bed. She was very pale and her fair hair was smoothed back from her forehead, otherwise she looked much as usual. Her eyes were closed and she might have been asleep. I drew nearer. A nun who had been sitting by the side of her bed moved noiselessly to the other end of the room.

'Elizabeth!' I whispered.

Very slowly her eyelids lifted. There came a faint weak smile of recognition.

'Hullo, Lyn,' she said.

I had to bend near her to catch her words.

'Darling, are you all right?' I asked. It was a silly question, but I just couldn't think of anything to say.

'Quite,' she answered. 'I'm not afraid.'

For the first time I felt that tears were near my eyes. There was something choking me, something in my throat that prevented me from speaking at all. I saw her lips moving again.

'Take care of Philip,' she said.

'You know I will,' I said.

She smiled again. Then her eyelids drooped as though she was tired. Blindly I groped my way towards the door, but the nun reached it before I did and opened it for me. Philip was waiting outside.

I took him by the arm, holding on to him so fiercely that I knew my fingers must be digging their way into his flesh.

'Listen,' I said. 'Elizabeth loves you, she has always loved you. Go in and kiss her, let her die happy.'

I couldn't see the expression of his face. The tears by this time were pouring down my face. I felt him move away from me. Then a firm cool hand took mine and led me down the passage.

'Come, dear,' the Mother Superior's gentle voice said.

We went down in the lift together. She led me into her own room.

'Drink this,' she said, putting a medicine glass into my hand.

I did as I was told, for I was quite incapable of argument. I felt sal volatile burn its way down my throat, and putting down the glass, I gripped my hands together to prevent the storm of weeping which I felt rising within me, threatening to overwhelm me.

'You must be brave,' the Mother Superior said, 'for I think that Elizabeth Batley is not unhappy.'

'It is not that, she has had so little in her life, so little happiness, that I would like her to have lived longer and perhaps found some of the things she has missed.'

'Perhaps her great happiness is coming to her now,' the Mother Superior suggested.

I looked at her and a question burst from my lips.

'You are quite certain there is an after-life?'

'Quite sure,' she said simply with a tender smile. And there was a sudden radiance in her face which made her, old and wrinkled as she was, seem almost a beautiful woman.

There was no time to say more for the door opened and Philip came in. He was very pale and I knew he was upset and desperately disturbed, despite his composure. He put a hand on my shoulder, as though to comfort me. Then he turned to the Mother Superior.

'Shall we stay?' he asked. 'Is there anything more we can do?'

'Nothing,' she answered. 'I think you would be wise to take your fiancée home. Lady Batley should be here in another three-quarters of an hour. If you would like to see her, I could telephone you.'

'Perhaps you will telephone if she needs me,' Philip answered. 'And anyway, would you let me know if there is any change?'

'Of course,' she answered. 'You will be at Chadleigh House?'

'We are going there now,' Philip replied.

I held out my hand to the Mother Superior.

'Good-bye,' I said, 'and thank you.'

'Good-bye, my child,' she replied. 'God bless you.'

In the street outside the hospital small boys were gathered admiringly round the car and being kept from touching the paint only by the stern admonitions of the chauffeur. We got in quickly and drove off. I made no protest when Philip directed the car to Chadleigh House. When he arrived he gave instructions to the butler that he would speak to Angela and also the people with whom we

200

were dining this evening. I don't know what he said because I went up to his sitting-room ahead of him and when he came upstairs, I was lying on the sofa with my eyes closed.

'I have put off the party tonight,' he said, 'and explained to your sister that you are here. I have ordered a little light dinner to be served up here on trays. I felt you would rather have that than any formality.'

I was grateful to him for his thought and care.

He lit a cigarette and came and sat down beside me.

'Shut your eyes, Lyn,' he said. 'Try and sleep.'

I didn't want to talk so I just smiled at him and shut my eyes as he told me, although I knew that sleep was the last thing that would come to me at that moment.

It must have been nearly an hour later when the ringing of the telephone startled both of us. Philip got up and walked over to his desk. I heard him say:

'Yes, it is Sir Philip Chadleigh speaking. Thank you for letting me know. Has Lady Batley arrived? She has gone home? Thank you very much. I will come round in the morning. Good night.'

I got up from the sofa.

'She is dead,' I said, making a statement rather than asking a question.

'She died quite peacefully about twenty minutes ago,' he answered. 'She slipped into unconsciousness soon after we left her. Her mother did not get to her in time.'

'I am glad,' I said, then added, because I felt that my words needed some explanation: 'Glad that you were the last person to see her. She loved you, Philip.'

'I know,' he answered. 'It was all so hopeless. What could I do?'

'I feel sure it wasn't your fault,' I said. 'Elizabeth's family were so keen on her making a brilliant marriage and you were kind to her. She told me all about it and she never blamed you in the slightest. She only loved you.' My voice broke.

Philip put an arm round my shoulders.

'Try not to be unhappy, Lyn,' he said.

'I'm not really unhappy,' I answered. 'I think that Elizabeth will regret very little of what she is leaving behind. It's just . . . oh, I don't know : . . it seems so useless to love, to suffer and just to pass on like that, for no reason.'

'Isn't everyone's life very much the same?' Philip asked.

'Perhaps,' I replied. Then I asked him the question I had already asked once that evening. 'Do you believe in an after-life?'

He released his hold of me and walked away and sat in one of the low chairs at the other side of the fireplace.

'I don't know,' he said.

I sat down on the hearth-rug at his feet and looked up at him.

'Why don't we know?' I asked. 'Why should someone like the Mother Superior have such complete faith, such absolute knowledge, yet you and I are uncertain?'

'I would give my whole life now, at this moment, if I could be certain,' Philip answered, and there was an agony in his voice.

'Why?' I asked the question almost beneath my breath. I was afraid to ask, afraid that he would turn away from me, yet I knew with an extraordinary clarity that the moment had come, the moment when Philip was going to speak to me, was going to tell me the truth about himself.

'Why?' he questioned. 'Because if I knew, I could be at rest. I could find peace and I could be free from the torture that I have been suffering now ever since she died.'

'Elizabeth was not afraid to die,' I said gently.

'I know,' he answered. 'But Nada was. She screamed, Lyn, and I have never been able to forget that sound.'

'Why did she do it?' I whispered.

'I don't know,' he answered. 'If only I knew, if only she would come back and tell me why she did it! Do you suppose I haven't been asking myself that question, day after day, night after night, year after year, why did she do it? We were not really quarrelling, in fact I thought she was teasing me. I thought she was testing my love, that at any moment she would smile at me and we would be in each other's arms. She had her moments of depression—what artiste doesn't? But they were transitory affairs—mere clouds in a blue sky of happiness. I loved her too much to ever treat anything she said to me lightly, but I knew how quickly she could change from tears to laughter. I was gentle to her, I said nothing that she could have interpreted wrongly. But suddenly she flung herself from the balcony in front of my eyes and as she fell, she screamed.'

'She must have had a reason,' I insisted. 'She must have.'

'But what reason?' he asked. 'Marriage, of course, is the

obvious one, but we had talked about it so often. She had been the one who said we could never get married. I can hear her voice now saying, "Philip, you have your career and I am so proud of it. I want you to succeed and I am content to be the shadow behind the throne, the woman in the background". Then that last day, that evening when she came to me, she started to talk about marriage. I thought she was joking. I swear to you, Lyn, that I thought she was joking. I told her that I had to go away, only for a short time, but I couldn't take her with me. While we were arguing, while we were still talking, as I thought half in fun, she fell.'

'It was an accident,' I said. 'Philip, it was an accident, it must have been.'

'If I could believe that,' he said, 'I could be at rest. But how can I ever know? She loved me, loved me as no woman had ever loved me before, or will love me again. If she loved me as much as that, or if she is still in existence—spirit, soul or ghost, would she not have given me some sign, have come to me, if only in a dream, to tell me that she did not kill herself because of me, that I was not her murderer?'

His voice was bitter and broken with the terrible rasping pain in it. It was more agonising for me than if he had shown me a bleeding wound.

'Don't,' I said. 'Don't Philip! Perhaps she can't. Perhaps it is impossible for her.'

'If anything is impossible to love,' he answered, 'then there is no God, there is no hope in the world, there is no salvation. Oh yes, you may think I am raving, but I have thought it all out. I have called Nada when I was alone until I thought that my very thoughts must materialise her before me. I have called her from the mountain tops and from the quiet places; I have pleaded with her, I have beseeched any God who had her in his keeping to let her free, just for one moment, to bring me some rest, some relief. But no, she is dead, she must be dead, or otherwise if she knew of my need I am sure she would come back. She could not fail me.'

He stopped and dropped his face in his hands.

'Oh my dear, my dear!' I said, but I dared not touch him.

24

The barriers were down. Elizabeth in her death had helped Philip as she had never been able to help him in life by her love for him.

I hardly dared to breathe, move, or do anything which might break the spell. At last Philip was talking to me; at last there was no longer that terrible restraint which had kept us apart all these long weeks and made us polite strangers. An overwhelming feeling of tenderness swept over me, and I knew I could now be both a help and a comfort to him.

There was a silence for what seemed a long time. The only sound in the room was the faint ticking of the clock on the mantelpiece, and far away in the distance, the gentle roar of passing traffic.

At last in a low and calm voice I said:

'Won't you tell me about Nada? I have often wished that I could have known her.'

Without looking up, without taking his hands from before his eyes, Philip answered me.

'She was a strange person; looking back now, remembering our many conversations together, I feel as though I accredited her with far greater intelligence and cleverness than she really possessed. For it wasn't what she knew, it wasn't her knowledge, which made her mean so much to me, apart from the love which we had for each other, it was something which is difficult to explain, yet such an intrinsic part of her that no one could try and describe Nada without mentioning it. It was, I think, her capacity for bringing out the best in anyone whom she came in contact with. She was a stimulant; there was something vital in the attention and interest which she gave to everyone whom she was fond of and to a great many other people who meant little to her, but certainly valued her friendship.

'From a man's point of view she made one ambitious; she made one want to succeed. My relations, my friends, thought I was wasting my time with Nada. It is laughable when I know that from her friendship came every ideal, every ambition, I have ever possessed. She drove me on, not exactly in words, but by just being with me, encouraging me, making me want—perhaps more than anything else—to lay the spoils of my victory at her feet.

'Even today after nineteen long years without her, her influence still touches all I do. When she died I tried to give up my career, to throw away the plans we had made together for my future; it was no use, I could not do it. I came back and when the Prime Minister sent for me the other day, his first words were, "Chadleigh, I have read the papers you sent to the India Office—you are the man we are looking for".'

'What papers?' I asked.

'A memorandum,' Philip explained. 'A memorandum started many years ago when I went to India to forget my misery and to escape from what life here was going to mean without Nada. I started then, because it had been the country of her birth, to study conditions, the people, their customs and their aspirations and, of course, in the years to come I continued. It was so interesting and so vitally important to the Empire. So today, through Nada, they want me to be Viceroy. It is funny if you think about it.' He spoke bitterly.

'She would have been proud,' I whispered.

'So proud,' he answered, 'that I can't believe that somewhere, somehow, she doesn't know, that she is not glad, glad and pleased with me.'

He got up abruptly from his chair and walked towards the window.

'I have no right to talk to you like this,' he said. 'Why do you let me?'

'You have every right,' I answered. 'When you asked me to marry you I knew about Nada—but I accepted you.'

'Lyn,' he said earnestly, turning round, 'you must believe me when I tell you that you are the only woman whom I could ask to share my life. From the moment I met you, you were different to all the others—it was not only your voice.'

'My voice is the same as hers?' I questioned.

'Exactly. It is uncanny, unbelievable,' he said. 'The day we met in the House of Commons, I went home that night and for the first time Nada was not alone in my thoughts. You were there too. One could not imagine two women more utterly different in appearance, yet, sometimes, I think that you have the same characteristics. You both invite one's confidence—you don't know, Lyn, how difficult it has been for me these last weeks, not to talk to you. I wanted to explain myself, to be frank with you. How stilted that sounds, but you have the gift of making people wish to open their hearts—Nada was the same. She also was frank, open and free from all pose and posturing. You are both very unlike the average modern woman.'

He stood looking down at me, but I felt he was seeing not my upturned face but another, a smaller, more beautifully-shaped one.

'You are perhaps surprised,' he said, although I had said nothing, 'that Nada was not more oriental. Due perhaps to her mother, she had a very English outlook on life. Her art was a thing apart—on the stage she was half-mystic, a creature inspired. Outside the theatre you would never have known that she was a star, she was too big, too much of a genius perhaps to bother with affectations. A child in many ways, but a child with every lovely feminine charm, one was never quite certain of her. Yet she said what she thought, and she had none of the tortured, twisted ways of thinking which makes the oriental such a difficult creature either to understand or to rule.'

It was immaterial but I was glad Nada had been like that. Now that I could no longer link myself with her, she had become again the frightening menace to my happiness she had been before. That I was not fighting someone steeped in intrigue and seduction, made it somehow easier. I could think of her as a girl, like myself, someone who had loved Philip simply and whole-heartedly, even as I loved him.

'Tell me more,' I said. 'Tell me how you met her.'

I knew now that he was glad to talk and I realised what I had thought long ago was right—all this had been bottled up inside him; he had no confidant, no one with whom he could discuss his own unhappiness, his loss and his utter desolation of heart. For him to speak was like the bursting of a dam when the water had been pressed against it with tempestuous strength for a very long time.

He sat down again.

'It was early in 1917,' he began. 'I had been in the trenches for over six months without leave. I came back to London in April, I can't tell you, Lyn, what it was like, to see green fields, trees that had not been shattered, torn and splintered by shells, gardens that were not ploughed up, strewn with barbed wire or dead bodies. There was the luxury, too, of baths, of clean clothes, of freedom from mud and the stench of death.

'It was just before the Easter holiday and so many people had gone away. I accepted an invitation to go to some friends in the country, but decided to spend a few nights in London before I went. The first night I dined with two men. We did ourselves well; one of them was on leave, another had just been discharged from hospital and was waiting for orders to return to France. We were young and all glad to be alive. We decided to paint the town as red as we could, to eat, drink and be merry.

'When dinner was over about ten o'clock, we went off to the Alhambra to see Violet Lorraine in the "Bing Boys". There wasn't a seat to be had, and we had dined too well to feel particularly cheerful about standing through the rest of the performance. We told the driver to go to the London Pavilion. There was a revue of some sort on there—we had no idea if it was good or bad.

'We managed to get three not very good seats and we had no sooner taken our places when the chorus, who had been singing and dancing as we entered, went off amidst a roar of applause. The stage was darkened. Very very softly, so that at first one was hardly aware of it, a strange flute-like music was played. It was the first time I had ever heard real Indian music. The front curtains of the stage parted to reveal a set all in silver, shimmering silver, which just caught here and there a glint of weird emerald-green light. Then, down the centre a figure seemed to float, rather than dance.

'I couldn't possibly describe Nada's dance to you. All I know is that the first time I saw it it held me spellbound, and that ever afterwards, even when I was seeing her practically every night, I could never escape that strange, almost hypnotised feeling which she aroused in me. One forgot everything; one moved in the same harmony that she did, driven by the strange music which accompanied her, into what was almost a trance-like excitement beyond

207

all reason. I don't think I was the only person to feel like that, for whenever Nada appeared in any theatre, however difficult the audience, it was hushed, and silence remained quite unbroken until she left the stage.

'What happened to my friends that night I shall never know. When Nada's turn was finished, I made my way round to the stage door. I sent in my card. Nada told me afterwards that never before in her stage career had she accepted an invitation from someone unknown to her. She came out to supper with me. I can't tell you about that evening. Afterwards it became one of many evenings, of days, weeks and months that we spent together. It was the prelude to much happiness and to an agony of unhappiness when I went back to the front.

'All I know is that we both meant something stupendous to each other—for me from that very first moment in the theatre, for her when she held my card in her hand and decided to see me. Of course, later, I was to have my doubts, my fears. I was to ask myself whether it was wise, whether I was throwing away my career.

'Nada was half oriental, but I don't think it would have made the slightest difference had she been a coal-black Negress. There was something between us far deeper than the superficialities of race or colour; we could not escape each other. From the moment we met we were tied together as surely as if we had been joined by the Church and the State.

'We had three years together—three years, Lyn, in which I grew up. I learnt what it was to live, to be alive to the intrinsic beauty of humanity, to know the best happiness this world can offer, when a man and a woman are really in union—mentally and physically. That is what I could never understand afterwards—that she could have been unhappy and that I should not have known it. She never pretended, never in any way tried to deceive me about herself. We discussed marriage so often. It was always she who said it was impossible.

'But what is the point of going over it all again? After nineteen years the question has never left me. I have tried every way to answer it, I have done everything in my power to find peace. Lyn, if you marry me, you marry a man who is haunted, not by someone he loved—that would be easy—but by a lack of understanding of himself, by a question to which he can find no answer.'

I said nothing, but I slipped my hand into his.

'I have destroyed her pictures,' he went on. 'I have burnt every one of them so that no one will ever see them again, but I can't destroy her memory, or pretend to you that I have forgotten her.'

'I don't want you to,' I said firmly. 'Don't you understand, Philip, that we can never build any sort of life together unless we are completely frank with each other? I am so grateful to you for having told me about Nada. I have wanted to know the truth. I want you now to promise me just one thing.'

'Yes?' he questioned.

'Promise me,' I said solemnly, 'that you will talk about her quite normally to me. Don't be frightened that I shall be jealous, resentful or anything silly like that. Tell me what she said, what she did and what she suggested to you. Say it quite naturally, "Nada and I did this together," or "Nada wanted me to do that." What does it matter? We are two women both loving you and perhaps she would like me to carry on the work that she started.'

He bent forward and put his arms around me.

'You are so very sweet, Lyn,' he said.

For a moment he pressed his cheek against mine.

'And so very lovable. It is not fair of any man to offer you the second best.'

'I shall be happy with whatever you offer me,' I answered. 'I love you, Philip.'

'Oh my dear, my dear,' he said humbly.

I felt close to him at that moment and extraordinarily happy, perhaps unreasonably so. Then the telephone rang. It was Lady Batley. As I heard Philip express his sympathy over the telephone, thoughts of Elizabeth came flooding back to me. I wondered, also, what Philip had said to her, but I felt that that was one of the things I could never ask him. Those last minutes were too intimate with someone so very near to death, someone who had loved him hopelessly for nearly eight years.

Poor Elizabeth! She had gone from the world unwanted and, to a great extent, unmourned. She would leave no gap in anyone's life. Her sisters might even be pleased that she was not there to be an encumbrance upon the exchequer and their various social activities. Lady Batley, I felt, had never loved her eldest daughter. She had only hoped that she would make a brilliant marriage and had been disappointed that she had failed.

How few girls in Elizabeth's class of life radiate any influence outside their own home. Lilies of the field, they are of little importance in a community, yet, I knew that had the opportunity come to Elizabeth, she would have made an admirable wife for any man, whatever his position in the world. She would have been a conscientious mother and she would have faced poverty and privation and suffering with a courage which came more from breeding than from any personal attribute. It was all such a hideous waste of life, and of being alive, and I questioned—as so many people must have done before me— whether the stratas of sociabilities into which civilisation tries to cramp mankind, were either wise or expedient for the whole.

Philip was still talking.

'But you must leave all that to me, Cousin Alice,' I heard him say. 'Please . . . you know I should be delighted to do it for the poor child. . . . Yes, just ask them to send me the bill and don't think about it again.'

I smiled cynically. Her daughter had not yet been dead many hours, but already Lady Batley was worrying about the cost of the funeral and was ensuring by her own methods that the expenses should not be hers.

'I will come round in the morning,' Philip went on. 'Now, don't worry, try and get a good night's rest. I know what a shock this has been to you. Good-bye.'

I made no comment on what I had overheard. Instead I said:

'What about dinner? It is nearly nine o'clock.'

'I told them I would ring when we were ready,' Philip answered wearily. 'Would you like something to eat?'

'I think it would be good for both of us,' I answered.

I was not hungry, but I was thinking of him. I felt now, more than ever before, that I must look after him; he was my trust and he had been committed to my care.

I suppose to every woman in love there comes the moment when her love becomes a two-edged sword, driving her on to a further and deeper sacrifice of self, so that ultimately there is no way that she can escape from her own love. At that moment I felt the same tenderness for Philip, the same anxiety for his well-being, as I would have had, had he been my son. I was well aware what it must

210

have cost him to break down the reserve of years. Emotionally he was exhausted; his vitality had drained away from him and he looked pale and tired.

When the butler brought the trays he asked Philip what we would drink. Philip looked enquiringly at me.

'I think champagne would do us both good,' I said.

It was a strange thing to ask for on the night of Elizabeth's death; champagne has always seemed to me a wine to be used for celebrating, but I knew that Elizabeth would understand and be glad.

25

As so often happens, one suffers reaction to shock and to emotion, not at the time, but later. Elizabeth died on Tuesday and it was not until Friday morning when I woke up aching in every limb, with a headache which almost prevented me from seeing and closed my eyes, that I knew Nature was taking its toll.

Friday was also the day of the funeral and I went with Philip that morning and watched Elizabeth carried to her last resting place in the little churchyard at her home, which was about an hour's run from London.

Lady Batley, hustling, inefficient and with what seemed to me a singular lack of sorrow, invited us both to stay to luncheon when the service was ended. But I insisted on coming back to London and we had a cold meal at Chadleigh House about two o'clock. When it was over, I felt so ill that I told Philip I thought I would go home and lie down.

'You are all right?' he asked anxiously.

'It is only a headache,' I replied.

It had become worse, due, I think, to the effort I had made at keeping my composure at the funeral. I have always despised people who make a scene in public and as the hymns were sung and the beautiful words of the burial service read over the narrow grave, I tried to think of Elizabeth as being secure from all the troubles and difficulties which were still for us here.

'If only I knew,' I said to myself again, 'what happened after death. If only I was sure that she was happy and at peace!'

I felt like Philip, as I raged against the impotence of not knowing, of asking an eternal question to which I could find no answer.

Philip motored me back to the house.

'Take care of yourself, Lyn darling,' he said. 'You are very important to me.'

He raised my hand to his lips. I was thrilled by his words; it was the first time he had called me 'darling', but since Tuesday night I had felt that he had begun to rely on me, to want me, to treat me with an intimacy which had never been there before. It was not love, I was quite aware of that, but it was tenderness and affection, and for the moment I was content.

I went up to my room and lay down, having first taken an aspirin. Later when I was asleep someone knocked at my door.

'Who is it?' I asked.

'Miss Henderson has called to see you m'lady,' the butler answered. 'She says she has an appointment.'

I had forgotten all about her.

'Oh Heavens!' I exclaimed. 'Ask her to come up. And bring tea up here.'

Almost irritably I remembered the letter I had written to the old maternity nurse. How long ago it seemed since Tuesday, the day that Elizabeth had died, the day that Philip and I had come to a new understanding. I propped myself up on the pillows. When Nurse Henderson was shown into the room I held out my hand in what I hoped was a cordial greeting.

'Will you forgive me for asking you up to my bedroom?' I said. 'I have had such an awful headache all day. I thought I would lie down.'

She was a short, plump little woman with snow-white hair which was swept up from her forehead in the old-fashioned Edwardian manner. Her hat was a severe felt and she was carrying an umbrella and mackintosh, although it was a hot, sunny day. Gold-rimmed pince-nez were clipped to her nose and attached by a fine gold chain to a circular guard on her chest. The lenses magnified her eyes which were surprisingly bright.

'I am quite used to bedrooms,' she answered with a smile. 'And it is very kind of you to see me, Lady Gwendolyn.'

'It was so nice of you to write to me,' I answered. 'I know my Mother will be most interested when I tell her. I expect to be going home next week-end.'

'I hope you will remember me to Lady Maysfield,' Nurse Henderson said. 'It is a long time since I have seen her.'

'I think you said in your letter that you had given up working now,' I answered. 'Do you like living in London?'

'Yes and no,' she answered. 'If you get my meaning. I live with my married daughter and her husband. I am comfortable, but I miss my job. It is hard to be idle after forty-seven years of continuous work.'

'It must be a change,' I said.

'I am over sixty-five, though you wouldn't think it, would you?'

'No, indeed,' I said politely.

'I have brought over three hundred children into the world,' Nurse Henderson said. 'That's private patients, of course. I don't count my hospital training.'

'And I was one of them!' I exclaimed 'What number was I?'

'Well, there Lady Gwendolyn, I can't answer that off hand. I should have to look it up in my book. I have kept a diary all the years I was at work, and very interesting reading it makes. I have often thought of publishing some of it, but perhaps it would be rather indiscreet.'

'Especially for the people who try to keep their birthdays quiet,' I smiled.

'Well, you don't have to worry about that as yet,' Nurse Henderson answered. 'Now let me see, you will be nineteen next Sunday, won't you?'

'You must confess that you looked that up,' I said. 'Don't tell me you have remembered the date after nineteen years.'

'Oh no! I admit that,' Nurse Henderson confessed. 'Although it should be easy to remember this year, as it was a Sunday on which you were born.'

'Was it?' I asked.

'When I read my diary I remembered it so well,' Nurse Henderson said. 'I only got back from a case on the Saturday. I was living then with my parents at Purley and on Sunday morning I got a call from the doctor asking me to come at once. It took a long time for me to get to the West End; the Sunday trains in 1920 weren't what they are to-day!'

'The West End?' I questioned in surprise. 'Why the West End?'

'Your Mother was at Park Lane,' Nurse Henderson answered. 'I remember being very impressed by the house

214

when I arrived. It was so big with lovely gardens at the back.'

'In Park Lane,' I said still mystified. 'But I thought I was born at Maysfield?'

'Good gracious, no!' she exclaimed. 'Fancy you thinking that, Lady Gwendolyn. We went down to Maysfield later as soon as your Mother was well enough to travel. They thought she would be better in the country air, away from the noise of London. She had a terribly bad time with you, but then, you were three weeks early. You know that, I suppose?'

'I know nothing,' I said. 'Tell me everything from the very beginning. I couldn't be more interested. You see Mother has never talked to me about my birth and I must say I have never troubled to ask her.'

Tea came in at that moment, and as soon as the butler had arranged it on a small table beside my bed, Nurse drew up her chair and, with every evidence of enjoyment, launched into her story.

'Fancy me being able to tell you all this!' she said. 'Well now, I will begin at the beginning. You arrived three weeks too early. Of course your Mother oughtn't to have been up in London, but your grandmother, Lady Corrimore, had wanted to see her and up she had come, just for a few days. Every arrangement had been made at your home in the country for the doctor to attend her there and a maternity nurse engaged.

'Well, as I was saying, the pains started suddenly on Sunday morning. Your Mother slipped as she was going through the hall to breakfast. It was one of those black and white marble floors. I have always thought they were bewildering, and I dare say the poor thing felt dizzy. They sent hastily for Dr. Cutler. He was a very well-known man in those days—he's dead now—and I was one of the nurses on his list. He generally sent for me if he was expecting a difficult confinement or any complications.

'Your poor Mother was in bed by the time I arrived and, of course, nothing was ready. There wasn't a thing I needed in the house, and every shop shut. However, Lady Corrimore's maid produced some flannel and cotton wool, and with bath towels and woollen vests, we decided that the baby could manage, at any rate until Monday morning.

'There wasn't much time to think. I was boiling water as

hard as I could and getting things sterilised for the doctor, and at the same time trying to help your poor Mother and keep her cheerful. It was a very hot day and the perspiration was running down my forehead and half-blinding me, for I have worn glasses all my life and I kept having to wipe them and put down whatever I was carrying to do so. It was a miracle that I got things ready in time, and, of course, the doctor didn't arrive until the last moment. He had another case on hand and was rushed off his feet, poor man.

'Well, you certainly weren't going to make things easy for us, Lady Gwendolyn. Everything that could be wrong with your entry into the world was wrong. When finally Dr. Cutler handed you to me, he said, "I am afraid it is dead, nurse".'

'Dead!' I ejaculated.

'Yes, that is what he said,' Nurse Henderson repeated. 'And I confess I hadn't been very optimistic for several hours. You were a miserable little object, a bad colour and not a sign of life in you. I slapped you vigorously, but without avail. Then, before I could do anything more, the doctor said, "Quick, nurse," and I had to attend to your Mother.

'I wrapped a bit of flannel round you and put you down on the other bed in the room, where I had arranged some blankets and hot water bottles. I remember thinking how disappointed your poor Mother would be when she came round. I hate a dead baby, it always upsets me.

'It must have been nearly five minutes later when both the doctor and I were startled by a sudden cry. He gave almost a shout of surprise and as soon as I could, I hurried over to where you were lying. It was a miracle; but you were alive! Your colour had changed; the grey-blue tones which we always associate with suffocation had vanished, your mouth was open and you were attempting to yell. I got to work pretty quick, I can tell you, and in a few seconds it was quite evident that you were not only very much alive, but determined to let us know it.

' "I can't understand it, nurse," Dr. Cutler said later and, of course, between ourselves, Lady Gwendolyn, we both knew he had made an error of judgment which might have proved fatal. If we had known there was the slightest spark of life in you, we should have got to work much quicker.'

'How strange,' I said, 'how very strange!'

216

My thoughts were busy; could there be any meaning in this? Could the sudden resuscitation of what had been an apparently dead baby, have anything to do with the theories and fancies that I had already put behind me and dismissed as absurd?

'Which was my grandmother's house?' I asked.

'Well, you know, that is what is so interesting,' Nurse Henderson replied. 'Of course it has gone now. It was pulled down only a few years after you were born, but it was next door to what will be your new home.'

'Next door to Chadleigh House?' I asked.

'It adjoined it,' Nurse Henderson said. 'I remember seeing Sir Philip's car waiting outside. I used to admire it when I went for a walk. It was a big blue Rolls Royce.'

'Do you remember anything about . . .' I stammered and hesitated . . . 'about the tragedy that happened at Chadleigh House? It must have been . . .'

'Well now, since you ask me,' she answered. 'Of course, I can't pretend to you, Lady Gwendolyn, that I don't remember it. The papers were full of it and naturally the servants at your grandmother's talked—you can't stop that class, can you? It was so strange happening just when it did, because it was at the actual time that you were being born.'

'The actual time?' I whispered.

'Yes,' Nurse Henderson said too intent on her story to notice the strangeness of my tones. 'The time of your birth was between half-past seven and eight o'clock in the evening. I couldn't be certain of the exact minute, but that was approximately the time. And it was then that the poor lady fell from the window next door. Dr. Cutler himself told me about it the next day. When he left the house there was still a crowd collected and he heard what had happened.'

'At the same time,' I repeated.

'It was terrible for Sir Philip,' Nurse Henderson said. 'I was sorry for him then, and ever since, when I have seen his pictures in the paper, I have remembered how sympathetic I felt for that poor young man. There were reporters and photographers round the house for days.'

It was too fantastic, too extraordinary, yet the conviction was growing on me that there was something in all this, there must be. It couldn't be coincidence; all these facts, all these incidents, piling up in a long array, forcing themselves upon me, refusing to be denied.

'Of course, it rather reminds me of another case I had. That was in the North of England,' Nurse Henderson was saying.

She talked on but I was thinking of a baby being put aside as dead, of another life coming to an end at that very moment, as Nada fell to the pavement outside. But had it come to an end? Had her life vanished into the ether from which it had come, or had it, that particular piece of life which belonged to Nada, entered the still body of the baby that was to become me? Everything that had happened to me in the last few months, every idea, every thought that I had on the subject of rebirth came crowding back to me, seeming to demand my judgment, challenging the decision which I had made and accepted without reservation beside Nada's grave in Highgate Cemetery.

It was with a great sense of relief that I heard Nurse Henderson say good-bye.

'You will excuse me, Lady Gwendolyn, I know,' she said. 'But I have got to catch a Green Line bus from Hyde Park Corner. If I miss the 5.30 there won't be another for two hours.'

'You certainly mustn't miss it then,' I said. 'It was very nice of you to come and see me. Is there any chance of you getting down to Maysfield for my wedding at the end of July? There will be a special train running from Victoria and I should be so glad if you would come.'

'Well now, that is nice of you,' she said. 'It will be a real treat for me, I can assure you, especially if I had a chance of seeing your dear Mother again.'

'Well, you must try to arrange it,' I said. 'You will get an invitation in a few days, we are addressing them as quickly as we can.'

'You will make a lovely bride, Lady Gwendolyn. I shall be proud indeed of one of my children.'

'One of the three hundred!' I said with a smile. 'Do you keep up with them all?'

'Oh dear no!' Nurse Henderson replied. 'Some of them have died, some of them have gone abroad, but I keep in touch when I can. It is a great interest to me now in my old age and often my daughter says to me when she is looking through the evening paper. "Here is one of your babies, Mummy, about to be married".'

'Well, goodbye,' I said, 'and thank you so much for coming. I have enjoyed our talk.'

218

'And so have I,' Nurse Henderson said. 'And I wish you every happiness, Lady Gwendolyn, every possible happiness.'

'Thank you,' I answered.

I rang the bell so that the butler would be waiting with the lift to take her downstairs. Then I lay back with closed eyes, pressing my hands against my forehead, trying to think, trying to control the chaotic excitement of my thoughts.

After a few moments I jumped out of bed and fetched my book from the drawer, but not even *The Evidences of Reincarnation* could help me judge the evidence which poured in on me. If only I could ask Philip, I thought to myself, if only I dare tell him what I hoped, what I half believed, but of which I was still uncertain. Yet I dared not take the risk. He might laugh, worse still, he might be horrified, shocked, disgusted at what might appear to him almost a blasphemy against the woman he loved.

No, I knew I must be quite certain, I must have some definite proof, something irrefutable before I could go to him.

Clutching my hands together I prayed passionately that that proof might be given to me and that through it I might find both Philip's peace of mind and my own happiness.

26

Philip encouraged by Angela decided that he must give a
party at Longmoor before our marriage. So besides all the
organisation required for the wedding itself, the sending of
invitations, the listing of wedding presents, and the letters
of thanks that we both had to write daily, we now had arrangements to make for an evening party on quite a big
scale.

As a lot of older people were to be invited, Philip
suggested that although it would be possible to dance, we
should not make it the essential part of the entertainment.
He engaged a string band to play in the reception rooms,
and asked several well-known artistes to sing during the
evening. Tables for bridge players were not forgotten, and
with the garden floodlit, and cushioned boats waiting on
the lake, there would be plenty for all our guests to do,
whether they were young or old.

Angela was as excited as a child about the whole
scheme.

'I have always thought,' she said, 'that a country party
was more fun than a London one. I simply can't wait to
find a house so that Henry and I can have our friends
down and give all sorts of parties, at all times of the year.'

'Haven't you seen anything you like yet?' I asked.

Every day stacks of photographs arrived from agents
and the house was littered with them, all of them showing
most inviting-looking places.

'There's always some snag,' Angela said. 'I can't think
how people can manage to be so uncomfortable. Why, the
house I enquired about yesterday had nineteen bedrooms
and only two bathrooms.'

'You can easily have some more put in,' I suggested.

'Of course I can,' Angela replied. 'But I want to get settled, and more than anything, I would like to have the

house before the summer holidays. I know how much Gerald will enjoy it, and Dickie too.'

It was really rather touching to see what a lot of thought Angela gave to her family these days, but I could not help being amused when on the morning of the dance she said to me:

'I have made Philip invite my new young man.'

'A new one?' I asked with raised eyebrows.

'Yes,' she replied. 'Charles Martin—you met him the other night.'

I remembered with difficulty, a tall, clean-shaven young man who danced well, but had little else to recommend him.

'Angela!' I said reproachfully. 'I thought you had settled down to domesticity.'

'I have,' she said quite seriously. 'At the same time I must have someone to dance with. No, don't look at me like that, Lyn, it doesn't mean a bit what you think it does. Henry and I are happy together now, happier than we have been for years, but he quite understands that I have to have a tame young man of sorts to run around with me and to keep me amused when he's too busy. Other women have pekingese—I prefer good dancers, even though they are dumb.'

'You are incorrigible,' I sighed.

'You wait,' Angela said darkly. 'Wait until you have been married ten years. By that time you will very likely have changed all your ideas and ideals.'

'I wonder?' I said.

'What will have happened to me in ten years' time?' I wondered as I came down to dinner at Longmoor, wearing a very bridal-looking white dress with gardenias in my hair and at my waist. The only touches of colour were their green leaves and the emeralds which Philip had given me. It was almost like being married to receive with Philip the guests who arrived in quick succession before dinner. I was proud to be at Philip's side, so proud that I was only afraid of letting him down, of failing his trust in me.

'You look lovely,' he said to me before anyone arrived.

'I feel terribly nervous,' I answered.

'You needn't be,' he said, taking my hand. 'I will look after you.'

I smiled up at him. There was a friendliness about him

221

these days which made our relationship easy and affectionate.

Angela came in before we could say more.

'Lyn,' she exclaimed in tones of dismay. 'Have you forgotten your gloves?'

Of course I had to dash upstairs, get them and come bustling down, hot and flustered, just as the first guests were announced in stentorian tones by the butler.

Dinner passed off quite well; it was, to my mind, one of those boring interminable meals with far too many courses and far too many people for real enjoyment. At the same time, everyone seemed happy and the food and drink were certainly excellent.

When the ladies withdrew to the drawing-room, I sat for a short while with the Princess (for one or two minor Royalty had come to the party), who was most gracious. Then I had a long talk with the wife of a Cabinet Minister, who gave me some exceedingly sensible advice on how to budget for a big household. I didn't want to disappoint her by telling her that I thought I should have very little to do with the running of Longmoor, or of any houses organised and managed by Philip's most efficient housekeepers and secretaries. But I listened attentively, and thanked her at the end of our conversation, with what I hoped sounded like grateful sincerity.

Afterwards Philip and I took up our positions again in the hall to receive the hundreds of guests who had accepted his invitation. They trooped past us, one after another; I hardly heard their names and could only smile politely or thank them for the good wishes which nearly all of them expressed as they shook hands.

Then I heard Philip exclaim:

'Marcus! I am glad you have been able to come. I was so afraid that something would prevent you.'

I looked up to see him greeting with both hands a tall, thin, grey-haired man with a lined face and quite the bluest eyes I have ever seen in my life.

'I landed this morning,' the stranger answered. 'You got my cable?'

'Of course I did,' Philip answered, then turning to me he said, 'Lyn, I want you to meet my oldest and quite my dearest friend—Marcus Cameron. One day you must get him to tell you some of our adventures together.'

Mr. Cameron took my hand and I felt that he was inspecting me critically, weighing me in the balance, passing judgment.

'I am so glad you were able to come,' I said politely.

'So am I,' he said simply.

Before I could say anything further, another guest was announced.

The dancing started about half-past ten. Philip and I managed to get one dance together somewhere about midnight.

'Are you very bored, Lyn?' he asked.

'Of course I'm not,' I replied. 'It is a lovely party.'

'I think the old people are enjoying themselves too,' he said with satisfaction. 'I went into the bridge-room just now and it was packed, everyone was settling down for a good fight with their partner in the traditional manner.'

'If you want to see a crowd,' I answered, 'go and look in the dining-room. I only hope you have provided enough supper. One would think that none of these people have had anything to eat for weeks.'

'You are too young to appreciate good food,' he said jokingly. 'That will come with age. It is almost the last passion left to our declining years!'

When our dance was over, we had no chance of talking together or of walking out into the garden as other couples were able to do. People standing about all seemed to want a word with Philip or with me. Soon we were separated, and I was claimed by another partner as soon as the music started again.

It was an hour or so later that I found myself able to enjoy a moment's respite. Someone cut my dance, either intentionally or because they were too busy in the supper room. The moment I realised that my partner was not coming, I did not make the mistake of hanging about the ballroom, where I should certainly have been asked to dance by someone else. I slipped through the open windows on to the lawn, and walked to the far end of the terrace which was in shadow, the fairy lights illuminating the flights of steps down to the gardens.

Below me on the lawns I could see people sitting on the chairs that had been arranged in twos under the arches of roses, or beneath the big trees. Beyond them again, I could see the lake, twinkling with lights as the boats moved slowly on its silver surface, with couples who preferred the peace of the warm summer's night to the noise and heat of indoors.

I leant against the cold stone balustrade, remembering that it was here on this very terrace Philip had asked me to marry him and that I had accepted him, a decision which had changed my whole life, and one which, so far, had brought me many things, but not the one supreme happiness for which I still hoped.

'I can wait!' I told the stars. I had gained so much already—Philip's confidence, a companionship which made me look forward to my marriage, if not as a radiant consummation of my love, at least as a union of interests and ambitions.

Philip knew now that I was reading and studying for the position he would take up at the end of next year.

'How many more surprises have you got for me?' he asked when I told him. 'I'm beginning to think I must have a memorandum on you before we go much further.'

'I want to help you,' I said timidly.

'You do,' he answered, 'more than I can tell you. I'm happier than I've been for—well, nineteen years—happier, and when you are with me, at peace. You have given me a new belief in myself. I'm grateful to you, Lyn, humbly grateful.'

I could only whisper my gladness at the time, but often when I was alone I would recall his words, the tone of his voice and the touch of his hands.

I was absorbed now in my memories when a step on the gravel made me start, and I looked round to see a tall figure standing beside me.

'Am I disturbing you?' a voice asked.

I recognised Mr. Cameron.

'Of course not,' I replied. 'I am playing truant and taking a moment's respite.'

'And Philip?' he asked.

'I expect that he is being the perfect host,' I answered. 'I haven't seen him for some time.'

'I can't tell you how glad I am to be here again,' Marcus Cameron said, indicating with a brief gesture the view in front and the house standing behind us. 'I have often thought of Longmoor, especially when, lying under a mosquito net, I have been longing for a breath of air which would help me to sleep.'

'Have you come from India?' I asked.

'I live there,' he replied. 'That is where I met Philip. Hasn't he told you?'

'Not a word,' I said. 'I am very angry with him. But tell me yourself.'

'It is ungrateful of him,' Marcus Cameron said. 'For our introduction was that I saved his life. He certainly wasn't very pleased with me at the time. When I got his temperature down and the fever left him, he cursed me with the last remnant of strength that was in his body and told me that he wished to die.'

'Poor Philip!'

'You would certainly have said that had you seen him at that moment,' Marcus Cameron went on. 'He was about four thousand feet up in the Himalayas with nobody with him but a couple of native servants on the verge of running away because they thought he could not live, and they didn't want to be left with a dead man on their hands.'

'Why were you there?' I asked.

'I am what is known as a travelling doctor,' he answered. 'I go all over the country carrying my operating theatre with me. It consists mostly of an old Ford car, a folding bed and a most unimpressive paraphernalia of implements and bottles. At the same time it is effective. My nurse is also my driver and my cook. He's a good boy and he loves the work, if it does often entail a twenty-four-hour working day.'

'What did you do with Philip when he was better?' I asked.

'Packed him up, bag and baggage, and made him come with me,' Marcus Cameron said. 'It was the best cure he could have had, to work, and work damned hard.'

I laughed, I could not see Philip in a travelling hospital.

'We were together for nearly eighteen months,' Marcus went on. 'One day I will tell you all about it, but I mustn't keep you now.'

'I want to be kept,' I said. 'I have been very dutiful all the evening, let me be selfish for a little while.'

He lit a cigarette.

'It is your turn to do the talking,' he said.

'Tell me,' I said seriously, 'as Philip's oldest friend, do you think I am capable of making him happy?'

If Marcus Cameron was surprised at my question, he gave no sign of it.

'I am used to making up my mind very quickly,' he said. 'I will answer your question in all sincerity. Yes, I think you are.'

'In spite of what you know about his past life?' I asked. 'Because, of course, you do know, you couldn't have been with Philip at that time without knowing.'

'Yes, I know,' he answered.

'You understand,' I went on, 'that he has not yet got over it—it still means a great deal to him, far more than I do.'

He turned and stared away from me.

'I often wonder,' he said reflectively, 'if we ever know how much things mean to us while we are in close contact with them. You may mean far more to Philip than he has any idea of at this particular moment.'

'I wish I could think that,' I said.

'You love him?' Marcus asked gently.

'That is why I am marrying him,' I answered. 'But I am not blind, neither am I pretending, even to myself, that the future is without its difficulties.'

'It is half the battle if you know what to expect,' he said.

There came one of those silences which can happen only between two people who are completely in sympathy with one another. I knew that I liked this man, that I could trust him, and I was glad, as I had never been glad with any of Philip's other friends or acquaintances, that I had met him and that he had come into my life.

'Tell me,' I asked, 'and please don't think that I am asking this question in any frivolous way, do you believe in reincarnation?'

He was quite still for a moment, then he replied.

'Of course! I have lived in the East too long to find a reasonable explanation for the misery, degradation and the injustice of this world save in rebirth.'

'Have you ever discussed it with Philip?' I asked.

'We must have, many times,' he answered. 'No one could be in India without coming across Karma in some form or another, practically daily. Besides, we still read our Kipling out there. You remember?

   ' "They will come back, come back again
     As long as the red earth rolls,
   He never wasted a leaf or tree,
     Do you think He would squander souls?" '

'Oh, but how can one be sure?' I asked. 'One feels instinctively, perhaps, but one is groping in the dark, trying to find something tangible to hold on to, something that will stand the light of day, that will defy the criticism and the laughter of unbelievers.'

'Could anything spiritual be so tangible?' he asked. 'My dear, you are asking an impossibility. This is third dimension. If any of us had such infinite minds that we could completely comprehend such things, we should certainly not be here. And as for knowing and being sure, surely you remember those words with which Rossetti greeted just the feelings which I am sure you are experiencing?

> "I have been here before,
>   But where or how I cannot tell;
> I know the grass beyond the door,
>   The sweet, keen smell,
> The sighing sound; the lights around
>   the shore." '

He said the words in a low, grave voice.

I answered him impatiently.

'I believe, I know and I am very nearly sure, but, unfortunately, that is not enough.'

My voice faltered on the last words. Marcus turned towards me and, putting both hands on my shoulders, looked down at me.

'Listen,' he said. 'One day you are going to tell me everything, but not yet, not until the moment comes, because confidence is like our happiness—it is either there because we cannot prevent it, or it has escaped us. Until then I want you to remember just three things. I am preaching you a sermon, but I know you won't mind. Just three things to linger in your mind and to carry you along the road that you are treading.'

'What are they?' I asked.

'Faith, Hope and Love,' he answered, 'and the greatest of these is Love.'

His hands dropped and he would have turned away from me.

'Please!' I said in agony. 'Please, you must help me. I must ask you one thing. Do you think that I could be Nada . . . come back?'

There was a moment's silence.

227

'I can't possibly answer that question,' he replied. 'There is no one that can answer it save yourself.'

'How can I be sure?' I asked. 'How can I be certain?'

'Only your own heart can tell you,' he said. 'But whatever the answer is, it is not important.'

'Not important?' I questioned.

'Not really! The question as to whether you can remember another life will not alter the fact that you are alive now, and that you must live your present life to the best of your ability.'

'It is important to me,' I said obstinately.

'No,' he said sternly. 'Rebirth is a natural law; memory is a very superficial thing which plays no fundamental part in it. The fact that you are Nada, or the reincarnation of someone, can be of importance only in so far as it affects the being that you are at this particular moment.'

'But can't you understand,' I said impatiently, 'can't you realise, how the idea tortures me?'

'Look at it this way,' he said. 'The key-note of Nada's last years was her great, overwhelming love for Philip. That was what was of importance in her life. That should be today, in your position, the main importance of yours. What matters then is love, not for yourself or for your own peace of mind, but for Philip. Think of him, it is he that matters.'

I was silenced; there was nothing more to say. While I stood before him, humble and without words, he bent down and taking both my hands, raised them to his lips.

'God help you,' he said gently.

Then he turned briskly towards the house.

'Come back to your guests,' he said in quite a different tone. 'You are neglecting them and I shall get the blame.'

A few steps and we were in the bright golden light shining from the windows. I glanced up at my companion and he smiled down at me.

'I shall dance at your wedding,' he said. 'Philip is a very lucky man.'

'You promise to come?' I asked.

'Nothing shall keep me away,' he promised.

We stepped through the door into the brilliantly lighted rooms, back into the laughing, chattering throng who were to continue enjoying themselves until the dawn broke, pale in a misty morning sky.

27

Three days before my wedding, I was looking forward to being Philip's wife with a queer excited joy which held in its happiness a touch of fear and apprehension.

But I was happy. A new calm had descended on me, a calm which came not from my heart, but from my mind. Marcus Cameron had brought me peace. Since his words on the night of Philip's party, I had tried with all my might to forget myself, to remember only the man I was about to marry and that I loved him. I felt, too, with a strange fatalism, that, sooner or later, things would right themselves and I would find the way out of the maze of emotions and feelings which encompassed me and which I still, as yet, did not understand.

The weather had become very hot and the last-minute rush of fittings, entertainments, and the sorting and arranging of presents, was most exhausting. I came back from a big luncheon party at which Philip and I had been the guests of honour, with a bad headache and a longing to sleep. It was thundery weather and thunder always affects me, making me feel heavy and depressed. I had not slept well the night before; London seemed airless and stifling and I was longing for the country and for the sea. We had planned to start our honeymoon cruising in a yacht lent to us by one of Philip's relatives.

But there was still so much to do that I knew it was unlikely that I could relax, even for a few moments. We were not going down to Maysfield until the night before the wedding, and as it would have been impossible to transport all the wedding presents which we had received to the country, Angela had arranged to give a huge pre-wedding reception for our friends to view the really marvellous collection of gifts.

Most of them were arranged on long tables in the drawing-room, while the jewellery—of which I had a considerable amount—was kept in Henry's safe, waiting until the arrival of the detective would allow it to be placed in a big glass cabinet which Philip had lent us from Chadleigh House. Angela and I had already spent several hours during the morning listing and placing presents and when I came in after luncheon, to find another pile waiting for me in the hall, I groaned audibly.

'Oh dear!' I said to the butler. 'Wherever are we going to put them all?'

'Her ladyship was asking the same thing, m'lady,' he answered. 'She is thinking of having another table erected in the boudoir.'

'That means more work,' I thought.

I was not really ungrateful, because people had been so extraordinarily kind and many of them, I felt, had spent far more than they could afford. It was just that such a superabundance was rather overwhelming and, of course, I was selfish enough to remember that I had to write and thank for each one.

I had done my best to keep my letters of thanks equal to the arrival of presents, but I had failed and already there were over fifty letters that I must finish before we went away on our honeymoon. I looked at the parcels; guessing their contents, and hoping they weren't flower vases: we had already received forty. Three of the small parcels looked interesting and I picked up the first that came to hand, a flat package which I thought might be a handbag.

I pulled off the string and paper, and inside found a thin green book. There was a note with it and one glance at the signature made my heart beat quicker. It was from Madame Melinkoff.

She did not start her letter conventionally, it just read:

I have thought of you so much since our meeting. I am sending you this book which belonged to my daughter, with my very sincere good wishes for your future happiness. Edith Melinkoff.

I looked at the title of the book. It was *The Garden of Kama*. Before I turned the pages, before I even opened it, I remembered the context of those lines I had quoted to

Philip that day in Richmond Park and which, innocent enough in themselves, had disturbed the friendliness of the day and had made him drive, furiously and in silence, back to London. I held the book to me, a strange excitement making me tremble, then I realised that the butler was still beside me.

'I will leave these presents,' I said, 'until her ladyship returns.'

I ran upstairs.

When I reached my own room I locked the door before I stood for a long time looking at the book I held in my hands. Slowly, with a timid yet sensuous kind of pleasure, I turned the pages. Every poem seemed familiar; every word found an echo in my memory. The book had been handled many times before. Some of the poems were marked and against one or two there were rough pencil sketches.

I cannot explain my feelings—they were too emotional to put into words, my heart knew definitely what my brain hesitated to affirm. It was my book and it was my hand which had scored and scribbled on the pages. I read each poem; here and there repeating a line or a verse out loud with my eyes shut.

It was like meeting a beloved friend after a long separation. Towards the end of the book one verse of a poem was not only underlined, but was also surrounded by a little design of pencilled leaves and flowers, as if to accent its importance. I whispered the words.

'And after death, through the long To Be,
    (Which, I think, must surely keep love's laws,)
I, should you chance to have need of me,
    Am ever and always, only yours.'

It was a message of love which echoed through the ages. Marcus Cameron was right—it was love that counted! Nada's words or mine? What did it matter, love would remain—unforgettable, invincible, eternal, long after we had passed away.

I went down on my knees with the book between my hands and I prayed as I have never prayed before. I asked that I could bring Philip real happiness; that I could find, not only peace for him, but with him, and that he might find again through me the love which he had once known.

How long I knelt I do not know, but when I got to my feet again I felt content, as though I had laid my troubles upon Another and the burden had been accepted.

Angela sent for me a few minutes later to come down and help her with the presents. We worked until it was six o'clock, and wouldn't have stopped then, except for some friends who dropped in on the chance of finding us at home.

Philip and I were to go that evening to a reception at the India Office, and we were dining first with the Secretary of State and his wife. Angela was not asked to dinner, only to the party afterwards, and Philip suggested that I should pick him up early at Chadleigh House so that we could have a few moments alone together.

'That would be lovely,' I had said to him. 'We are asked for half-past eight, so I will come to you about three-quarters of an hour earlier. I shall be glad of a few moments' rest, I can promise you.'

'Poor Lyn,' he said sympathetically. 'But don't let it get you down. This time next week we shall be on the high seas, without even a telephone bell to disturb us.'

'Thank heaven for that!' I answered.

Actually I left for Chadleigh House about half-past seven—I was early because I literally ran away. I was tired of being asked questions, of talking on the telephone, of making arrangements and of writing letters. It was impossible even to have a bath without someone banging on the door and asking me my opinion or demanding my signature.

A further complication had been added to the general confusion by the fact that Gerald had now, not only recovered from his operation, but after a week at the sea, was well enough for Angela not only to want him to be at the wedding, but also to be a page. At the same time, she didn't wish him to come to London to be fitted, so that we had to choose the page's costume, have it made, order the shoes and all the other paraphernalia, entirely from the measurements sent to us by his governess. I was, of course, delighted to have Gerald, but it didn't seem possible to get everything finished to time.

Another crisis arose while I was dressing, on this occasion because Mother, in her usual absent-minded way, had asked half a dozen people at the last moment to come to the wedding, but had forgotten to let us know either their names or addresses. Now she had written quite an annoyed letter to Angela because they hadn't received invitations.

'What are we to do?' Angela asked limply as I sat doing my hair in front of the looking-glass.

'Wire Mother and telephone or telegraph to her friends,' I answered.

'That's a good idea,' my sister said approvingly. 'I'll tell Miss Jenkins. Look in and see me on your way down in case there is anything else.'

'All right,' I replied.

But I did nothing of the sort. As soon as I was dressed I crept past the drawing-room so that Angela wouldn't hear me. I was quite certain there would be a hundred and one more things to see to, but I had gone on strike. I got a taxi for myself, and felt, as it drove off, the elation of a school-boy playing truant.

When the butler opened the door to me at Chadleigh House he looked surprised.

'Sir Philip is not back yet, m'lady,' he said.

'I suppose he has been kept at the House,' I answered. 'Never mind, there's no hurry. When he arrives tell him I am here and I will go up to the sitting-room.'

'Very good, m'lady.'

He opened the door of the automatic lift.

'I will take myself up,' I said and, closing the gates, pressed the electric button.

The lift moved swiftly and noiselessly. When it stopped I opened the doors and let myself out on to the landing. I turned to the left, opening the green baize door which led to Philip's apartments. It closed behind me with a little thud and I turned the handle of his sitting-room.

For a moment I stood too startled to exclaim or even to move: the room was empty and dismanteled, the floor carpetless, the windows without curtains. I gazed round me bewildered, until, looking out of the further windows, I noticed that there was only a narrow parapet instead of the usual balcony. Then I understood. I had come up a floor higher. This was not Philip's room.

But it had been. The panelled walls were the same as in the room he now occupied. There were the marks on the walls where the pictures had been removed. There were empty shelves which had once held his books. There was

233

the open grate, identical to the one in the room below, where he burnt logs rather than coal.

I stepped into the room, closing the door behind me. Irresistibly I was drawn towards the windows. They were level with the floor and opened outwards even as Philip's did now, but here on this floor, the small leaded roof was protected only by a low tessellated stone parapet. I stood with my hand touching the framework of the window. Then the headache, which had throbbed across my forehead all day, seemed to get worse. I felt it clamping me like iron bands. I tried to resist it; tried to fight against the pain and the kind of suffocating drowsiness which swept over me . . . I struggled . . . but. . . .

I came into the room. I was aware of my own lightness, of the freedom with which I moved. I was wearing a dress of rustling emerald-green silk and the silver lace which banded the bodice, left my shoulders bare.

'Philip!' I called.

He opened the door between the bookcases and came towards me from his bedroom.

'Darling,' I said. 'I am early!'

He held out his arms and I flew into them. I was so small, so tiny that he had to bend to hold me. I put my head against his shoulder, I could feel his heart beating and I knew that his lips were seeking mine. I raised my face and knew the ecstasy of his kiss; the passion and fire of it made me a little breathless.

'Oh, my dearest,' I murmured.

'What a surprise,' he said. 'I wasn't expecting you for another hour.'

'You're glad?' I asked.

'You know I am!' His voice was deep with a vibrant note.

'How I love Sundays,' I whispered. 'We have got the whole evening together. Just you and I together alone.'

Still holding me close to his heart, he took my hand in his, and loosening my fingers, pressed his lips against the open palm.

'I love you,' he said simply.

I moved in his arms, holding out my other hand.

'I've got another surprise for you,' I said. 'It came yesterday, but I couldn't bear to part with it so I kept it until tonight. It is you—what I have always told you you look like.'

'What is it?' he asked puzzled, taking the little package and undoing the tissue paper.

Inside, lying on a bed of cotton wool, was a small but exquisitely made charm. It was a tiny black panther of black enamel with emerald eyes.

'A portrait,' I said softly. 'Of my black panther.'

Once again Philip caught me in his arms. He held me so tightly that I gave a cry, half of pain, half of ecstasy.

'Thank you, my angel,' he said. 'I shall keep it always.'

'I'm not certain I can bear to part with it,' I said taking it from him, and laying it against my cheek.

'It will bring me luck,' he said, 'when I am away from you.'

I felt a sudden fear.

'When you are away from me?' I repeated slowly. 'You are going away?'

'I have got to tell you, darling,' he said. 'I have dreaded this moment all day, but I must tell you. I got the letter last night. The Foreign Office have asked me to go on a trade commission, which is being sent to the Balkans next month. It is a compliment that I have been chosen and it is almost impossible for me to refuse. What excuse can I give? Indeed, what excuse is there, save that I cannot bear to leave you!'

'How long will you be away?' My voice was trembling.

'Two months at least,' he answered. 'Perhaps longer. Oh darling! Don't look at me like that. If you only knew how miserable I have been ever since I knew! I had an inkling some weeks ago that I might be one of the members to go, but I hoped so much that I was wrong, that someone else would be chosen in my place.'

'Two months!' My voice expressed only a little of the agony I was suffering. 'Oh Philip! I can't bear it. I can't do without you all that time. Let me come too.'

'If only you could,' he answered.

He tried to put his arms round me, but I pushed him away.

'Don't touch me,' I cried. 'I can't bear it at the moment. Already I feel as though we were separated. I am lost—lonely—afraid!'

'Nada, darling,' he said. 'You mustn't feel like that. You know I love you more than anything else in the world. If you want me to give up my constituency I will do so

235

tomorrow. I have offered to so many times, but always you have refused to let me.'

'If I let you,' I replied, 'how unhappy you would be. You would have nothing to do, nothing to think about.'

'I should have you,' he answered.

I smiled, a sad, rather bitter little smile.

'Would that be enough?' I asked. 'Could any woman be enough for a Chadleigh?'

'Don't darling, don't be cruel,' he pleaded. 'You can't think that I want to leave you.'

'I'm thinking of myself,' I replied. 'How can I stay in London alone without you? How can I dance when my heart is breaking, when I'm desperate, miserable and so terribly lonely?'

'Nada, Nada,' Philip pleaded. 'You're making things worse by talking like this.'

'I shall kill myself,' I whispered. 'I cannot live without you.'

Almost roughly he seized my shoulders and forced me to face him.

'You are not to talk like that! Never, never say things like that, not even to tease me. If you really want me to stay I will stay, you know that.'

I peeped up at him from under my eye-lashes.

'You are hurting me,' I said, but in a very different tone of voice to that which I had used before. I felt a new delight, a new happiness within me. How terribly, how desperately he loved me, this man of mine, who meant all the world to me! But a feminine instinct prompted me to think: 'He must not have things too much his own way.'

He would go, of course he must go on this commission, it was important, it was part of his career, it would help him towards the fame I had planned for him, but at the same time, he should suffer a little now, even as I would suffer when he had gone.

I was afraid when I thought of those long dreary days without him; the nights when, after the theatre, he would not be waiting to take me out to supper, when I must go home alone, but not for one moment would I have interfered. I was too proud of him, too ambitious for this brilliant lover of mine.

I longed to throw myself into his arms, to put mine around his neck, to feel his dear sweet face, and in the touch of his lips know that we were one as we had always been. But not yet! That unity, that rapture would come later. For the moment I would tantalise him, I would make him a little miserable, perhaps a little afraid.

'You are hurting me,' I said again and only then did he relax his grip of my arms.

He let me go and I turned away from him, moving across the room towards the windows.

'Give me the letter,' I said. 'Let me see what it is that is of so much importance that you must leave me alone.'

'It is in my bedroom,' he said.

He went towards the door, but before he got there he turned and held out his hands.

'Nada,' he begged, 'be sweet to me.'

'Get me that letter,' I said severely, and he obeyed.

When he was gone I opened my hand and looked down at the little black panther I had given him so joyously a few minutes ago.

'You shall take care of him,' I murmured and I pressed my lips against it. Then an amusing mischievous idea came to me. I would hide the charm somewhere in the room and he should find it. When he found it, the reward would be my kisses.

I looked round. The bookcases were too obvious. I had to be quick, for in a moment he would be back. Between the two windows I saw a narrow strip of moulding jutting out a bare inch from the walls. Standing on tiptoe, reaching as high as I could, I pushed the little charm on to the top of the panelling. It was secure there and quite invisible. I had hardly hidden it before I heard Philip in the doorway and, to cover my movements, I walked through the open window and on to the lead-coping outside. I sat down on the parapet, arranging my green silk skirt around me.

'Don't sit there,' Philip said sharply. 'It is dangerous. You might slip and fall.'

'And why not?' I answered, making my voice low and mournful. 'Would it matter so very much? You want me no longer. What is there for me to live for when our love is not more important than a trade commission to the Balkans?'

'Nada,' he said, 'come in. I want you.'

I shook my head.

I knew that he was debating with himself whether to

237

come out and fetch me. He was frowning; he looked worried; somehow I loved him all the more because I had such a power over him. He was so childlike in many ways, this dear, dear man of mine, to whom I had given myself so completely that had he but known it, he held me utterly captive, his slave.

'No!' I said, forcing a pout to my lips, a stubborn expression into my eyes.

'Please darling,' he pleaded, holding out his arms. I could not resist any longer. He was so handsome, so compelling and so irresistibly lovable.

I moved to obey, to go back to him, to obey his command. My foot slipped, I felt the heel of my shoe slither on the lead beneath it. I made one convulsive effort, with every nerve and pulse in my body strained, to regain my balance. I felt myself topple over the parapet.

I fell! I screamed and as I screamed I felt with every atom of my consciousness that I must not die, I must live, I must live for Philip. . . . Philip! . . . But I was falling . . . down . . . down . . .

My heart was throbbing. It seemed so loud that I wondered at the moment what the sound was. Then I realised it was my own heart that I heard beating, as I sat crumpled up on the floor, my face hidden in my hands. I raised my head: I was alone in an empty room. What had happened? Where had I been? What had I seen and felt?

Weakly, half-dazed, I rose to my feet. I held on to the window-frame. The window was closed. For a moment I stared at it, remembering that just a second before it had been open, and that I had passed through it.

'It is true then!' I said out loud, and I threw back my head gasping for air. My voice echoed in the empty room. I was afraid. In a mirror built into a panel opposite me I saw my face, white and strained. I looked at myself for a long time.

Slowly I turned to where between the windows was a small moulded panel of wood, the top of it jutting out barely an inch from the wall. I reached up my hand. There was no need for me to stand on tiptoe.

I felt a quiver of fear. Suppose it was not there, suppose, once again, my faith was shattered, my hopes were disappointed?

Tentatively, trembling, my fingers searched. There was

something hard, something small there, thickly covered in dust. I took it down. It was a tiny black panther.

I think I gave a little cry of happiness. I only know that as I walked towards the door, the whole world seemed golden and glorious around me. I had found the answer to my own questions and to Philip's. I held in my hand the key to peace and to happiness.